THIS DARK EMBRACE

IN THE WALTER McDUMONT MYSTERY SERIES

BY PAUL STUEWE
This Dark Embrace
BY PAUL STUEWE & HUGH GARNER
Don't Deal Five Deuces
BY HUGH GARNER
Murder Has Your Number
Death in Don Mills
The Sin Sniper

THIS DARK EMBRACE

Paul Stuewe

A Midnight Original Mystery

THE MERCURY PRESS

Copyright © 1996 by Paul Stuewe

ALL RIGHTS RESERVED. No part of this book may be reproduced by any means without the prior written permission of the publisher, with the exception of brief passages in reviews. Any request for photocopying or other reprographic copying of any part of this book must be directed in writing to the Canadian Reprography Collective (CANCOPY), 214 King Street West, Suite 312, Toronto, Ontario, Canada, M5H 3S6.

The publisher gratefully acknowledges the financial assistance of the Canada Council and the Ontario Arts Council, as well as that of the Government of Ontario through the Ontario Publishing Centre.

Edited by Beverley Daurio
Cover design by Orange Griffin
Composition and page design by TASK

Printed and bound in Canada by Metropole Litho
Printed on acid-free paper
First Edition
1 2 3 4 5 00 99 98 97 96

Canadian Cataloguing in Publication Data
Stuewe, Paul, 1943-
This dark embrace
ISBN 1-55128-037-X
I. Title.
PS8587.T846T54 1996   C813'.54   C96-931712-3
PR9199.3.S78T54 1996

The Mercury Press
137 Birmingham Street
Stratford, Ontario
Canada   N5A 2T1

Los Angeles, January, 1934

CHAPTER ONE

Idly tapping his fingers on the taxicab's steering wheel, McDumont watched the little man in chauffeur's livery struggling with the Great Dane. The dog had been to the vet's across the street, hadn't liked it, and was in no mood to get into the black limousine quietly. When the chauffeur tried to pull him into the back seat, the big animal stuck his feet out and refused to move. The chauffeur stepped back and glared at the dog. The dog licked its chops and looked placidly at the chauffeur.

Another little guy, this one in a grey tweed jacket and dark slacks, came sauntering down the block. He passed the limousine, gave man versus dog an amused glance, kept on to where McDumont was parked, stopped, thought about it, and then hopped into the back of McDumont's taxi. "Follow that limousine when it pulls out," he said.

"I'm your man," McDumont replied. Ahead of him the chauffeur had changed tactics and was trying to push the Great Dane into the front seat. The dog still wasn't buying it. McDumont hadn't had a tail job since he'd started pushing a hack for Frank's Taxi, but he'd heard some of the other drivers talking about them: jealous husbands, mostly, and things could get rough if it turned out the little lady was on her way to see a boyfriend. But this must be something else, unless the fare got his kicks from economy-sized dogs or pint-sized chauffeurs.

McDumont glanced back at his passenger. A mild-looking character, natty suit, glasses, a little less than average height, a businessman maybe. What the hell, if the guy wanted to play tag with some fat cat's pooch that was his business. McDumont wasn't going to mess up the first job he'd had since arriving in Los Angeles. There was a Depression on and he'd had enough of hopping freights and sleeping in hobo jungles to last him the rest of his life.

"They're pulling out, driver."

"Yes sir, I got him." McDumont eased away from the curb. There were already two cars between his cab and the limousine. When he started to edge left so as to pass at least one of them, the fare tapped him on the shoulder and said, "No, that's all right, we don't want to get too close." McDumont shrugged and settled back against the lumpy front seat. His passenger had some kind of English accent, not the just-off-the-boat English you often heard in McDumont's native Toronto, but definitely English all the same. This was getting interesting, for a slow Thursday afternoon in one of L.A.'s posher neighbourhoods.

For that matter, the neighbourhood was getting positively ritzy. The road was starting to wind in and out among houses that had gates and fences insulating them from the world outside, with expensive cars in their driveways and gardeners labouring on lawns as immaculate as well-brushed billiard tables. Then they were going uphill and the fences became solid brick walls, with only the occasional heavily barred entranceway admitting to the presence of human habitation. McDumont could hear his passenger whistling and tapping out some kind of jazzy, complicated rhythm on the upholstery; Ellington's "East St. Louis Toodle-oo," sounded like. Well, the guy might look like a square, but at least he was musically hep.

Suddenly, they ran out of road. The limousine had stopped in front of a massive gateway, next to a guard booth occupied by a man in security-service uniform. The guard came out, spoke with the driver of the limousine, and then went back into the booth. McDumont braked and pulled over about twenty yards behind the limousine. The gate swung open and the limousine accelerated quickly through it. The security guard stepped out of the booth again and looked at McDumont's cab, then went back inside, picked up a telephone, and had a brief conversation with someone at the other end. Then he put the phone down and began walking toward the taxi.

"What do you want to do?" McDumont asked.

"Let's see what he has to say. We're still on a public street, at least it appears so to me."

The guard, a tall, well-built man with a shiny black holster on his right hip, walked up to the driver's-side window. "Help you fellows?" he asked.

"Just out for a little drive," McDumont replied. "Nothing illegal about that, is there?"

The guard looked down the road for a moment before answering. "Nothing illegal maybe, no. But I think the police are going to want to talk to you anyway."

"Surely that's not necessary," the passenger interjected. "We'll be on our way if you're going to make a federal case out of it."

McDumont heard the roar of an approaching engine. In the rearview mirror he watched a black sedan pull across the road behind them, effectively blocking the narrow street. Two large, beefy men got out and sauntered toward his cab. If they weren't cops, McDumont was Little Lord Fauntleroy out on a toot.

The pair split up, one walking up to McDumont's window and the other leaning against the right rear door frame. "Let's see your license, buddy," drawled the florid-faced bruiser who had chosen McDumont's side of the taxi.

"You guys cops?" McDumont asked.

"No, we're members of the Ladies' Garden Club out on a sightseeing tour. Now cut the gab and let me see your license."

"Sorry, I'd like to see some identification first," McDumont replied. "You guys could be a heist crew or something."

"Hell, Larry," said a voice behind him, "show Mr. Taxi Driver your ID. You remember how the Captain lectured us about improving our relations with the public."

"I'll show the little prick some ID, all right." A snub-nosed revolver materialized in Larry's right hand and was thrust into McDumont's face. "How do you like that ID, buddy?"

"I really don't think that's necessary," said McDumont's passenger. "It was a perfectly reasonable request. But since you don't seem to be capable of behaving in a civil manner, I suppose the driver had better do as you demand."

Larry snorted. "Holy Christ, what have we got here? You just get off the boat from England or some place, pal? What do you think, Lou, should we run these guys in for illegal immigration? They don't seem to understand how we do things in the good old U.S.A."

"Nah, let's just check them out and get out of here. I don't think they've got a full deck between them."

McDumont stared at the revolver. "Can I put my hand inside my jacket?" he asked.

"Just do it nice and slow," Larry said. "I ain't shot anybody yet today, and you're the kind of guy makes my trigger finger get itchy."

McDumont took out the temporary license that he had been issued by the Taxicab Authority, pending approval of his application for permanent status. He handed it to Larry.

"Jesus, Lou, this here is Walter McDumont, and he ain't even a real cabdriver. Where are you from, McDumont? 'Torinto?' Where the hell's that, Italy? With a name like McDumont you can't be no wop."

"I'm from Toronto," McDumont answered. "That's in Canada."

"Canada," Lou repeated. "We haven't got enough people out of work around here, we have to bring them in from Canada. How'd you get this job, mack? You related to the mayor or something?"

"No, I was just going past the office and they had a sign out, 'Drivers Wanted.' It's no great job. You pay the company for the cab, you pay gas, then you work eighteen hours a day to make enough to eat in some greasy spoon and flop in a rooming house on Figueroa Street."

"Aw, that's too bad," said Larry. "Ain't that too bad, Lou? You ever heard a sob story that bad in all your life?"

"Yeah," said Lou, "that's a crying shame, that is. He should talk to my brother. Last job he had was selling apples down by the market there. Bunch of kids jumped him, beat the shit out of him, stole everything he had. Even stole the goddamned apples. Yeah, things are tough all over."

"Well, I'm going to show Mr. McDumont how we handle these things in L.A.," Larry said. He held up the temporary license, took a cigarette lighter out of his pocket, and set the paper afire. He watched it burn for a moment before dropping it on the ground and grinding his foot into it. "Gosh, I'm sorry about that, Mr. McDumont. Now I'm going to have to arrest you for driving a cab without a cab-driver's license."

"I think things have gone quite far enough," the passenger interjected. "You had better have a look at this card before you go on with this farce." He handed Lou a business card.

Lou stared at it and frowned. "You better take a gander at this, Larry. Back at the car."

The two men walked toward their sedan, obviously disagreeing as to what they should do next. "I'm very sorry about this," the passenger said. "I seem to have gotten you into a spot of trouble."

"Oh, don't worry about it," said McDumont. "I wasn't planning on spending the rest of my life driving a cab."

Lou came back alone. He handed the passenger back his card and said, "Okay, just get the hell out of here. You don't report this, we won't report it, nobody needs to know anything." He looked at McDumont. "But if I were you, mack, I wouldn't try to drive cab in this town any more. Once Larry gets a hate on for a guy, he can be one mean son of a bitch. Now the two of you scram, and don't come around here again."

He went back to the sedan, got in, and pulled it over so that the taxi could get by. McDumont used the driveway to turn around and drove slowly past the shiny black car. As they went by, Larry pointed his gun at them and yelled, "Canucks and limey bastards, you'll get yours."

"Where now?" McDumont asked.

"I don't know about you, but I think I could use a drink. Could I buy you one? No, I suppose you have to keep working."

"No, I'll take a drink, but I'd better get this hack back to the office before L.A.'s finest think of something else to arrest me for. Some of the joints around there aren't too bad, if you don't mind associating with us down-and-outers."

"Oddly enough, that happens to be just exactly what I would very much like to do. But I have the advantage of you, Mr. McDumont. You don't know anything about me. Let me introduce myself. My name is Chandler, Raymond Chandler. I'm doing what you might call some research, some research into local mores. And I think you may be able to help me."

After returning the cab and paying off what McDumont owed the taxi company— which Chandler insisted on taking care of— the two men walked around the corner to the Shanty Lounge, where they settled into a back booth and ordered draft beers. When they came, Chandler took a sip of his and regarded the glass with a bemused expression. "I still can't get used to what Americans call 'beer,'" he observed. "It reminds me of beer, and if I drink enough of it I may forget that it isn't beer, but deep down inside I know it's one step up from dog urine."

"I know what you mean," said McDumont. "Canadian beer has a little more to it. This stuff tastes watered."

Chandler glanced around at the Shanty Lounge's faded booths and battered tables. "Not an unlikely eventuality, I should think. I do know Canada a bit, actually. I was in the Canadian Army in the Great War. Went up to Victoria to enlist and was overseas before I knew it."

"I hopped freights out there last year," McDumont replied. "Nice country, but no work. I didn't make it to Victoria, but I can tell you that the good citizens of Vancouver sure hustled us bums out of their fair city in a hurry. I spent most of the winter in a work camp near Kamloops, that's a ways east of Vancouver, working on the Trans-Canada Highway. Twenty cents a day and military discipline. Jeez, it was rough."

"So this year you decided to head south for the winter. How do you find the United States?"

"It's one hell of a place. I've seen hoboes beaten nearly to death by the railroad bulls, and I've been fed square meals by some of the nicest people you'd ever want to meet in your life. It's hard to figure sometimes— it's like the minute you put a uniform on someone, they turn into one of Hitler's punks."

Chandler looked at him thoughtfully. "You're obviously a very intelligent fellow, Mr. McDumont, and you've seen a bit of the world. I liked the way you stood up to those policemen— if more of us did that, they might not take such unconscionable liberties. Tell me, would you be interested in working for me on this research I mentioned?"

"Research? Are you a sociologist or something like that?"

Chandler smiled. "No, I'm something even odder. I'm an out-of-work businessman with an urge to write fiction."

"Oh, I get it," McDumont said. "What the communists call 'social realism,' the kind of stuff you see in *New Masses*? Well, I've seen my share of social realism, all right."

"I'm sure you have, but that's not quite what I'm after. I'm more interested in the kind of detective fiction *Black Mask* is publishing, writing that grabs you by the throat and puts you in a world where good and evil are clearly defined, and where good doesn't always win. The best of it makes those old what-time-was-the-butler-in-the-hallway? mystery stories seem like ancient history."

"I've read some of that pulp-magazine stuff," McDumont said. "Bimbos with big bazooms and private eyes who got their heads beaten in and could still put a bullet through the bad guy's right nostril at a hundred yards. That's what you want to write?"

"I don't dispute the accuracy of your observation; there certainly is too much of that sort of thing. But I've been corresponding with the editor of *Black Mask*, Joseph Shaw. I've sold him one story, actually, and I think he's after something better— writing that both entertains readers and has something to say about the kind of world we live in. That's what *I* want to write, in any event."

"So where do I come in?" McDumont asked.

"I haven't thought this out completely, but I am going to need help in exploring parts of society that I don't know anything about. That card I showed the policemen? I was given that by an oil-company executive I know, a fellow who's had occasion to use private detectives in several court cases with which he's been involved. I talked to two of them, and they turned out to be police officers who had been dismissed from their jobs, for excessive brutality and bribe-taking, respectively. I don't want to have anything to do with people like that— you could smell the corruption on them."

McDumont stared thoughtfully into his beer glass. "I don't really know what I could do for you," he said after a while. "The only real crooks I ever met were guys I bumped into in jail, times I was in a day or two for vagrancy. You'd hear them bragging to each other about jobs they pulled, that kind of stuff, but they wouldn't say much to guys like me."

"I don't think I want a hardboiled criminal, Mr. McDumont, even if I knew where to get one. No, what I need is someone who doesn't look out of place in the Shanty Lounge, and is also intelligent enough to understand the different kinds of things I might want him to do. You're perfectly well-qualified in those terms; and I certainly feel a sense of obligation to you, given that I seem to be responsible for your losing your job. Would ten dollars a day and expenses be adequate?"

McDumont grinned and shrugged his shoulders. "'Adequate' isn't the word. Okay, you can't say I didn't warn you. I'll sign up. Now where do we go from here?"

Chandler smiled and extended his right hand. "First of all, let's properly introduce ourselves. I am Raymond Chandler, 'Ray' in this relentlessly informal society, and you must let me know how you prefer to be addressed."

"I prefer 'Walter,'" McDumont said as they shook hands. "'Walt' always makes me think of that guy who does the cartoons, Disney, and I get enough Mickey-Mouse crap without having to be reminded of it all the time."

"Very good, then, 'Walter' it shall be. It seems to me that we've got one very interesting possibility for investigation staring us right in the face. Those people who set the police on us certainly reacted in a very suspicious manner. What do you think about looking into their background? I'm sure they're not criminals, but we might turn up something interesting."

"Yeah, okay. How do you get started on something like that?"

"Well, it's quite remarkable what you can find out about people in the library. On our little excursion we ended up at the last address on Mountain Drive. Let's find out who lives there."

They took a cab to the Los Angeles Public Library. The Reference Room was a vast, poorly lit mausoleum, most of whose tables seemed to be occupied by shabbily dressed men staring blankly at newspapers. "You can stay here as long as you don't go to sleep," McDumont said. "But if you fall asleep, those sourpusses over at the Reference Desk will call the security guards and have you thrown out. I know, I fell asleep here last week."

"Perhaps that's why the gentleman behind the desk is staring at us," Chandler replied. "He seems extremely interested, one might even say concerned, as to what we might be doing here."

"He's just an old poop. You might not believe this, but I did once work at a library in Toronto, the branch in my neighbourhood. We didn't have much in the way of reference books, but we did have a city directory. You'd figure L.A. would have one, too."

"Exactly the place to start, I should think. Let us inquire of your acquaintance of the crabbed disposition."

They walked over to the desk. "We're looking for the Los Angeles Directory," Chandler said to the librarian, a balding, elderly man whose pursed lips suggested that he was either a misanthrope or made a habit of sucking lemons.

"And what would be your purpose in consulting such a directory?" The gentleman could raise his eyebrows, too.

"That's our business," said Chandler. "Are you trying to make our business your business?"

"I'm sure your business is no concern of mine. However, the person accompanying you was recently ejected from this library for gross misbehaviour. You can't blame me for being suspicious of anyone who comes here in his company."

"'Gross misbehaviour,'" McDumont snorted. "I dozed off over the want ads and the next thing I knew the Cossacks were hustling me out the door. Who does this guy think he is, anyway?"

Chandler looked at the nameplate on the desk. "Mr. Peter Waldgrove, Reference Librarian," he read. He took a pen and pocket notebook out of his sport jacket. "I must make a note of that. Mrs. Vanderhoven is always so interested in matters pertaining to the library. I'm sure she'll want to bring it up at the next board meeting."

Waldgrove cleared his throat. "Just a moment, please. If there has been any misunderstanding, I apologize. The directories are in the bookcase to the right of the doorway, over there."

As they crossed the room, McDumont stared at Chandler with admiration. "You really get around," he said. "How do you know this Mrs. Vanderhoven, anyway?"

"I don't know her from Adam," Chandler replied. "I just made up a name that sounds like it belongs on the library board. Stuffed shirts of Waldgrove's sort usually back down if they think they're outranked." He chuckled. "I was at a posh night club a few weeks ago, doing a wild lindy hop with a lady smoking a big cigar, and a waiter grabbed her and told her she couldn't smoke on the dance floor. She turned up her nose and said, 'Do you know who I am?' The poor fool looked worried and said, 'No, who are you?' 'My daddy is the City Fire Commissioner and he can close you up just like that,' she told him, lying through her teeth, and he fell all over himself apologizing to her and spent the rest of the night deluging us with free drinks. She had some nerve— but she got away with it."

"That's a good one," McDumont said. "I'll have to remember that the next time I get rousted for sleeping on a park bench."

Chandler laughed. "Certain minimal standards of appearance and deportment apply, of course. As far as that goes, Walter, would you be offended if we paid a visit to my tailor? We might get you something more... umm... conventionally respectable, given that you may be moving in more... umm... conventionally respectable circles."

"You mean like places where drunk ladies attack you with big cigars?" McDumont replied.

"Nicely put," Chandler said. "Yes, exactly those sorts of places."

"Okay by me. As long as I don't have to wear one of those monkey suits with white tie and tails and all that jazz."

They stopped in front of a massive bookcase topped by a sign for "City Directories." Chandler took out the most recent volume of the Los Angeles Directory, for 1932, and turned to the listings for "Mountain Drive." "The highest number is for a 'Bronson, Paul,' no occupation listed. There is a Mrs., Estelle; one daughter, Penelope; and a son, Paul, Junior. And that's about it. No phone number listed, either."

"What do we do now?" McDumont asked.

"We'll try *Who's Who*, that should give us a little more information. Then I want to go to the newspaper room. There's an index to the Los Angeles *Times*, and I'd be surprised if the Bronsons don't turn up there somewhere."

Who's Who revealed that Paul Bronson was fifty-two years old, a banker, president of the Western Fidelity Trust, born in Boston, educated at Harvard and the Wharton School of Finance. He had married Estelle Simpson in 1907. Penelope was born in 1911, Paul, Jr. in 1922. Bronson had begun his career with Massachusetts Savings and Loan, and by 1925 was an executive vice-president. Two years later he had assumed the presidency of Western Fidelity Trust in Los Angeles.

He was a member of the Golf and Tennis as well as the Century Club, and served on the board of several philanthropic organizations. His address was given as care of a Brentwood law firm.

"Suspicious guy." McDumont said. "Doesn't want people turning up at his door looking to borrow the odd tennis ball. You sure you want to keep on with this?"

"Let's dig a little deeper. *Who's Who* isn't exactly a scandal sheet. Come on, the newspaper room is down this way."

The Los Angeles *Times* index for 1927 referred them to a story on Paul Bronson's assumption of his new job, and subsequent volumes listed several society-page items on Mrs. Estelle Bronson's involvement with various charity balls and fundraisers. There were also a few entries for her husband's pronouncements on financial matters, including a 1933 story headlined "Depression can't last, says bank exec." But nothing suggested skeletons in the closet or reasons for calling the police when a stranger's car stopped at the end of the Bronson's street.

"What now?" McDumont asked. "The *Police Gazette?*"

"Not a publication in which I should expect to find the Bronsons. No, they spent most of their lives in the east. Let's see what else we can find in the newspapers."

They found it in the Boston *Globe* index for 1923. "Banker's Son Kidnapped" was the first story, and you could read the outline of what happened after that in the subsequent headlines: "Ransom Paid; Family Waits"; "Still No Word on Kidnapped Baby"; "Hope Fades for Abducted Child." Chandler filled out requisition slips for the issues listed, and after a quarter of an hour a library aide brought the newspapers over to the large oaken table where he and McDumont were sitting.

According to the *Globe*, on April 23, 1923, one-year-old Paul Bronson, Jr., had been taken out for a ride in his baby carriage by his nurse, Margaret Robinson. Three blocks from the Bronson home a black sedan pulled across the sidewalk, almost hitting the carriage; two men got out of the car, pushed the nurse to the ground, and took the baby away. There was only one other witness to the kidnapping, an elderly gentleman out for a stroll, and he had been unable to give the police any helpful information. Margaret Robinson had been so terrified by the sedan's near-miss of the baby carriage that she had noticed little about either the men or the car, although she did state that one of the men had a long scar on the right side of his face.

The ransom demand came by telephone that evening. The sum of one hundred thousand dollars was to be left at an abandoned farm north of Boston, after which Paul Jr. would be returned to his parents. The kidnappers had emphasized that any sign of police involvement would result in the infant's death.

"I don't believe this story," McDumont said. "It's as if they were trying to panic the kidnappers by telling everybody what was going on."

"You've got to remember that this was before the Lindbergh baby was kidnapped," Chandler replied. "The newspapers made such a circus out of that one that the police and the courts have clamped down on them. But in 1923, there would have been reporters living on the Bronson doorstep trying to get a scoop."

The ransom had been paid, but the child had never been returned. A check of the *Globe* indexes for the following years gave no indication that either Paul Bronson, Jr., or his kidnappers had ever been found. There were several follow-up stories on the kidnapping, the most recent less than a year ago, all of which alluded to the continuing mystery of the boy's whereabouts.

"Funny that he's still listed in the directory and *Who's Who*," McDumont observed.

"Hope springs eternal. If the lad's body was never found, he could still be alive. You can't blame his parents for wanting to believe that."

McDumont thought for a moment. "How do we know he isn't living with his family?" he mused. "You could come up with all kinds of possibilities if you worked at it. Could there have been another demand for money, maybe this time insisting that everything be kept secret? The kidnappers figuring that they could get away easier if the police didn't know the baby had been returned? What about the Bronsons' move to California? Is that connected to what happened?"

Chandler stared at him and then smiled. "Perhaps you should be writing the mystery stories, Walter— I couldn't dream up a plot that complicated if my life hung in the balance. Not that some of the butler-in-the-passageway school wouldn't be up to it. But you're right, there are other possibilities, and we'll have to look into them."

"How? We can't just call up the Bronson house and ask if their son is there."

"No, we can't, although some of the hardboiled detectives in the cheaper pulp magazines wouldn't be beyond it. No, I think we'd better try for a more oblique approach." He paused. "What we need is someone who knows the family but isn't emotionally involved with them. Someone who knows what's going on and won't mind talking about it."

"Like a newspaper reporter?" McDumont asked.

"Like a newspaper reporter," Chandler affirmed.

Perusing the indexes and back issues of the Los Angeles newspapers suggested two possibilities. The *Herald*'s society columnist, Bethany Chambers, had written several stories about Estelle Bronson's social and charitable activities; the *Examiner*'s business reporter, Harvey Pearl, had quoted Paul Bronson extensively in a series on current economic conditions. Chandler proposed that they each tackle one of the reporters.

"Me and a society columnist?" McDumont protested. "What do I talk to her about, the correct fork to use when eating Christmas dinner at the Salvation Army? I wouldn't know what to say."

"Process of elimination," Chandler replied. "My background is in business, and I can think of all sorts of plausible reasons to want to talk to Mr. Pearl. Ergo, you get the Chambers lady. You're a handsome young devil, and from that picture they run next to her column I don't think handsome young men are a salient aspect of Miss or Mrs. Chambers's life. All you need is a little preparation— and a new wardrobe."

"I was afraid you were leading up to that," McDumont said.

The clothing salesman seemed genuinely pleased. "I must say, Mr. McDumont, I had my doubts when you walked in the door. But you look quite the gentleman. I'll prepare your bill, Mr. Chandler." The salesman walked off toward a cash desk larger than the furnished room McDumont was renting.

McDumont stared at his reflection in the mirror. An embarrassed, expensively dressed young fellow looked back at him. The young fellow was wearing a dark blue blazer and grey wool slacks, and his dazzlingly white shirt was set off by a red-and-yellow striped necktie. Gleaming black brogans completed the ensemble.

"I wouldn't have believed it," Chandler said. "From cab driver to Beau Brummel in less than an hour."

"Can I take this stuff off?" McDumont pleaded. "I'm getting stiff from trying not to move and break the illusion that I'm just off for a weekend at my country estate."

"Yes," said Chandler, "Pygmalion has nothing on you. Stick a cocktail in one hand and a tennis racket in the other and you could crash one of Mrs. Vanderhoven's parties with no one the wiser."

McDumont snorted. "Okay, okay, can I peel the glad rags now? I'm about ready to sock Mrs. Vanderhoven in the eye if I don't get out of these duds."

"Now, now," Chandler replied, "that would never do. What would Bethany Chambers think if that nice young man who's writing a book on Los Angeles society behaved in such a manner? No, the fellow who's going to take her to lunch at the Ambassador would never do that."

"The Ambassador? That swanky hotel where the doormen have doormen? Jeez, they look funny at me when I drop off a fare there. You expect me to eat lunch at that joint? Couldn't I drop into her office with a bottle of hooch and tell her I've fallen madly in love with her picture in the newspaper?"

"No, only in the cheaper sorts of detective fiction does the private eye operate like that. You're going to play up to her in a different way, by asking her to share her unparalleled knowledge of the local social world with a starry-eyed young fan. There aren't many people who can resist being treated as an expert. You could even go so far as to say that the way to most persons' hearts is through their egos."

"You could say that," McDumont replied, "but as far as I'm concerned this job of yours is beginning to look like work." He glanced at the returning salesman and grimaced. "Oh, well, in for a penny, in for a pound. Take me to a telephone while I'm still dressed in these swell duds— I'm going to need all the moral support I can get."

CHAPTER TWO

On the telephone, Bethany Chambers was first aloof, then cheerfully condescending, and finally downright friendly. She seemed to find it perfectly understandable that a young journalist writing a book on L.A.'s upper crust— "The better sort of people" was how she phrased it— would be anxious to interview her. And she didn't waste any time when McDumont suggested lunch.

"The Ambassador? Yes, just ask René for my usual table. Thursday? Twelve-thirty? Delighted, Mr. McDumont. Until then, *au revoir*."

McDumont put down the receiver with a shrug. "Oh reveille yourself, toots. It's all set up," he said to Chandler. "Thursday. Now all I have to do is memorize Emily Post and practise my parley-vooing."

"You won't need any more French than the typical Los Angeles *nouveau riche*," Chandler said. "*Bonjour, enchanté*, and *au revoir* will see you through. Toss in *cherchez la femme* if you want to seem really sophisticated. You'll find that the waiters at the local French restaurants are either Italians or Mexicans; I once took a French businessman to lunch at one of them, and he nearly fell out of his chair when he heard them try to speak his language. As for restaurant etiquette, just do whatever Bethany Chambers does— except for powdering your nose and freshening up your lipstick."

On Thursday morning, Chandler told McDumont not to worry. "It's only lunch," he emphasized. "You eat lunch every day of the week, don't you?"

McDumont grimaced in a way intended to suggest that this was probably not the smartest thing to say to someone who had hoboed across large tracts of North America without consuming regular nourishment.

Chandler shrugged. "Well, you do *eat*, I've seen you. You eat quite a bit, actually, you certainly polished off those pancakes at the diner this morning. So how can you object to a very nice lunch at a very nice restaurant in a very nice hotel?"

"It's not that," McDumont snapped. "I don't know what very nice things to say to her."

Smiling now, Chandler punched him lightly on the shoulder. "Don't be silly, it won't be that difficult. Remember: you're a bright young fellow who's thinking about writing a book on the local social whirl. You're going to ask this Chambers woman about a few of the really posh families— I'd suggest the Huntingtons and the Carrolls— and then you're going to bring up the Bronsons, perhaps because you're a great admirer of Paul Bronson's ideas about economics. After that, just play it by ear."

"You can sing that in soprano," McDumont said. Then he chuckled. "Why did you have to pick my cab for your little adventure, anyway? What did I do to deserve it?"

"You were the right man, in the right place, at the right time. How much luckier can you get?"

Watching Bethany Chambers deftly tuck away a stevedore-sized portion of filet of sole, McDumont had to admit that Chandler had been right. She nodded sympathetically at McDumont's story about researching a book, and obviously assumed that she was the fount of all wisdom on the subject of local society. The really remarkable thing, McDumont decided, was her ability to shovel down the grub while yacking away to beat the band. At the moment, she was expounding on the differences between "old money" and "new money."

"Old money is so comforting, don't you think? It's simply there and it's sure of itself and nobody frets about it, that's not to say people don't *care* about it, of course they do, but they don't *worry* about it, do you see what I mean?" McDumont nodded and tried to think of something intelligent to say, but after a quick gobble Chambers was off again. "Now new money, that's something quite different. They *are* worried about hanging on to it, but of course they don't want to be *seen* to be worrying, so they spend it as if it were water, in the silliest ways sometimes, you wouldn't *believe* some of the things I have to write about in my column, pet birthdays and parties for utterly *impossible* relatives— they must import these people from outer space or the Midwest— you'd think with a Depression on, the new-money crowd would be a *little* more discreet, but no, they're going to let the rest of us *know* that they have it or die trying." She paused to skewer another forkful of sole.

McDumont decided that it was now or never. "Where would you put the Bronsons?" he asked.

"You mean people who come from old money back East but are

new to Los Angeles?" she said. "That's a good question." It also wasn't what McDumont had meant, but Chambers seemed ready to pick it up and run with it anyway. "When they're as intelligent and sophisticated as the Bronsons, it isn't a problem. They bide their time, they learn who is worth knowing and who isn't, and eventually they fit in very well. There are others, I won't name names, but I *could*, mind you, oh, yes I could, who act like Columbus discovering America, they're bringing civilization to us heathens and won't let us forget it. But the Bronsons aren't that sort, they've fit in nicely." A thought visibly passed across her brow. "Are they friends of yours?"

"No," McDumont answered, "but I have been impressed with Paul Bronson's understanding of current economic conditions. He seems much more intelligent than your typical businessman." McDumont mentally substituted "capitalist exploiter of the working class" for "businessman" and swore that he would donate his day's salary to the local branch of the Communist Party.

"Yes, I quite agree. It runs in the family, did you know that?" McDumont was just able to shake his head before she continued: "They're a very *intellectual* family. Paul paints and Estelle has her theatre group and Penny, well, quite the young authoress I understand, poems and stories in the little magazines and they *say* she's writing a novel that will make Main Street look like Rebecca of Sunnybrook Farm. And then of course she teaches at the settlement house. I gather that her mother isn't *entirely* happy about that; one does encounter a rougher element in such places."

"I should think so," McDumont agreed. "Although some of them are better than others— do you know which one she teaches at?"

Chambers thought for a moment before replying. "I imagine it's Harrison House. Estelle is on the board there and has hosted several benefits for them. Of course she's involved with any number of charities. I can't imagine how she finds the time, her schedule must be *so* exhausting."

McDumont realized that he'd never have a better chance to ask her about Paul Bronson, Jr. "Is there a son? Or am I confusing them with someone else?"

"There's a son, all right, but he's been a bit of a problem. Asked to leave several schools for reasons that one gathers were rather serious, given that the Bronsons *are* people of substance and influence, and the boy is goodness, what, not even a teenager yet. A shame, really, such a *nice* family, but these things do happen. What about *your* family, Mr. McDumont? You haven't said a word about yourself."

"There isn't much to say, really. Father lost all his shares in the 1929 crash, and so it's been journalistic work rather than law school for me." Not really lies, McDumont thought to himself; he had spent three months as a copy boy at the Toronto *Star*, he had written a few paragraphs for the newspaper's "Around Town" page before being fired for insubordination, and his father had owned a few shares of some worthless penny gold stock. As for law school— he'd been serious about it until he'd been a witness to a traffic accident at the age of 16, and had been asked to perjure himself by lawyers for both the defendant and the plaintiff.

"What a shame. What sort of journalism have you done?"

"I was at the Toronto *Star*, but currently I'm freelancing. I'm hoping I can interest a publisher in a book about Los Angeles society."

"I should think you'd have a very good chance, it's quite an interesting little part of the world." She glanced at her watch. "I must run, Mr. McDumont, deadlines and all that, it's been delightful talking to you. Thanks so much for lunch— it's always a pleasure to meet a refined young man, so many roughnecks on the streets these days. Ta-ta!" She rose and made a beeline for the door to the lobby.

As he paid the cheque, McDumont reflected that it hadn't really been so bad after all. And the business about the Bronson boy seemed to be cleared up. With any luck, Chandler's curiosity would be satiated and they could move on to something more interesting than the Bronsons' petty problems.

"Splendid work, Walter, just splendid. I think you may have missed your calling— an enterprising young gigolo can do very well in this part of the world." They were sipping draft Pilsener at Rumplemeyer's, a German-style beer garden two blocks south of the Ambassador.

McDumont grinned. "If I thought you were serious, I'd knock your glasses off and paste you one." He took a sip of the cold, pungent brew. "That's that, anyway."

"What do you mean, 'That's that'?"

"I mean there's no more mystery. After what the Bronsons went through with the kidnapping, they're naturally suspicious of chumps who come prowling around the family estate. Or did you get some hot scoop from that business-writer guy?"

"No, I can't say that I did. Mr. Pearl has a very low opinion of the oil business, not that I blame him. I don't think my story about looking for capital for a South American venture made much of an impression on him. Not that he didn't believe me, but the woods are full of chaps with preposterous schemes these days. Still, there was something odd about the way he spoke about the Bronsons— he actually went to Bronson's home to interview him for this series of articles, you see. What was it he said... yes, it was when he was describing the way Bronson responded to questions. He was very slow, not just careful as you would expect him to be, but it seemed to Pearl that he was very concerned about something else, something that preoccupied his thoughts even when he was responding to questions about general economic conditions. Pearl said it was disconcerting— like interviewing a person who had recently been bereaved."

"Well, maybe he'd recently been bereaved."

"Perhaps, but you would think he would have declined to be interviewed if he were that upset. No, I think there's something about the Bronsons that isn't quite right. What about the son, for example? The Boston paper runs stories about his never being found, and yet here he is living with his parents in Los Angeles. Doesn't that strike you as odd?"

"Maybe, but I bet the Bronsons are so sick of the whole business they don't want to talk to anybody about it. Hell, you're the boss, it's your money. Where do we go from here?"

"I think it's more a question of where *you* go from here. You said that the Bronson daughter, Penelope, teaches a course in writing at Harrison House. It seems to me that a young chap who's trying to write a book might want to take a course like that."

"It does, does it? Listen, why don't *you* take the course, you're the one who's so hot to be a writer."

"True. But you'll fit into the settlement house atmosphere better than I would, and I'm conceited enough to think that I don't have a great deal to learn from Miss Bronson— I'll bet *she* hasn't sold a story to *Black Mask*. I haven't mentioned this before, Walter, but when I was a young cub in England I did do a bit of literary journalism— reviewing in some of the literary quarterlies, that sort of thing. I'm not quite the authorial novice I may seem to be; in fact, if fate hadn't intervened, I might have become some sort of newspaper writer, cranking out editorials for the London *Times* or whatever. In any event, the people who would be taking this class are... probably more your sort of people than mine."

"That's the truth. There was a settlement house not too far away from where I grew up; you went there when there was nothing doing at the YMCA or the parks. I remember the social workers distributing Christmas hampers to the poor, you had to register for them and be interviewed to make sure you were poor enough to be eligible. Some old fart would come around and make sure your furniture was falling apart and there were the right number of bugs in your beds. Bunch of nosy parkers if you ask me."

"I'm sure you're right, Walter, but let's give Miss Bronson and Harrison House the benefit of the doubt. Perhaps it really will be a worthwhile class."

"Yeah, and maybe it'll snow tomorrow." McDumont looked around at the convivial crowd quaffing their steins of beer and said, "Just when

I was beginning to enjoy this job, too. Okay, I'll do it; but if Penelope Bronson is some young snot of a social worker, it's no dice."

"Fair enough. This looks like a bit of a long shot, I admit. But let's see how the class goes. Who knows, perhaps you'll even learn something."

Worthwhile or not, McDumont thought, Harrison House's "Advanced Creative Writing" class was one mixed-up group of people. There was definitely a genteel element present, some of whom wore frayed, visibly out-at-elbows garments as well as aloof, I'm-just-here-on-a-whim facial expressions; a couple of real down-and-outers, guys who smelled of cheap alcohol and were avoided by the others; and a small knot of young men and women in freshly pressed working clothes, who sprinkled phrases such as "class consciousness" and "bourgeois morality" into their very loud conversations with one another.

McDumont smiled to himself and returned to reading the *Story* magazine Chandler had bought him as preparation for the role of aspiring young writer. He was surprised by how good many of the stories were— he'd been expecting the kind of artsy, pretentious crap that most of the little literary magazines featured. But this was different: good, solid realistic writing that had something to say and said it with precision and directness. McDumont had always been a reader, had obtained a library card as soon as he was old enough, had even paid hard-earned cash to rent *Lady Chatterley's Lover* from what most Torontonians would have described as a "dirty" bookstore in the city's red-light district. Lately, though, he'd become dissatisfied with most of what was being published. Nobody seemed to realize that there was a Depression on. Millions of people had seen their jobs and their dreams of a happy life go up in smoke, and the whole social and economic system was being questioned in a way that would have been unimaginable before October, 1929.

A sudden lull in the conversation announced the arrival of their instructor. A young woman in horn-rimmed glasses, her black hair pulled severely back behind her head, dressed in clothes that McDumont decided were either conservative-but-tasteful or tasteful-but-conservative, walked briskly to the front of the room. She dumped a pile of books and a briefcase on the desk, and in sweeping cursive script wrote "Advanced Creative Writing" on the blackboard. Underneath this she printed "Penelope Bronson" in smaller capitals.

She turned to the group and said, "My name is Penelope Bronson, and I will be your instructor for this class. We will meet on Tuesdays and Thursdays, for two hours, for the next ten weeks. I want to emphasize that this is *not* a course in remedial English, or in basic composition. If there is anyone here who is looking for courses such as these, Harrison House does offer them." She surveyed the room with a sharp, almost aggressive glance. "Very well, then, let's begin. In a course such as this, motivation is very important. I'm going to be asking you to do quite a bit of reading as well as writing, and those who cannot keep up will be encouraged to leave." She paused again, then smiled quickly. "I do sound awfully *fierce*, don't I? But I really do care about literature, I care about it passionately, I suppose I get carried away. But what about you? What do *you* expect from this class?" she asked, looking at her students expectantly.

One of the young men McDumont had identified as a Communist-Party type spoke up in loud, strident tones. "I believe it is the writer's role to instill revolutionary consciousness in the working class," he avowed. "Only the overthrow of the capitalist system will allow the state to wither away and true democracy to be established in the United States. By portraying the social realities of the class struggle, the writer can help to bring about the triumph of the proletariat."

"Quite a responsibility, I should think," Bronson said. "Do you all agree with that?"

There was a general shifting and scraping of chairs, but no one seemed to have anything to say. McDumont couldn't stand it. "I don't agree," he said, and immediately wished he hadn't spoken.

"You don't?" Bronson queried. "You had better explain yourself, sir. You don't mean to tell me that there is a young would-be writer in this room who does not follow the party line on this question?"

McDumont felt his face turning red as he fumbled for a response. "What bothers me," he finally said, "is how everybody seems to know what the working class should do. Well, I'm from the working class, and I don't intend to leave my blood on a barricade just so some middle-class intellectual can lead a revolution." He paused and wiped his forehead. "I support the Communist Party, even though I'm not a member. I agree with most of their ideas, but I don't accept Lenin's theory about the vanguard role of the Party. The Soviet Union had its revolution in what, 1917, and seventeen years later they're still one hell of a long way from allowing the state to wither away."

"A Trotskyite," the young man who had spoken first sneered. "Takes the right position on everything except the need for violent revolution. When you come right down to it, just another kind of social fascist."

"Watch who you're calling a fascist," McDumont said heatedly. "If you ever came closer to the working class than ordering your servants around, I'll be a monkey's uncle."

Now it was the young man's turn to flush. "What do you know about it, you *lumpen* layabout? It's people like you who make it impossible to organize a revolution in this country!"

Penelope Bronson regarded them with amusement. "I think that's enough political discussion," she said. "No matter what your ideas are, you will need to be an effective writer to convince others to agree with you. And one of the best ways to learn is to take a piece of good writing and analyze it word by word to see how the author puts together sentences and paragraphs and then the piece as a whole. After that, you might want to try imitating the author's style when expressing your own ideas. And finally, of course, you hope that what you've studied becomes an organic part of you, a valuable addition to all the other thoughts and experiences that are part of what makes us unique as individuals. I thought that for our first exercise we might take a short story by Ernest Hemingway and try to see just how he achieves his effects."

She turned and picked up a stack of papers. "I've mimeographed copies of 'Soldier's Home,' one of Hemingway's most interesting stories, and I would like you to read it and analyze it." She began to pass out copies to those at the head of each row of desks. "Remember, what we're looking for is the way the story is put together, how it is constructed. I don't want to know how you *feel* about it; it may seem terribly unsympathetic on my part, but I really don't *care* how you feel about it— that's between you and the author. What I want to do is give you some idea of how good writing works, of how style and structure can work together to create something that goes beyond the dictionary meaning of the words."

The middle-aged woman to McDumont's right, whom he had immediately typed as one of the "genteel" element, abruptly raised her hand. "Where is inspiration in all of this?" she asked in a high, warbling voice. "I do not see how one can speak of great literature without acknowledging the role that inspiration plays in the lives of the great authors. For we poets, for example, the muse must be invoked, must be propitiated, must be prepared for by putting aside mundane pursuits and making ready to receive the truly spiritual forces that can be sensed by minds of the higher sort. I do not see why we should bother with this person Hemingway, whom I understand to be very dubious morally. What of Keats, Shelley, Browning... why can we not read them?"

Bronson smiled. "If you're going to make personal morality one of the main criteria for great literature, I'm afraid you have some unpleasant surprises awaiting you concerning Keats and Shelley, in particular. My own view is that inspiration comes, if it comes, as the result of hard work. All the authors you mentioned worked very hard on their poetry; if you look at their original manuscripts you can see how they experimented with different words and tried out different expressions before they were satisfied with what they'd written." She paused. "Goodness, I seem to be doing nothing but making speeches tonight. Are there any other questions or comments? No? Very well then. For our next class

I'd like you to read the Hemingway story and try to understand how it works, what he's doing, how he's getting to where he wants to go. Good evening. I'll see you on Thursday."

On his way out of the classroom, McDumont exchanged menacing glances with the ardent young Communists, who were talking about him in uncomplimentary terms. Well, the class might be full of jerks, but he had to admit that he was really impressed with Penelope Bronson. For a society babe, she was one smart cookie. Too bad about those horn-rimmed glasses; they made her look like some librarian, although you never could tell with women. McDumont had lost his virginity at the age of sixteen with a classmate who sang in the church choir, was president of his school's Red Cross Club, and generally acted like Miss Goody Two-Shoes, so he'd already learned not to try to tell a book by its cover. And there was nothing about glasses, even horn-rimmed ones, that said they couldn't be taken off.

"Hemingway, eh? You're a lucky fellow— I'd have thought Pearl Buck or some other do-gooder would have been more in the settlement-house line. But what do you make of Penelope Bronson? You've told me how smart she is, but we're not founding a literary society here. Do you think you're going to be able to get to know her more intimately?"

"For Christ's sake," McDumont said, "it wasn't exactly an intimate situation. What am I supposed to do, hit her over the head with a poetry book and carry her off into the sunset? I mean, I think she took what I said seriously, but she didn't ask me back to her place to look at a few etchings. Besides, why should it all be up to me to find out what's what with the Bronsons? What about your social connections and your important friends? Why don't you give them the third degree if you're so damned crazy about it?"

Chandler frowned. "Calm down, calm down. It may be news to you, old chap, but I'm not exactly on the Bronsons' social level. When my wife was well, she might have been able to arrange something; but she's very ill, and I'm afraid the Chandlers aren't up to much in the socializing department these days."

"I'm sorry, I didn't know..."

"That's quite all right. It's not something I like to broadcast, but my wife is a good deal older than I am and is in rather poor health. And I really don't care to discuss it further." He paused. "I'm sorry, Walter, I got a bit carried away there. Things are not well between my wife and myself. I haven't been a very good or even a very faithful husband lately, and I spend much of my time feeling either angry or guilty about the situation. We'd best avoid the matter entirely."

Neither said anything for the next few minutes. Then Chandler seemed to snap out of his depression as suddenly as he had fallen into it. "So, Hemingway it is, then. Now let me tell you how I view his use of a non-Latinate vocabulary..."

By Thursday McDumont felt that he knew "Soldier's Home" better than its author. He'd read *The Sun Also Rises* and *A Farewell to Arms* years before, had enjoyed them while finding them somewhat frivolous in their respective treatments of decadence and romance, but he'd missed most of Hemingway's short stories; and boy, was he impressed. "Soldier's Home" was a bleak story, its protagonist completely alienated from his post-war home and society, but there was also something about it that struck McDumont as exactly accurate, dead on target. The characters seemed absolutely real, their implicit moods and feelings flowing naturally out of the precise details of what they said and looked like, and finally you felt that in his world Hemingway had moved beyond questions of good and evil. This was how it *was*, no more or less than that, and while you could take it or leave it, there was no way that you could ignore it.

His classmates didn't seem to feel that way, however. On Thursday evening the class was dominated by the young Communists, who had obviously prepared a little ideological theatre for their fellow students' enlightenment. One of the radicals would make a statement about Hemingway's "individualism" or "elitism" or "incorrect understanding," after which the others would chime in with additional examples, or sometimes just fervent agreement. When they weren't running their little circus, the woman who had heard that Hemingway was morally "dubious" was deploring his lack of moral fibre; at one point she even asserted that he should "face up to his problems and be a man." McDumont tried to talk about how skilfully Hemingway used simple words to suggest complex realities, but he was immediately attacked for "bourgeois mystification" and other assorted ideological sins, and it didn't take him long to decide that there was no point in trying to express such an unpopular point of view.

Penelope Bronson took little part in the discussion, although her facial expressions suggested that she found much of it either painful or downright unbelievable. "That was certainly very interesting," she said at the end of the class. "I would like to see everyone participate, however"— McDumont thought she glanced at him— "even if your ideas are different from those of the others." She rubbed her forehead. "Now I think it's time for you to do some of your own writing. Hemingway doesn't seem to have appealed to most of you, but as an exercise I do want you to try to write about your own experiences in the way that he does: simple words, realistic speech, no complicated grammar to make it seem 'literary.' Don't worry about length, just take something that happened to you and see if you can write it down in that sort of style. Have your composition ready by Tuesday and we'll discuss what you learned in the process. Good evening."

McDumont went back to his room and started jotting down ideas. He had some dillies, no doubt about it. There was that teenaged hooker in Cairo, Illinois, taking everybody on at twenty-five cents a go; the kid who'd gotten his arm caught in some machinery hopping trains on the Prairies— McDumont had never seen so much blood; the Texas town where a tall sheriff with two gleaming pistols had told him to "get out of here before the sun goes down." Sure, but he couldn't write about stuff like that for a woman teacher he didn't know. What the hell, he'd write about the Toronto slums. He'd pretend that he was some hotshot author reliving his impoverished youth. Hemingway had written quite a bit about Toronto when he was a reporter at the *Star* in the 1920s, although most of it was about parts of the city that were foreign territory to McDumont. Maybe, just maybe, a young guy *could* show him a thing or two; anyway, he was going to try.

"Cabbagetown?" Chandler asked. "Why on earth was your neighbourhood called 'Cabbagetown'?" He looked around at Rumplemeyer's clientele. "I've always associated cabbages with Germans—we called them 'Krauts,' that's German for 'cabbage,' in the Great War, you know. Are there that many German immigrants in Toronto?"

"Toronto's got a little bit of everything," McDumont said, "but it doesn't have anything to do with the Germans. If you came from the English mill towns, you would have grown up in some crummy little house with a really tiny yard. People grew vegetables everywhere they could, and front yards were better since they usually got a little more sunlight." He snorted. "You could tell when somebody got promoted to foreman; they ripped out the vegetables and put in grass and a few flowers. They'd become respectable."

"Seems very sensible, when you put it like that." He chuckled. "You're certainly right about the middle class, though. My relatives would have starved to death rather than grow vegetables where the neighbours could see them." Chandler chuckled again and took a long draught from his stein. "Well, I don't know that Holmes and Watson have anything to fear from us, Walter, but I do know that I've learned a lot about all sorts of things since we started on this. What do you think?"

"It's been a learning experience, all right. But how much longer do you want to keep on with it? I don't see anything funny or weird about the Bronsons."

"No, you're probably right. Still, in for a penny, as you so nicely put it." Chandler glanced at his watch. "I must go, I'm afraid, and you have a spot of writing to do. Shall we meet here for dinner on Tuesday?"

"You're on," McDumont replied. "Cabbagetown, here I come— how does that song about California go, 'Right back where I started from'? I know what it was like, that's for sure; I just hope I don't make a fool out of myself trying to write about it."

CHAPTER THREE

McDumont spent most of the weekend writing about growing up in Cabbagetown. He was surprised by how smoothly his recollections flowed once he had jotted down a few concrete images from the past. Using short, crisp sentences consciously modelled on those in Hemingway's short stories, he wrote of what it had been like to grow up poor in the Toronto slums:

The people get orders for clothes at the relief office.

These are taken down to the central clothing depot and are filled by a man behind a wooden partition, who glances at the order forms and retreats behind rows of high shelves. The room smells like an army quarter-master's stores, and the recipients line up in front of the wicket. There are benches around the walls where shoes may be tried on. These are unnecessary as none of the shoes ever fit. The attendant ties up the order in brown wrapping paper and the recipient hurries from the office and down the street, looking straight ahead until he is clear of the neighbourhood.

He ate dinner with Chandler at Rumplemeyer's. Chandler read McDumont's assignment and was very complimentary; McDumont was flattered, tried to be modest, but still found himself talking on and on about what a wonderful experience it had been to try to recapture his past. He knew that what he had written wasn't entirely his own, that it was to a large extent derived from Hemingway and lacked the emotional reactions which had made the real-life Walter McDumont an angry young rebel rather than the cool, detached observer of his essay; but he still felt a sense of accomplishment that was incredibly exhilarating.

He talked so much to Chandler that he was almost late for class. Walking briskly, McDumont turned the corner onto the block where Harrison House was located and stopped short. A black sedan was just pulling up behind the black limousine that was parked in front of the settlement house. The sedan braked harshly to a halt and the driver jumped out. It was Larry, the cop who had given McDumont such a hard time outside the Bronson estate. McDumont ducked down behind a trash can and cautiously poked his head out.

Penelope Bronson was about halfway up the steps when Larry caught up to her. Larry said something— something she didn't much like from the expression on her face— but she didn't reply. Larry raised his right hand and slowly, almost obscenely, drew his index finger across her throat. She glared at him, but still said nothing. Larry turned and walked back to the sedan, a big grin on his face. Bronson shrugged her shoulders, looked up at the sky, and then went into the building. The black sedan roared past the limousine, saying goodbye with two derisive bleats of its horn.

McDumont shook his head. What in the name of God was that all about? He wished he'd been able to hear what Larry had said. It looked like the son of a bitch was propositioning her, but was that really very likely? Penelope Bronson wouldn't give a guy like Larry the time of day, you could tell from the way she looked at the man, as though he'd crawled out of a swamp. But what really bothered McDumont, bothered him more than he felt comfortable admitting, was the way Larry had spoken to her and touched her; there was contempt there, and something between them that allowed the policeman to treat her like a cheap tramp.

So what do I know? McDumont said to himself. Maybe she is, maybe she isn't, it's no skin off my nose. Just the same, he'd like to get Larry alone in a dark alley one of these nights. He'd like that one hell of a lot.

Class was torture. Every time McDumont looked at Penelope Bronson, he saw the big cop slowly drawing his finger across her throat. Once she called on him, asking him something about what he had written, but he couldn't get the words out, couldn't focus on the handwritten sheets of paper in front of him. She made light of it, saying, "Your mind must be somewhere else tonight," and moved on to another student, but he noticed her glancing at him frequently during the remainder of the class.

At the end of class, when he handed in his assignment, she looked at the name on the first page and said, "Thank you, Mr. McDumont." He replied, "You're welcome" automatically, like a dunce; she must think he was a complete jerk for Christ's sake; it wasn't as if he was doing her a favour. How dumb could a guy get? Next thing he'd be bringing her an apple, maybe then she'd let him be teacher's pet.

He went back to his room and, after tossing and turning for a while, finally fell asleep. He dreamed about a long string of freight cars slowly clanking across the Prairies... grain hoppers swaying through endless fields of wheat... sun glaring down on a tiny figure who ran hard along the tracks behind them but could never catch up to the slowly receding train.

McDumont had never seen Chandler look surprised before. "Larry did *what?* Are you sure you saw him do that?" He put down his coffee cup and stared at McDumont.

"It wasn't dark yet and they were standing on the steps. I could see them perfectly. She could have been a hooker walking the streets as far as Larry was concerned."

Chandler looked around the Fremont Street diner and then took a long sip of coffee. "What about Larry's partner, Lou? Where was he while this was happening?"

"I didn't see him. I don't think he was in the car. Anyway, it wasn't cop business. It was something between Penelope Bronson and Larry, something that gave Larry the right to touch her like that without her trying to stop him."

Chandler shrugged. "There could be something between them, you know. There are some very... odd... relationships in this town between bored, wealthy women and men from the lower classes. Some of the film stars, even, if the gossip columnists know what they're talking about... "

"No," McDumont interrupted, "I am not going to take Bethany Chambers out to lunch at the Ambassador Hotel, or anywhere else, and ask her about it. If you want to go down that road, the pleasure is going to be all yours."

Chandler chuckled. "What a shame, Walter, when the two of you were getting on so well. No, not to worry. I suspect it's merely your friend Larry's incredibly boorish manners coming to the fore here."

"I hope so. But you wouldn't think that was all there was to it, if you'd seen it. I've seen how cops treat hookers, and that was exactly the way he treated her. She took it, and she's not the type of woman who would do that unless she figured she had to."

"Could he be blackmailing her? That's always a possibility with people who have money."

McDumont thought it over. "Maybe," he said reluctantly. "Hell, it could be anything. Maybe Larry is a former student who has a crush on her. Maybe that's what it is."

Chandler looked at him appraisingly. "Unlike any of her current students, of course."

McDumont blushed. "Why would I have a crush on some society dame who wouldn't give me the time of day? No percentage in that. She comes to class in a limousine, for Christ's sake. I can just see myself asking her for a date— 'Excuse me, Miss Bronson, would you like to down a few cold ones at the Shanty Lounge? Or would a burger at the White Tower be more to your liking?' Yeah, no percentage in that at all."

"Come on, old chap, I was only joking. In any case, this business with Larry comes under the heading of what the more melodramatic fictional detectives would describe as 'The plot thickens!' I think we may be on to something here."

McDumont stared into his coffee cup. "Maybe you're right," he said after a while. "But I'm beginning to think I don't want to know what it is."

As it turned out, McDumont didn't have to ask Penelope Bronson for a date.

At the end of Thursday's class, during which the young Communists were if anything more talkative than usual, she asked him to stay behind for a moment. When the rest of the class had left, she said, "I was extremely impressed with your essay, Mr. McDumont. You're a very talented writer. Is this the first piece of serious writing you've ever done?"

He couldn't help blushing. "I did work on a newspaper once. I wrote a few things there, but nothing much, really."

"Well, I think you have a definite gift for it. Are you going to send your essay out for publication? I think you should. There's a lot of interest in this sort of thing at the moment."

"No, I hadn't thought about it. Do you really think it's that good? You're not just being polite, are you?"

She smiled. "If you could see what I said about most of the other essays, you'd know that I don't believe in 'just being polite' where good writing is concerned." She checked her watch, and looked him directly in the eye. "There's a coffee shop just down the street and I'm positively famished. Come and keep me company while I eat something."

Penelope Bronson ordered a Western sandwich and a pot of tea. McDumont wasn't hungry, but he ordered a cup of coffee so that he'd have something to do with his hands.

He had to admit that he was a little afraid of this friendly, chatty young woman who had replaced the no-nonsense teacher of creative writing. Talk about false pretences— here he was, spying on her, making like a detective to satisfy the silly fantasies of some would-be mystery writer, and she was treating him like he was a hotshot young author. To make it even worse, he could now see that behind the glasses and the professional manner there was a very attractive female sitting across from him, and yet he didn't dare endanger this new relationship by coming on to her.

And she certainly wasn't coming on to him, at least not in any way that he was used to. She was simply being very friendly, and he hoped he could respond to that as someone who wasn't exactly flush with friends, rather than like a wise guy on the make.

Bronson didn't say much while polishing off her sandwich. That accomplished, she poured herself a cup of tea and leaned back against their booth's padded banquette. "That was just what I needed. Now you are going to have to talk to me, Mr. McDumont. I want to know what you've been doing since growing up in Toronto. I'm particularly curious as to how you developed such an effective literary style. Over to you, sir."

"There isn't much to tell. I always have loved to read, but I haven't done a lot of writing. I left school at sixteen, worked as a copy boy at the Toronto *Star*, got fired when I wouldn't take a group of snotty high-school kids on a tour, and had a bunch of stupid, dead-end jobs after that. Last year I decided to bum my way out West hopping freights; you can get work on the prairies at harvest time. But the winter was tough and I got stuck in a work camp in British Columbia, so this year I decided I'd try the States. And I haven't done any better as far as finding work goes, although I guess I have had some pretty strange experiences."

"Strange? In what way?"

McDumont blushed. "Some I couldn't tell you about, they were things I'd never seen before and I hope I never see again. Things people do when they're at the end of their rope and they have nowhere to go. Oh, hell, you know what I mean. I don't have to spell it out for you."

"I don't know about that." She poured herself another cup of tea and then looked at him steadily. "Let's face it, Mr. McDumont, I would like the world to treat me as a very wise, sophisticated woman, but most of what little I know about human behaviour is taken from books. I attended a very proper private school for young ladies, followed by a very proper and emphatically non-co-educational small college that viewed men as dangerous if unavoidable nuisances. Since then, I've done my best to remedy those deficiencies in my education, but it hasn't been easy."

She sipped at her tea. "Actually, it's been pretty goddamned difficult," she sniffed as tears gathered at the corners of her eyes. "Excuse me. Why am I saying this to you, why should you care? Let me get a handkerchief and I'll be all right." She dabbed at her eyes with a square of white linen.

"But I do care." Jesus, where did that come from? Was it true? Well, he'd said it. Now he had to live with it.

She looked puzzled. "Do you mean what you just said?" she asked. "Or are you just being kind to a damsel in distress?"

"I'm not being anything. What I said, it just came out. You want me to think about it, I could probably come up with some song and dance about how you're a good teacher and kind to bums in your class and so on, but then I would be trying to con you. No, take it or leave it, I don't know anything about you except that I think you're okay. If that's a crime, sue me."

Bronson smiled. "All I'm going to say is 'Thank you, Mr. McDumont, for a very pleasant and very surprising evening.' And then I'm going to very demurely shake your hand, and ask if I can give you a lift anywhere."

"I'd just as soon walk," he said, shaking her hand. "I've got a lot to think about."

It was a long walk back to his rooming house on Figueroa Street, but McDumont felt like a long walk. He wasn't sure what he was feeling, but whatever it was made him want to kick up his heels in the air and break into song. Puppy love, that's all you could call it, and he didn't care how goddamned silly it was. It felt great. Sure, Penelope Bronson was just being nice to him, but what the hell, it had been a long time since he'd had anything to do with a woman who didn't immediately let him know that she was selling it, giving it away, or saving it until she got married.

McDumont knew he was a good-looking guy. Women came after him and he usually made the most of his opportunities. But he was also aware that things like that didn't have anything to do with who he was or what he wanted to become. This was different. This was about liking somebody, getting to know them, maybe becoming friends.

It took him almost three hours to walk home. Tired as he was, he thought about Penelope Bronson for a long time before he got to sleep.

Chandler was delighted. "You've surprised me before, Walter, but this time I'm amazed. You have to ask her out, you know— this is just too good an opportunity to pass up."

"She's not a bloody 'opportunity,' damn it, all she's doing is being nice to me. I don't see why I have to ask her for a date— that could queer things. Maybe it really is just my writing that interests her."

Chandler stared into his beer stein. "Perhaps. I'm not saying that

Miss Bronson is anxious to make closer acquaintance with your manly charms. But if you don't do anything more than have coffee with her after class, you'll be missing a marvellous chance to find out more about the Bronsons."

"Not necessarily, Ray. I can always ask her about herself and then bring the conversation around to the family. That's a normal thing to do."

"That's a possibility, but it would be even better if you managed to see her at home. We've had a couple of indications already that there's something odd about the Bronson household; and this is probably the best chance we'll ever have to see what things are really like. No, I want you to ask her out on a date, and I want you to pick her up at home. I'll rent you a car; you can tell her you borrowed it from a friend."

"You want a lot of things tonight, don't you? Maybe they're things I don't want to do. Or maybe you'd like to come along. You can play the organ while I make like your pet monkey and do tricks. No, Ray, listen, this isn't just a job any more. Penelope Bronson is a decent human being, she could be in some trouble, and I'm not going to spy on her. Not for you, not for ten bucks a day, not for anything or anybody!" McDumont was almost shouting, and several of Rumplemeyer's patrons were staring at him.

"Calm down, calm down." Chandler raised his eyes to the ceiling and frowned. "Listen, Walter, think about the way the situation is likely to develop. Let's say you and Penelope Bronson get into the habit of having coffee after class. What happens when the class is over, which it will be in a little more than a month? That will be the end of it. You'll probably never see her again. And how intimate a conversation can you have in a coffee shop? I tell you what will happen: you'll have a delightful time discussing your favourite books and authors, and you won't find out anything about the rest of her family."

Chandler paused and cleared his throat. "I'm sorry if my curiosity offends you all of a sudden, but the object of this exercise is to find out if there is anything in the Bronsons' past that they're trying to hide. And you won't find that out if you and Penelope Bronson spend all of your time together extolling the merits of Ernest Hemingway."

About thirty seconds went by before McDumont said anything. When he did speak, the words came out slowly, as though they were difficult to say.

"You're probably right. But I do feel bad about taking her out under false pretences, as if I were an undercover cop or something. If she ever finds out what I'm doing, I'm going to feel like a real bastard."

"But you like her, don't you? You really are interested in getting to know her better, right? If you weren't helping me with my little game, you wouldn't hesitate to ask her for a date, would you?"

McDumont groaned. "No, but this is different. Jesus, I don't know what I think. All right, I'll give it a try. But don't be surprised if she says nix— for all I know she's just kind to stray writers and stray dogs."

"I don't think so," Chandler replied. "I have a feeling that Miss Bronson needs help. And if you do get to know her better, you could be the one she asks to help her."

"Yeah, sure," said McDumont, "and maybe we'll all become famous writers, have our books made into movies, and live the life of Riley in sunny California."

Chandler grinned. "Tell me, old bean, can you think of any reason why we shouldn't?"

Next Tuesday's class was agony, too, but at least it was for an entirely different reason than the previous Thursday's. Penelope Bronson asked McDumont to read his essay to his fellow students, and the young-Communist element was ferociously critical. "Petty-bourgeois sentimentality" was about the kindest thing they had to say for it, with "absence of class consciousness" turning up so often that McDumont suspected it must be the latest slogan popularized by the Communist Party newspaper, *The Daily Worker*.

Some of his older classmates, on the other hand, found his essay "depressing" and "cheerless," although there were also a couple of positive comments about how realistic and believable a description of Cabbagetown he'd written. Penelope Bronson certainly wasn't affected by what most of her students had to say; at the end of the class she remarked, "It wouldn't surprise me if Mr. McDumont became a very successful author," and then glared furiously at the audible sniggers this produced from the young radicals.

Afterwards, at the coffee shop, she was still angry about the class's reactions. "They're so disgustingly predictable," she said as she chased a tea bag around a pot of hot water. "Not an original thought in the bunch of them, just clichés and catch-phrases that they've picked up from lazy minds and sloppy thinkers. The art-for-art's-sake crowd are as bad as the would-be proletarians— they're all living in dream worlds that don't have anything to do with life as it is."

She stopped and made a visible effort to collect herself. "That's a laugh, 'Life as it is.' What do *I* know about it? You must think I'm as misguided as the rest of them. What *do* you really think, for that matter? You can tell me, I won't bite your head off. I'm just a fellow-travelling liberal with a guilty conscience."

McDumont smiled. "Anyone who thinks I might make it as a writer is okay by me, you better believe that."

He took a sip of coffee. "But when you're poor, you learn right away not to be honest with people who have more money and power and social position than you do. The welfare workers who came to our house, most of them were nosing around because that was their job; they were supposed to nose around. But some of them gave you a big song-and-dance act, they really cared about you and wanted to help you, and they were the ones you really had to watch out for." He paused, started to pick up his coffee cup, then put it down again.

"Maybe some of them really were sincere about helping people, I don't know; but what would happen is, they'd be so nice that people would confide in them, tell them things they shouldn't have told them.

Some single mother on welfare, say, would admit that she did know where the father of her children was. Then welfare would go after the guy for child-support payments, next thing you know the guy would come around and beat the living hell out of the woman before skipping town for good. So after a while, you learned to keep your mouth shut— what people didn't know, you couldn't get hurt with."

He could see that he'd shocked her, even though he'd tried to soft-pedal how he felt.

"So there's nothing to be done, then? The poor can't be helped? Those of us born with silver spoons in our mouths should just go on our hedonistic way, eating and drinking and being merry until we die?"

"No, I wouldn't go that far. But you have to realize that most of the problems poor people have could be solved with one very simple thing: money. When I was a kid, I didn't steal stuff because I liked stealing; I stole because I couldn't afford to buy what I wanted. It was either go without or take it. So I took it. My mother worked her fingers to the bone keeping a roof over our heads and food on the table, but there was never enough money for clothes, let alone things like candy bars or going to the movies."

He paused, and looked at her without blinking. "I don't think I've ever told this to anyone— my mother never even knew about it. But when I was a teenager, a bunch of us got arrested for vandalizing a freighter in Toronto harbour. The judge really read us the riot act, told us we'd be put in reform school if we ever did anything like that again. He really put the fear of god in me. And since then, I've walked the straight and narrow— except for a couple of times when I've been thrown in jail for vagrancy."

"Vagrancy?" she repeated. "I thought that's what they did with derelicts and hoboes." She blushed slightly. "I'm sorry, I didn't mean to imply that you were that sort of person."

McDumont laughed. "Well, you might as well, that's the sort of person I am. These days, a lot of places use the vagrancy laws to protect themselves against what they call 'derelicts' and 'hoboes.' They pass a law that says you have to have some big sum of money in your pocket— fifty or a hundred dollars, maybe, which most people wouldn't carry around with them— and then they arrest us bums for not having that much money in our possession. You spend a few nights in a cell, jammed in like sardines with a bunch of other guys, and then they kick you out with a warning that they'll send you to a prison farm or something if they catch you again."

"But surely that wouldn't stand up in court," Bronson interrupted. "It's an obvious case of discriminating against people because they aren't wealthy."

"Sure," McDumont said sarcastically, "next time it happens I'll get my lawyer to take it to the Supreme Court." She bit her lip and looked down at her plate. "I'm sorry, Miss Bronson, I know you didn't mean anything by it. I'm just a loudmouthed jerk who isn't used to civilized conversations."

"No," she said after a moment, her voice almost irritated now, "that's certainly not true. And for goodness' sake don't call me 'Miss Bronson.' I'm not your maiden aunt. I'm only two years older than you are."

McDumont was surprised. "How do you know that? I didn't say when I was born in my essay."

"I looked at your registration card, if you must know." She blushed again. "Anyway, you can call me 'Penny,' that's what my friends call me, and I'm going to call you 'Walter.' Or do you prefer 'Walt'?"

"Walter is fine." He stared at her. "Penny, I know I'm not the kind of guy you're used to, but could we go out on a date some time? I bet you're really busy and everything, but maybe some time in the fu..."

"I thought you'd never ask," she interrupted. "What about this Friday?" When he nodded, she said, "Perhaps it would be easier if we met somewhere. My family lives in a very out-of-the-way place, it's right at the end of a street called Mountain Drive..."

"Oh, I know where that is," McDumont said. She looked surprised, so he said the first thing that came into his head. "I had a temporary job on a landscaping crew out there not too long ago. I know where it is."

"You'll have to check in at the gate, but I'll make sure they know you're coming. Why don't you come by at seven... if you're sure you won't have any trouble finding it."

"I'll be there." He paused and smiled. "Should I wear a tie and jacket, or do you want to go slumming?"

"You'd better wear the tie. My parents are... well, let's just say that if you don't, they're liable to send you around to the servant's entrance. You can always take it off later." She giggled. "Now that really does sound forward, doesn't it?"

McDumont laughed. "But you won't get the jacket off me without a struggle. You know, Penny, you're what my Yorkshire ancestors would have called 'a bit of all right.' We're going to have a good time on Friday."

"Yes," she said, "I think we are."

McDumont looked around at Rumplemeyer's lunchtime crowd and said, "I did it."

"Did what?"

"Asked her for a date."

"And? Come on, get on with it."

"She even said she thought I'd never ask. I'm going to pick her up at her home tonight."

"Splendid! Simply splendid. After we've finished eating, I'll rent you a car— there's a place not far from here. Where do you think you'll go?"

"I thought I'd better ask you about that. She knows I'm just an average Joe, she wouldn't expect me to take her to some fancy night club. But I can't take her to some flea trap, either— she's a good kid, but I don't know if she's ready for a dump like the Shanty Lounge."

"I shouldn't think so. I don't think of myself as being excessively fastidious, but I do prefer a place where they wash the glasses before reusing them. Let me see... one of the Central Avenue jazz clubs might be a possibility. It's a Negro neighbourhood, not an area you'd want to wander about in, but the jazz clubs cater to white audiences. How does that sound?"

"Sounds great to me. But what if Penny doesn't like jazz?"

"If she's the young intellectual you've told me about, she'll either really like it or feel that she is supposed to like it, so that shouldn't be a problem. No, the more I think about it, it's the perfect kind of place for you to go; you can dance, you can drink, and the ones I've been in were so dimly lit that a little hand-holding and so on and so forth seems to be positively encouraged."

McDumont chuckled. "Don't get me wrong, Ray, but that isn't the kind of joint I can imagine *you* going to. I'd figure you to be more the Paul Whiteman type, you know, music for tired businessmen whose wives want to be trotted around the dance floor."

"As you probably aren't aware, you arrogant young twit, Paul Whiteman gave musicians such as Bix Beiderbecke and Frankie Trumbauer a wonderful opportunity to play for millions of people. Why, he has Jack Teagarden in his current band, although I don't suppose that would impress you."

"Okay, you've made your point, you're hep. Any particular place in mind, oh great jazz authority?"

Chandler thought about it. "I think the Sapphire Club would do very nicely. It's a bit on the raucous side, but I've been there with some rather conventional people and they found it quite entertaining. One suspects that the Negroes who run the place are putting on something of an act for their white visitors, but it's still tremendous fun. Yes, the Sapphire Club should be just right."

"Lead me to it," McDumont said with a laugh. "One way or another, I think this is going to be a night to remember."

CHAPTER FOUR

The guard at the gate knew that he had seen McDumont somewhere before. But he didn't know where, and that bothered him. He did know he hadn't seen McDumont in a sporty red roadster, and this seemed to bother him even more.

"Yes, sir?"

"Walter McDumont to see Miss Bronson."

"Yes, sir. I'm sorry, sir, the name again was...?"

"Walter McDumont. *Mister* McDumont." He tried to put a little force into it, even though his nerves were screaming for him to slam the car into reverse and get the hell out of there.

"Yes, sir." The guard walked back toward the booth, then stopped and began to rub his chin with a large, meditative paw. Jesus H. Christ, thought McDumont, it isn't that I can't get to first base with the Bronsons; I can't even get up to the plate.

He put his head out the window. "I'm in a bit of a hurry, I'd appreciate it if you could be quick about it." Who was that? Ronald Colman, Leslie Howard, some la-di-da aristocratic twit letting a member of the lower classes know who was who. If I weren't in this up to my neck, McDumont thought, I'd be ashamed of myself. He glanced down at his snazzy new attire. But I'm not myself, that's for damned sure.

His new self now seemed to be aces with security, in any event. The guard trotted off to his booth, spoke into the phone, and nodded his head a few times. The gates opened smoothly, noiselessly, as if in deference to McDumont's handsome new image. The roadster accelerated up the drive, and then the gates closed quietly behind it.

Penny was at the door. "Hello, Walter. It is Walter, isn't it? Or have you sold your soul to the devil and turned yourself into the sort of young man my parents expect me to go out with?"

McDumont blushed. "Can we go? I don't know how much longer I can stand the strain of holding up these clothes. And if you want to see me act really devilish, just keep bugging me about the new threads." He paused and wiped his forehead. "I'm sorry. I'm a little nervous. You've got to remember that I'm not really what I'm trying to look like."

"Well, you look very nice, whoever you are. And no, we can't leave without introducing you to my parents. Come along, they won't bite."

Easy for you to say, McDumont thought as he was introduced to Estelle and Paul Bronson, but I think the lady of the household could sink her teeth into me without batting an eye. Estelle Bronson obviously did not number any people named McDumont within her circle of acquaintances, and seemed disinclined to change that attitude. That this very dubious young man was not familiar with her Toronto friends appeared to strike her as a perfectly natural, as well as thoroughly damning, phenomenon, and she clearly interpreted his confession that he was "between jobs, for the moment" as conclusive proof of gross social inferiority. "I hope you know what you're doing, Penelope," Estelle said with a contemptuous fling of her head as she left the room.

Paul Bronson, on the other hand, although somewhat reserved at first, was friendly enough, and seemed genuinely interested in McDumont's experiences as a citizen of the road. McDumont had suggested to Penny that they might gloss over his chequered background with some little white lies, but she had insisted on telling her parents the truth. "Mother isn't going to like you anyway, your blood isn't blue enough, and Daddy couldn't care less about where people come from— you should hear him go on about the idle rich and their worthless children. In his own very Republican way he's something of a social critic." McDumont could see now that she was right, although this still didn't make him feel any better about the serious deception he was playing on her, and on her family.

"You're going to think this is ridiculous, Mr. McDumont," Bronson said in a confiding tone, "but I've often thought that I'd like to put aside the hurly-burly of this social and economic rat race and go sample the kinds of adventures you're having. I wasn't born with a silver spoon in my mouth, you know— I waited tables in the university dining room and worked two jobs during the summer in order to get through college— and Estelle and I had some lean years before things began to work out. Oh, I know it's a pipe dream, one of those the grass-is-always-greener fantasies, but there are times when I could leave all this behind and get out there and rough it. I really could."

McDumont chuckled. "Well, sir, if you ever decide to do that, I hope you'll consider trading places with me until you change your mind. I'll even throw in some free lessons about how to hop a freight and which towns have the best soup kitchens."

"You don't think I'm serious," Bronson said, frowning slightly. "But I mean it. All this"— he gestured expansively with both hands— "doesn't mean anything more than a few bodily comforts, for sale to anyone who can pay the price. It's just a place, more comfortable than most, but just a place."

"Speaking of places," Penny said, "Walter and I should be going. We won't be late."

"You just have a good time, honey." Bronson spoke thoughtfully, as if such a conventional remark might contain deeper wisdom. "As if he'd recently been bereaved," the business reporter Chandler talked to had said, and now McDumont thought he'd caught a glimpse of what that meant; there was something melancholic and uneasy, something you couldn't quite put your finger on, in Paul Bronson's conversation. Bronson had lost something, and he didn't look as though he expected to get it back.

Central Avenue was jumping. On the blocks south of Washington Boulevard the Club Alabam, the Turban Lounge, the Last Word, and the Down Beat competed for business with aggressive doormen who commanded squads of satin-jacketed car jockeys. The doormen and the car jockeys were all black, those getting out of the cars all white. Los Angeles's Chief of Police had publicly declared that the city was not ready for what he'd called "mixed audiences," and so white visitors to this jazz ghetto were zealously protected from having to sit next to blacks— at the same time as they listened to music played by black musicians, dined on food prepared by black chefs, and drank liquor served by black waiters.

Those who owned and managed the clubs, on the other hand, were all whites, although most of them certainly hadn't been selected for their executive skills. The recent repeal of the Prohibition Amendment had put hordes of liquor-smugglers and strong-arm men out of work; and while organized crime looked for new worlds to conquer, it continued to look after its own by investing dollars and muscle in the booming night club business.

McDumont pulled up in front of the Sapphire Club. "I've never been here, but a friend of mine recommended it. What do you think? We don't have to go here."

"Oh, look," Penny said, reading the Sapphire Club's pulsating neon marquee, "'Curtis Mosby and His Kansas City Blue Blowers.' They're wonderful. I've heard them before, here or somewhere else. Let's go in, this is one of the nicer spots."

"So you're a fan of Mr. Mosby's," McDumont said after they had been seated at a tiny table for two and begun to nibble on their gin and tonics. "And this must be him now." The musicians were slowly filtering on stage, led by a tall, angular man who passed out sheet music and spoke briefly to the other members of the band before sitting down at his drum kit. He picked up the microphone and grinned broadly at the audience.

"Good evening, gentlemen and ladies, he-cats and she-cats and all those cats in between. We'd like to kick things off with a little blues I wrote on my way over to the club tonight, don't even have a name yet, what say we call it 'Central Avenue Blues' because Central Avenue is where we are and Central Avenue is where it's at." He nodded to the bass player. "Glide for me, Clyde."

The bass laid down a slow, walking tempo quickly picked up by Mosby's shimmering brushes and the pianist's heavy block chords.

Then trumpet, sax, and trombone joined in with simple, repetitive statements that hadn't yet decided to become a melody, but weren't going to let that stop them from commenting on what was happening. After the horns' progressively more intense unison passages had culminated in a joyous collective shout, they suddenly stopped playing and the pianist began to sing:

*I was down on Central Avenue,
Saw my baby with another guy.
I was down on Central Avenue,
Saw my baby with another guy.
She said "Honey, how you doin'?
This here's the preacher, Mister Sly."*

The other members of the band chuckled, hooted, shook their heads. "You better go home, girl," Mosby interjected to general laughter. "That preacher never saw the inside of no church 'cept when he was robbin' the poor box."

*I said "Mister Sly, Mister Sly,
You don't look like no preacher man."
I said "Mister Sly, Mister Sly,
You don't look like no preacher man."
"I can't help that," said Mister Sly,
"I'm doin' the best that I can."*

Another chorus of remarks, this time dominated by "Uh-huh" and "Uh-oh," greeted the second verse. "That man going to need to preach," yelled Mosby. "He going to need to preach the best sermon he ever preached in his life!"

*I said "Baby, baby, baby,
Why do you do me thisaway?"*

I said "Baby, baby, baby,
Why do you do me thisaway?"
She said "What you want from me, sugar,
When you don't bring home no pay?"

"That's it," Mosby said. "You don't pay the freight, you don't carry no weight."

So I shot 'em down like dogs,
Wasn't nothing else this man could do.
So I shot 'em down like dogs,
Wasn't nothing else this man could do.
You want to make your mama do right,
Keep her 'way from Central Avenue.

"That's right, that's right," was the collective verdict of the band as the song ended with flurries from the horns and a crescendo of drum rolls. "Mr. Roosevelt Sykes on piano," Mosby announced. "Roosevelt Sykes, let's give him a nice hand." The audience applauded wildly, with war whoops, whistles, and the odd "Bravo!" adding to the general clamour.

"You're right," McDumont said as Mosby introduced the next number, "that's one great band." He turned toward Penny. She was frowning. "What's wrong?" he asked. "Don't you feel well?"

"It's kind of sad, don't you think? All that business about the woman cheating on her man and the man killing her and her lover— I mean I know that blacks haven't had an easy time of it in this country, but you'd think that they wouldn't want to dwell on that sort of thing." Her voice was tense, almost strident. "And why is it that it's always a woman who gets shot or stabbed or beaten up or slapped around? Does this make men feel better or something? Does it make *you* feel better? Does it do something for the masculine ego?"

McDumont stared at her. Penny was saying something very important to him— no, that wasn't it, she was saying something very important to her, something that he just happened to be overhearing. The image of Larry slowly drawing his finger across her throat slammed into his mind. Was that what she was referring to? He didn't know her well enough to understand what she was talking about. But he had to answer her somehow.

"No, it doesn't make me feel better. And I don't think you're right about that 'It's always the woman' stuff— you listen to Bessie Smith and Ma Rainey, they sing about how bad all the men they've ever known are. Not that two wrongs make a right. But everybody has times when they feel like singing the blues, that's what you do, you sing about it. It doesn't mean you're going to go out and kill somebody."

He paused. "And if you don't think blacks should be so concerned with such things, I'd like to take you back to some of the nice little old Southern states I've bummed through. I'd like to show you people living in conditions that make my good old Anglo-Saxon slum in Toronto look like easy street." He tried for a lighter tone. "We're pretty good at making speeches to each other, aren't we? You and your high artistic standards, me and my proletarian tirades. Maybe we could put together a vaudeville act or something."

Penny didn't say anything for some time. Then she looked at him very intently. "You're an awfully nice person, Walter. But you don't know me at all. And if you knew who and what I really was, you wouldn't want to know me."

"I'll be the judge of that," he replied. McDumont tried to be flippant, even though he felt as if he'd just been punched in the stomach, felt as though there were something evil and vicious at the table with them. But he had to pretend she was just being flirtatious. "I think we're ready for another drink." He looked around anxiously for a waiter, doing his best to avoid the frank, almost mocking stare of this complicated person he was beginning to care so much about. Who the hell was she? And what the hell was he supposed to be to her? 'I'm damned if I know,' he said to himself. 'I'm damned if I know.'

"We're going to take a little break, ladies and gentlemen, and then we'll be right back." As Mosby and the other musicians filed off the bandstand, McDumont thought that he had better ask Penny if she wanted to leave. Her aggressive self-deprecation had been replaced by silent withdrawal. He guessed that this masked thoughts she couldn't, or wouldn't, share with him— not that a night club was the place for true confessions. They should have gone somewhere else, he reflected. Yeah, maybe a morgue or a cemetery. That would match the collective mood they'd managed to work up.

McDumont turned to speak to her, but Penny's eyes were focused on a short, nattily dressed, fiftyish man who was making a beeline for their table. A warm smile played across his craggy features as he took Penny's hand.

"You've been a bad girl, Penny. I haven't seen you in ages. No doubt it's the fault of your handsome friend— aren't you going to introduce me?"

McDumont could see that she was making a conscious effort to observe the social niceties. "Walter, I'd like you to meet Jack Diamond. Jack, this is Walter McDumont."

The two men shook hands. "A pleasure, Mr. McDumont," Diamond said. "Even though you're escorting one of my favourite ladies. I've often told Penny that her intelligence and beauty are wasted on the younger male— it takes a mature man to appreciate the value of such qualities."

"Oh, you really are impossible, Jack," Penny replied, smiling. "But you're sweet, too." She glanced around at the packed tables. "And not doing badly, I should say. You'd never know there was a Depression on from this crowd."

"Some of your friends are here, too," Diamond said. "Sally Roebuck and the Ramsdale twins, Fred Lawrence, a few others. Oh, I almost forgot, Larry Harmon was in earlier. He asked me to tell you that he was looking for you if you happened to come in."

McDumont saw her wince, but her voice was still smooth and

unruffled. "That's nice, Jack, but I'm not really in the mood for table-hopping tonight. I'd appreciate it if you wouldn't say anything to anyone."

Diamond glanced at McDumont and then smiled at her. "Whatever you say, gorgeous." He looked over their heads and frowned. "Now you'll excuse me. Crusher Kerrigan just came in and I'm the only one who knows how to handle him."

"Crusher Kerrigan?" McDumont said quizzically. "Who's that, some fighter?"

"Not exactly. He's sort of a local legend, this big mountain-man type who's carrying the torch for a black singer, Cookie something or other. And Cookie won't have anything to do with him, but he's nuts about her and roams up and down Central Avenue day and night on the lookout for her. It wouldn't be so bad if he were the size of a normal human being, the bouncers would be able to handle him, but he's *huge*—I've seen him absolutely destroy a room when he's in a bad mood; even the police are afraid of him."

"He must be some guy," McDumont said, "but it seems as though your friend Diamond has the knack, all right. Take a look."

Diamond had his arm around as much of Kerrigan's waist as he could manage, and was talking to him in an earnest, friendly way. Kerrigan listened intently, and then a smile played across his broad, weathered face at something Diamond said. It was like watching a sheet of plywood crinkle.

"Diamond's a natural diplomat," McDumont observed. "Although I suppose you have to be in a place like this. Anyway, do you want to go? You don't seem to be having a very good time."

She looked at him, at first seriously, and then her face broke into a shy grin. "No, you're wrong about that. I'm having a very good time. But as Einstein said, everything's relative. I'm so used to having a terrible time with terrible people that it takes me a while to adjust to someone who's nice."

"Someone who isn't Larry Harmon," McDumont said before he could stop himself.

"What do *you* know about Larry Harmon?" She leaned toward McDumont and her voice was sharp, inquisitive.

"I know him. He pulled me over for a minor traffic violation. We got into a beef, and he ended up making a federal case out of it. I talked to some of the other cabbies about him and they said he'd done the same to them. He's got it in for taxi drivers for some reason." That sounds incredibly lame, McDumont thought, but it's the best I can do on the spur of the moment.

Penny glared. "Oh, so he persecutes poor little taxi drivers, does he? What an awful, rotten shame!" Her voice broke and she began to cry, short little sobs at first and then longer gulps of anguish. McDumont took both her hands in his and began to caress them, saying, "It's all right, Penny, it's all right."

After a while she stopped crying, wiped her face, and composed herself. "Walter, you must think I'm crazy. I'm not crazy. But crazy things have been happening to me and my family. I haven't been able to talk to anyone about them. I don't know if I should talk to you about them. But I've got to talk to someone."

He grasped her hands firmly. "You can talk to me, Penny. I know something's wrong. But before you say anything, I've got a confession to make." For a moment he thought of telling her everything that he was concealing from her, but he couldn't face that right now. "I saw you and Larry Harmon in front of the settlement house last week."

She didn't say anything right away. Then she stared directly into his eyes. "Did you hear what he said to me?"

"No. But I saw the way he was treating you. And it wasn't right."

Disconcertingly, she laughed. "'Wasn't right'? Surely you exaggerate, Mr. McDumont. He didn't hit me, did he? He didn't shoot me down like a dog, did he? I'm not some poor black woman, he wouldn't dare treat me that way." Her voice was rising in pitch, verging on hysteria.

"Penny, Penny." He stroked her hands, trying to put all his affection and desire for her into this simple act of touching. "I want you to tell me about it. You've got to tell me about it."

Her shoulders slumped and her head fell. Looking at the surface of the table, she began to talk in a quiet, monotonous tone. Her hands returned the gentle pressure of McDumont's.

"I can't tell you all of it, Walter. I wish I could, but there are too many people who could be hurt. Larry Harmon knows there's something strange about my family, something terrible, and he's trying to use it to... put pressure on me. He wants me to..." She stopped, before going on in the same lifeless tone. "I can't say it. But you know what I mean."

McDumont was stunned. Not by what she'd said— he'd figured that something like this was going on— but by her telling him. By her trusting him. McDumont, the guy you could confide in, also the rotten little worm in the apple who was going to share her secrets with someone else. Or was he? What the hell *was* he going to do? He had to say something to her right now, that was what he had to do.

"I won't let that happen."

Penny shook her head and pulled her hands away. "Walter, this isn't a movie. This is Los Angeles, where the only way you can tell the police apart from the gangsters is that the police wear uniforms. Larry Harmon could walk in here right now and shoot you in the back of the head and he'd get away with it." She paused and smiled, very slightly. "No, that's not quite true. Larry would be afraid of Jack Diamond. Larry tried to work some kind of protection racket on the Sapphire Club last year, and Jack wouldn't stand for it. I heard him tell Larry that he'd sic Crusher Kerrigan on him if he had to, and that shut Larry up right away. Everyone's afraid of Crusher because they know he isn't afraid of anything. But Larry would get you somewhere else. They say he's killed several men and gotten away with it."

"Not if I killed him first," McDumont said. His conscious mind told him this was cheap theatrics, something a pulp-fiction hero would say to a good-girl-gone-wrong heroine. But it was also precisely what he felt.

Penny was angry. "You don't know what you're talking about. And what if you did? Do you think you could get away with it? And it still wouldn't change the... the problem with my family. No, Walter, you don't want to become involved in this. I shouldn't have said anything, I'm sorry. Perhaps we'd better go."

McDumont took her hands again. "I don't care what happens, Penny, I want to help you. Maybe I was talking through my hat about trying to be a tough guy, but there must be other things we can do. Sometimes just talking about it can help— and you know I'm a good listener."

She couldn't help smiling. "You're certainly right about that. Very well, Mr. McDumont, based on your wonderfully sympathetic ears, you are hereby enrolled in the Penelope Bronson Fan Club. Duties to consist of listening to said Bronson bemoan her mixed-up personal life while squiring her about the fleshpots of Los Angeles. Raise your right hand and say 'I do!'"

McDumont threw his right hand into the air and repeated "I do! I do!" A waiter immediately materialized at their table and asked, "What can I get you folks?" Penny and Walter collapsed in laughter. "We certainly can't complain about the service," McDumont said weakly when he'd regained control of himself. "Just the cheque, please," he added in a steadier voice. As the waiter bustled off, McDumont assumed a gruffer tone and said, "I hope you realize that we're now man and wife— that waiter heard two 'I do's' and he's going to come back with a marriage certificate."

Penny laughed. "And wouldn't you be shocked if he did? I can see the headlines now: 'Trapped into Marriage, Idealistic Young Writer Runs for Cover.' Don't worry, Walter, I won't hold you to it."

"Darn it all, just when I thought you were beginning to like me, too. Better luck next time."

She looked at him steadily, seriously. "And I suppose there will be a next time?"

"If there isn't," he said, "you're never going to hear the end of it."

The Club Alabam was directly across the street from the Sapphire Club. As Penny and Walter came out on the sidewalk, something large smashed through one of the Alabam's front windows, slammed against a telephone pole, and thudded to the ground. It was a large black man dressed in a tuxedo, who groaned loudly and tried to stand up before collapsing onto his hands and knees. The club's front doors opened and a small mob of anxious whites came boiling out, then scattered in all directions.

Jack Diamond suddenly appeared behind Penny and Walter. He stared at the man on the sidewalk, who had stumbled to his feet and was shaking his head as if he couldn't believe what had happened to him. "Jesus, Jess Izzard's one of the best heavyweights west of Chicago— nobody but Kerrigan could put that bouncer down," he said. "Someone must have told Crusher that Cookie was going to sing the last set at the Alabam. Now there's going to be hell to pay." He ran across the street and went into the club.

"Do you think we should phone the police?" McDumont asked Penny. "Maybe call an ambulance for Izzard?"

"I wouldn't phone the police unless you want to see some people get shot. And you won't get an ambulance to come to Central Avenue at this time of night— a man died here last year, bled to death inside the Down Beat. They called for an ambulance but it didn't come. At the inquest, the coroner said he didn't blame them, he wouldn't come down here, either. No, let Jack see if he can handle it."

They stared at the pink stucco walls of the Club Alabam. Screams and sounds of furniture breaking reached a crescendo, then subsided. Two black men wearing waiters' clothes ran out the front door, gawked at Izzard, and scurried away down the street. One of them was holding a bloody towel against his forehead.

For a moment, there was almost complete silence. Then Crusher Kerrigan stepped out onto the sidewalk. He glanced at Izzard, shrugged his shoulders, and then fixed his eyes on Penny and Walter. Although his clothing was rumpled, as if slept in, he didn't look as though he'd been in a fight. He was carrying a suitcase with one arm. Under the other, a small, very pretty, and very frightened black woman wriggled ineffectually.

"Ain't she a honey?" Kerrigan said, apparently addressing Penny and Walter. "She's the sweetest little thing old Crusher ever set eyes on. She sure is a Cookie, she's good enough to eat." He put down the suitcase and fondled her hair affectionately. "You sure give old Crusher a hard time though, babe— how come you're always running away from me? You know I'm going to treat you good."

Cookie looked up at him. "Crusher, please put me down right now. I swear I won't run away. Come on, sugar, put me down, don't do me this way."

Kerrigan laughed. "No, babe, we played that scene. I'm going to take you home, show you how sweet I can be to a woman who treats me right. I got you, and I'm gonna keep you."

Frowning and shaking his head, Jack Diamond hurried out of the Alabam. "You really did it this time, Crusher. Sid is just about ready to have you bumped off. I told him you were good for the damages, but you can't keep doing this, big fella. I don't care how tough you are, one of these days somebody is going to take an elephant gun and put you down for the count." He went over to Izzard and looked at Kerrigan critically. "Well, at least you didn't kill this guy, that's something."

Kerrigan looked abashed. "I'm sorry, Jack. It's Cookie drives me crazy, I can't think straight on account of her." He looked at her ruefully. "What am I going to do, baby? I can't live without you, and you can't live with me. What am I going to do?"

"Let me go, you big goon. How do you think I like it, always being pawed and grabbed and followed around? Why don't you get back, man, let me breathe? You ain't the ugliest guy in the world, you know— maybe we could get together if you ever gave me a chance to think about it. But right now, you let me go!"

Crusher's forehead wrinkled in visible thought. Then he grinned and, with surprising grace, gently set Cookie on her feet. "I'm sorry, babe. I shouldn't treat you that way. But just give me a chance. I'm crazy about you, I want to be good to you."

Cookie's exasperated expression softened. "I know, Crusher, I know. But you just can't come at me that way, man. I ain't some tootsie working a hot-pillow joint, I want to make it with the music and get out of that roach hole I been living in. You got to respect that, man, and you don't act like you do!"

Kerrigan's massive frame slumped, and his voice was much lower, almost strangulated. "I hear you, babe. I'm sorry. Later." He started to walk away.

"Crusher!" Cookie's strident voice stopped him in his tracks and spun him around.

"Yeah, babe?"

"You get your ugly self back here. I ain't walking home alone at this time of night!"

As the unlikely pair sauntered off arm-in-arm down Central Avenue, Jack Diamond crossed the street to where Penny and Walter were standing. "How do you like that?" he said. "Mutt and Jeff got nothing on those two." He scratched his head. "They're so different, maybe they have something in common."

Penny and Walter looked at one another. He smiled. She seemed sceptical. "Opposites may attract," Penny said. "But can they stay together?"

"There's only one way to find out," McDumont said. "Surrender to the magnetism of the moment and see where it takes you."

"Poetic cuss, ain't he?" Diamond commented. "Well, children, I've got to get back to my joint and make sure that the help hasn't gone south with the cash box. Blessings on you, young people, and you watch out for Penny, Mr. McDumont— she's a special friend of this establishment." He went into the Sapphire Club, then popped back out and said, "I'll send a boy for your car."

"'Magnetism of the moment'?" Penny queried. "What's a staunch social realist like you doing with such flowery sentiments?"

"Just continuing the metaphor of polar attraction, oh teacher of literature. Looking on the positive side despite your negative comments. Clever, eh?"

She laughed. "Clever, but out of character, I'd say, unless you're really a romantic poet in disguise. Which, given that you've already displayed some of the characteristics of the dissolute young night-club hopper, would not surprise me in the least."

"Time to hop you back home, anyway," McDumont said as the roadster wheeled up in front of the club. "After the night we've had, it wouldn't surprise me if this car turned into a pumpkin."

McDumont wanted to kiss her goodnight, but he was afraid to break the relaxed, quiet mood they'd fallen into on the drive home. They walked to the front door of the Bronson house in silence. Penny took out her key, and then turned to him.

"I had a wonderful time," she finally said.

"I'm nuts about you," McDumont replied.

Then they were in each other's arms, kissing passionately, pulling apart to regard one another and then embracing again.

Estelle Bronson opened the front door. "I'm sorry to disturb you two lovebirds," she said harshly, "but Penelope has a very busy day tomorrow. There's so much to do about Sunday's party, darling, we really must get on with it."

Penny frowned, then smiled quickly. "Yes, I was just mentioning it to Walter. I'm so pleased that he'll be able to come— aren't you, mother?"

"Charmed, I'm sure," she replied in a tone that suggested she was anything but. "Now come in, Penelope, there's a chill in the air."

"Two-ish, Walter," Penny said. "And thank you for a marvellous evening." She stepped through the doorway.

"The pleasure was all mine. Until Sunday, then. Good evening, Mrs. Bronson."

"Good evening, Mr. McDumont."

She closed the door abruptly.

And the best of British luck to you too, toots, McDumont thought as he walked back to the roadster. Then he thought about Penny, how she'd felt in his arms, the taste of her lips, the smell of her hair. He thought about it all night long.

CHAPTER FIVE

"What *do* you wear to a Sunday afternoon shindig at the Bronsons?" McDumont asked. For the last two hours they'd been holding down a booth at Rumplemeyer's while he gave Chandler a highly edited version of the previous evening's events.

McDumont had told him about Penny's problem with Larry Harmon, but he tried to put it in a way that played down the growing emotional intimacy he felt with this wonderful, complicated woman. But the whole situation was becoming ridiculous— here he was holding out on Ray, while when he was with Penny he couldn't tell her the whole truth, either. What the hell *was* he doing?

Chandler stared intently into his beer stein. "Damned if I know," he finally replied. "It would have been straw boaters and white linen jackets in my day, but my day was a couple of centuries ago. But that's what one's tailors are for— drink up, old chap, we'll just get there before they close."

McDumont groaned. "If I'd known I was going to have to turn into a clothes horse for this deal, I'd have stayed in Toronto and settled for a nice job sweeping the streets."

"And miss all this fun and excitement? Look at what that Kerrigan chap did last night, there's a scene right out of pulp-magazine fiction for you. Don't be silly. We've fallen into an adventure story of our very own."

"Yes, *we* have, haven't we? But somehow I seem to be doing most of the dirty work. I know you're paying for it, but I don't want to seem greedy— why don't you go out and seduce Estelle Bronson or something, make yourself useful?"

Chandler grinned. "From your description of said lady fair, I think that might be beyond even my remarkable powers. But enough gay repartee. Time and tailor wait for no man, so let us hie ourselves to a haberdashery and select the latest disguise for our hero." He hiccupped. "Goodness, I seem to be rather drunk."

"That's the understatement of the year," McDumont agreed. "And boy, do I wish I could say the same."

"Something refined but *sportif*, don't you think?" the salesman said thoughtfully. "A touch of elegance with perhaps just a *soupçon* of raffish charm."

"Quite, quite," Chandler agreed, trying very hard not to laugh, and barely succeeding.

"Hold the raffish charm," McDumont put in. "I'm raffish enough for this crowd already. Let's concentrate on the refinement."

"As you say, sir, refinement is never out of fashion. Let me see... yes, this should do nicely." The salesman took a maroon silk sport jacket off the rack and held it up against McDumont's chest. "There'll be no time to do alterations, but you're a perfect 38 long, sir. Perhaps you'll try this on for me."

McDumont put it on. It was surprisingly light, and cool and

sensuous where it touched his skin. He felt himself becoming more refined by the minute.

"Yes, just the thing," Chandler observed. "And your grey slacks will go with it very well. Now, the shirt... we'll need something in yellow, I should think. And a new tie, too. Something dark and not too flashy."

The salesman cleared his throat. "Might I suggest an ascot, Mr. Chandler? They're quite the style this season. All the gentlemen are wearing them."

"Maybe all the gentlemen know how to tie them," McDumont said, "but I sure as hell... I'm afraid I don't." If the guys back in Cabbagetown could see me now, he thought, they'd bust their guts. You saw men wearing ascots in the movies, but their names were usually Lord This or Earl That, and they spoke and acted as if they were far too good for the rest of us crumb-bums. He'd be a monkey's uncle before he was going to wear one of those things.

"Yes, perfect, whatever you think suitable," Chandler said. As the salesman bustled away, he turned to McDumont. "Walter, you don't have to say it. I know this is cruel and unusual punishment. But think of it as camouflage, something that will help you to blend in with the rest of the guests. You're going to be nervous enough about socializing with the Bronsons without worrying about whether you're dressed properly."

McDumont grimaced, opened his mouth, then closed it without speaking. Finally he said, "I still don't know how to tie the goddamned ascot."

"Not to worry, I'll pop round before you go and do the necessary. And believe me, it *will* help you feel more at ease."

Although Estelle Bronson was still glacial, her husband did seem genuinely glad to see Walter. "Nice to have the pleasure of your company again, Mr. McDumont. I'd like to talk to you for a moment." Bronson took his guest by the elbow and steered him off into a quiet corner. What is this, McDumont wondered, the polite version of the shotgun wedding? Or maybe it's the genteel equivalent of the bum's rush: the back door opens and I get thrown out on my keester.

"I've been giving some thought to your employment situation, Walter— you don't mind if I call you 'Walter,' do you?"

"Certainly not, sir."

"Good. As I was saying, I've been thinking about what a shame it is that an intelligent young fellow can't find a decent job these days, and something has occurred to me."

"Actually, I'm not really looking..." McDumont started to say, but quickly shut his mouth. No, he thought, I'm already employed spying on your family, sir, and I won't be available until I've finished looking for all the skeletons in your closet. Contact Mr. Chandler for references.

"Now hear me out, Walter, hear me out. I've felt for some time that the banking community in general, and Western Fidelity in particular, has done a very poor job of explaining why we operate the way we do. Before the Depression it didn't really matter. Everyone assumed that banks were the rocks on which you built a strong economy, but in the last few years that attitude has changed. And not without some justification, I might add— too many of my colleagues were making poorly secured loans, getting caught up in the euphoria of a skyrocketting stock market. We know what happened as a result. But now that the smoke's cleared and we can assess the damage, I think it's time for banking to reassert its importance as the foundation of a strong financial system. What do *you* think?"

"I'm sure you're right," McDumont replied, "but I don't see how I..."

"Now don't jump ahead. That's the problem with you young fellows, you don't stop to look at the big picture. Let me tell you what I have in mind. My daughter informs me that you're a very talented writer. Well, banking— and here I mean Western Fidelity, of course— is very much in need of people who can write about it in an articulate, persuasive way. I suppose you could call it 'public relations,' although that usually doesn't seem to mean anything more than smiling at your customers and contributing to the local Community Chest. But what I'm talking about is more philosophical, a vision of what banking could be in a recovering economy." Bronson paused and took out a cigarette. "I'm not very good with words myself, I have lots of ideas but I'm not very good at expressing them. But I think that if I collaborated with an experienced writer we could produce something that would give Western Fidelity a real shot in the arm, and show the banking community how to protect its own best interests. Would that kind of thing interest you?"

McDumont didn't know what to say. No, he knew what he *should* say— something along the lines of "I'm not for sale and I detest this corrupt and rotten capitalist system" would be a succinct expression of what he really felt— but you could hardly say that to the father of the woman you were falling in love with. And whose family you were spying on. Christ, what a mess!

"I'm flattered that you would think of me, sir, but... but... I'm not really that sort of writer." That was it, go for the I'm-an-artist-not-a-businessman line. Any father of Penny's should have heard that one before.

Bronson slapped him firmly on the back. "Nonsense, Walter, you're just being modest. I want you to give what I've said some thought, because this could be the opportunity of a lifetime for the right fellow. A salaried position, working directly under me. Not a bad way to start out on your career, eh?— and I know a certain young lady who might be impressed by it."

I think I know a certain young lady whose behind I'd like to tan, McDumont mused. "That's very generous of you, Mr. Bronson, and I appreciate what a wonderful opportunity you're offering me. But I've just learned that my mother is quite ill"— sorry Ma, McDumont thought, you're as strong as a horse, but it was the first thing that came to mind— "and it's possible I may have to go back to Toronto shortly. Could I have some time to think about it? It would be a big change for me, it's not something I'd want to decide on the spur of the moment."

"Of course, of course," Bronson replied, smiling. "I've come at you out of the blue. But think it over seriously, Walter, because this is not the sort of proposal I'm in the habit of making to every young man I meet." His facial muscles expressed something midway between a twinkle and a wink. "And I think you might want to discuss it with Penny. She's not the sort of girl you can take out on the town on a taxi driver's salary, you know."

"I will, sir. And if you'll excuse me, I do want to talk this over with Penny." Boy, did he want to talk this over with Penny. Bronson had him working in the bank, married to his daughter, and probably next in line for membership at his clubs. McDumont wondered how many children he and Penny were supposed to have— well, he'd probably find that out soon enough, the way things were going.

He felt a strong urge to tear his clothes off, run out the door, and make a beeline for the nearest railroad tracks. All of a sudden, life was too complicated.

Penny was nowhere in sight. McDumont found his way to the garden and circulated among his fellow guests, most of whom were engaged in animated conversations. The occasional idle glances he received sparked no immediate calls for his expulsion, so he figured he was doing all right in the disguise department, anyway.

McDumont was beginning to think that he'd better go back to the Bronsons and ask about Penny's whereabouts when a warbling female voice from behind him called out, "Yoohoo, Mr. McDumont!" Since he assumed that only the Bronsons knew who he was at this clambake, the first thing that occurred to him was that Estelle Bronson must have suddenly taken up yodelling.

But the reality was even more terrifying. Bethany Chambers was bustling toward him, a broad smile on her puss, and was that... yes, it *was* something like a conspiratorial wink twisting her facial features into bizarre contortions. For the love of Mike, McDumont realized, she thinks I'm here researching my book on the upper crust. As if things weren't screwed up enough...

"Such a pleasure, Mr. McDumont, so delightful." She performed another complicated facial manoeuvre that looked to McDumont like a smirk, although a harsher observer— Edgar Allan Poe, say— might have described it as a ghastly grin. Whatever it was, it seemed to imply that Bethany Chambers and Walter McDumont were working the same journalistic beat. And even though what she thought she knew wasn't exactly what he was really up to, it would still take only a well-placed word or two for her to torpedo his chances with the Bronsons. Something along the lines of "So kind of you to help Mr. McDumont with his book, Estelle," for example. And if she said anything to Penny, Penny who thought he was aces because he seemed to genuinely care for her— which he did, of course, but if she thought he was really just nosing around doing investigative research... cripes, McDumont didn't even want to think about *that* possibility!

No time to waste, then. "I'm very pleased to see you, Miss Chambers, but I would like to ask you not to..."

"Darling," she interrupted, speaking to someone behind him, "what a marvellous party. Have you met Mr. McDumont?"

Christ, McDumont thought, some other old busybody. He put his best company smile on and turned around. Penny looked at him quizzically.

"Yes, we have actually, Walter is the star student in my writing class at Harrison House." McDumont could see that Bethany Chambers had picked up on the "Walter," was probably tucking it away under the "New Romances to Keep Track of" category of the gossip columnist's mental files. And any second now she'd be spilling the beans about his supposed book on Los Angeles society, no wonder he was Penny's star student, blah blah blah.

He had to do something. So he said, "Excuse me, Miss Chambers, but Penny was going to lend me some books about writing, and I'm anxious to obtain them. Could we go get them now?" He tried to put a pleading look into his expression as he gently nudged Penny toward the door into the house.

"What books do you...? Oh yes, I remember now. Do excuse us,

Bethany, but if I don't do it right at this moment I may not have another chance." She smiled at McDumont. "Keen students are so few and far between. One doesn't want to disappoint them."

"But of course, dear, I understand perfectly." There was that smirk again. Chambers had them at it hot and heavy in the library or she was no judge of human nature. "We'll chat again, Mr. McDumont, I am so interested in how you're getting on."

"What was that all about?" Penny asked when they were out of earshot. "And how do you know Bethany Chambers, anyway? Is she your long-lost aunt or something?" She spoke lightly, but McDumont could tell that Penny was surprised.

He had to come up with an explanation, and he had to do it fast. He could say that he was beginning a career as a professional gigolo, and Bethany Chambers was his first conquest. No, that didn't bear thinking about. Or maybe just that she'd used his taxi and they'd started chatting, become friendly. Weak, but the best he could do on the spur of the moment.

Penny seemed to accept it, but now she was curious about why he'd so abruptly rushed her out of Chambers's presence. That was a lot easier. "Because I wanted to see you alone," he said, as soon as they were inside the house and by themselves in a small room off the main hallway. "And because the minute I catch sight of you I want to do this." He kissed her.

She laughed, kissed him back, then broke away. "That's all very well, Walter, but you've forgotten that I have to be a gracious hostess. Now you go back to Bethany Chambers and butter her up a bit. She's a silly old thing but she's really very sweet, and I know my mother wants to keep on her good side."

"What about the books?" he said, playfully ruffling her hair. "We'll have to go up to your room to get them, and who knows how long they'll take to find?" He kissed her. "Now that I think of it, I've always been interested in browsing your bookshelves. 'Keen,' one might even say, were one the sort of person to say 'keen,' which of course I am not, although I have been described as such by a young lady of my acquaintance."

"That young lady isn't falling for that old line, Mr. Smoothie. No, you just stay here a minute and I'll go find a couple of books, then it's back to Bethany Chambers for you." She strode purposefully out the door.

A moment later, a boy came running into the room. He was carrying what looked like a tommy-gun, the fast-shooting weapon that cops and criminals alike used when volume of fire was more important than accuracy. He pointed it at McDumont and said, "Stick 'em up or I'll drill ya!" in a shrill voice.

McDumont put up his hands. He'd heard that Americans liked to have lots of guns around the house, but this was ridiculous. "Take it easy, son. You wouldn't want that thing to go off. I'm not a burglar or anything, I'm a guest of your parents. Why don't we go and find them?" The little twerp didn't look to be more than twelve or thirteen years old, but he was waving the gun around so crazily that it might go off at any moment.

"Nah, you look like a gangster to me." McDumont watched in horror as the boy took careful aim and pulled the trigger. A thin stream of water hit McDumont in the face and then dribbled down to his ascot and shirt front. This punk kid had just shot him with the world's biggest squirt gun.

McDumont took out his pocket handkerchief and wiped his face. The boy was convulsed with laughter. Should I break the bloody gun over my knee, McDumont wondered, or would a good old-fashioned spanking be more appropriate? Another few seconds staring into that goddamned thing and my pants would have been wet, too.

"Paul? Paul Junior?" Estelle Bronson burst into the room, put her cocktail glass down on an end table, and grabbed the gun away from the boy. Her face was flushed and she waved her arms frantically, erratically. "How many times have I told you to stay in your room when we have company?" she screamed. She slapped the boy across the mouth and raised the toy high over her head, as if she were going to smash it down on him.

"For god's sake, Estelle, what do you think you're doing?" Her husband angrily snatched the squirt gun away from her and put his arm around his son, who was now sobbing violently. "What's going on here?" Then Paul Bronson noticed McDumont. He blushed, clearly embarrassed by the situation. "All right, young man, you go to your room. We'll talk about this later."

"Sure you will," his wife said in a mocking tone. "You'll have a nice heart-to-heart chat, like all good daddies do with their sweet little boys, and afterwards he'll be the same little brat that he's always been." She looked away as Paul Junior left the room. Then she laughed and said, "What will Mr. McDumont think, Paul? If we don't watch out, he won't want to have anything to do with the Bronson family." She made a visible effort to compose herself. "I am sorry, Mr. McDumont, Paul Junior does get out of control sometimes. Now if you'll excuse me, I'm going to get something to settle my nerves." She picked up her glass and stormed out of the room.

Paul Bronson collapsed into an easy chair. His face was ashen, his speech slow and halting. "He's not a bad boy, Walter, he's not. But he's had some problems growing up, problems not of his making, and I don't know what to do about it." He paused and wiped his forehead. "Estelle has given up on him, but I'm not ready to do that. He's only twelve years old. You can't give up on someone who's only twelve years old." His voice faltered as he got to the end of this sentence, as if he didn't completely believe what he was saying.

"No, I was a hellion at that age, I know what it's like." McDumont was embarrassed to have witnessed this scene, wanted to get out of there, but decided that he'd better wait for Penny to return. "I wouldn't worry about it too much," he continued, "it's probably the sort of thing he'll grow out of."

"Yes, I'm sure you're right. Ah, Penny." Bronson rose from the chair. "Come give your old dad a hug, he needs one."

"What was all that commotion?" Penny asked as she embraced her father affectionately.

"Oh, nothing really, Paul Junior decided to use Walter for target practice and your mother overreacted. But no harm done, eh, Walter?"

"Of course not. Are those the books, Penny? I'd better go find Bethany Chambers, she'll think I'm avoiding her." Any port in a storm, McDumont thought.

"Yes, you do that. I want to talk to dad for a minute."

As McDumont left the room, he glanced back over his shoulder. Paul Bronson seemed to be leaning on Penny, his body frail and vulnerable as he talked to her quietly, while she looked at him as though he were telling her something very important. McDumont wondered what they were saying.

Bethany Chambers was loading up her plate at the buffet table, balancing two hefty lobster tails on a mound of assorted goodies. "It all looks so delicious, doesn't it?" she said as McDumont joined her. "I know I shouldn't indulge myself so dreadfully, but what's a poor girl to do?" She lowered her voice. "Confidentially, this is one of the best things about being a society columnist. I'm going to have such a good time tomorrow comparing notes with the other reporters at the *Times*. There was a fundraising banquet last night for Alderman Phillips, that means someone on the city desk dined on rubber chicken and canned peas. And I believe the Angels are playing a double header today, so the boys in sports will be recovering from too many hot dogs, too much beer, and"— she glanced upward— "a case or two of sunburn. Well, that's not our worry, is it, Mr. McDumont? Come keep me company while I do justice to this."

They found an unoccupied table and sat down. "I wanted to say before, Miss Chambers, I'd appreciate it if you wouldn't say anything to the Bronsons, or anyone else for that matter, about this book I'm working on. You know how people can be about journalists— they always think we're only interested in scandal or whatever."

She smiled. Yes, he thought, ghastly grin would be the phrase, all right. "Of course, Mr. McDumont, I know *just* what you mean. You can imagine the kinds of things I come across in writing a society column, sometimes I think that I should start a scandal sheet and tell people what really goes on behind these façades of gracious living." She sighed and attacked one of the lobster tails. "But I don't suppose I ever will, although after I retire... I'm years away from that, of course... yes, I'll have to think about some sort of exposé, goodness knows I have the material."

She smiled her peculiar smile again and patted him on the shoulder. "I suppose that means I'll have to be very careful about what I tell *you*, Mr. McDumont. I can't have you revealing my secrets ahead of time, can I?" She lowered her head in a gesture that implied mutual conspiracy. "Although we could think about a joint effort, couldn't we? We could become *collaborators*..."

I'd volunteer for the salt mines first, McDumont thought. But she probably did know a lot about the Bronsons; maybe he should play footsy with her. No, here was where he drew the line. "Perhaps after I've finished my book," he said, "we might think about it then. After you've decided about your retirement plans, of course."

"Lovely, yes, let's do that. Oh, hello, Margot, so nice to see you."

A statuesque blond woman in a tight yellow dress sat down next to McDumont. She was stunningly beautiful, her delicate facial features contrasting with a bold, curvaceous body that seemed to exude sensual invitation. She crossed her legs and displayed several inches of well-bronzed thigh.

"You won't mind if I join you," she said languidly, "everyone else is so remarkably tedious. We haven't met before, have we?" she said to McDumont. "I'm sure I'd remember if we had. I'm Margot Stevenson. My husband is on the board of Paul's bank." She laughed. "*Board* is right, spelled b-o-r-e-d. God, they're a dull bunch. And you are...?"

He couldn't help staring at her. She was several years older than he was, but the perfection of her appearance made it difficult to guess what her exact age might be. He wondered if she was a movie star or something; he hadn't seen many films lately. "Walter McDumont," he said. "I'm Walter McDumont, I'm pleased to meet you."

"Yes," she said, shifting slightly to reveal a further expanse of smooth, lustrous skin. He tore his eyes away from her and glanced at Bethany Chambers. She was looking at him with a wry smile; she'd probably seen Margot work her way through legions of callow young men. Odd how Margot did make him feel callow— he'd been around, but he'd never met anyone like this before. He felt completely tongue-tied.

But good old Bethany came to his rescue. "Mr. McDumont is a recent arrival to our fair community, Margot. He's from Toronto originally, a very talented young journalist."

"Canadian, are you?" Margot mused. "I don't think I've ever... *known* any Canadians before." You could have cut the sexual innuendo in her voice with a knife.

McDumont felt like an exotic specimen about to be captured by a voracious collector. He wondered if he would put up much of a fight. Somehow, he didn't think so.

"Margot is certainly one of the most... *active* members of Los Angeles society," Bethany Chambers observed. Hooray for Bethany, McDumont thought; she does have a sense of humour and she wants me to know what Margot is. Not that any fool with eyes and a normal quota of male hormones couldn't figure it out. "I haven't seen you all that often lately," Chambers continued. "Have you been away or...?"

Margot Stevenson blushed, very briefly, but McDumont was glad to see it— it made her seem more human, less perfect. "Oh, no, I haven't been away, I've been involved with one of my... projects," she responded. Am I going to be one of her projects, McDumont wondered? It wasn't up to him, anyway. He was trapped in the headlights. Any time she wanted to Margot could take his hand and lead him off to a quiet bedroom and...

"Penny!" Bethany Chambers enthused, "so there you are. And with Mr. McDumont's books, too." Penny sat down between Walter and Bethany and said, "Yes, I'm back. Good afternoon, Margot. We haven't seen much of you lately."

"Margot's been working on one of her *projects*," Chambers said quickly. "And you know what Margot's like when she's working on one of her projects."

"Yes," said Penny, "I heard that you were interested in that young sculptor, what is his name, Raphael or Roberto?"

"Rudolfo, actually," Margot replied, "Rudolfo Martinez." She seemed less self-possessed now. "Rudolfo is a very gifted young man, he just needs a little encouragement."

Penny's laugh was discreet, but still a laugh. "Well, I'm sure you've given him that." She moved her chair closer to McDumont's and put her hand on his elbow in a gesture of intimacy and possession. "Walter is my latest discovery, a marvellous young writer." She increased the pressure of her hand. "I've been showing him around town a bit. We had a delightful evening on Central Avenue last Friday."

"I see," Margot said. She glanced at her watch. "Well, I mustn't keep Rudolfo waiting— I said I'd drop by and help him choose what to exhibit in his next show. It's been so nice to meet you, Mr. McDumont." She gave him her hand and he pressed it, gingerly. He was painfully aware of Penny's fingers digging into his other arm.

"Yes, I must be on my way as well," said Bethany Chambers, rising. "Such a pleasant party, but my deadline beckons. Ta-ta, all."

When they were by themselves, Penny took her hand away and Walter rubbed his elbow vigorously. "I knew you were crazy about me," he said, "but I didn't know that you wanted to take me apart piece by piece."

"I'll do more than that if you ever let Margot Stevenson get her hooks into you. Now listen, Walter, I know she's attractive, but she's almost old enough to be your mother and she's a complete tramp. Why her husband puts up with it, I don't know, but I can tell you that I won't stand for it!"

He looked at her affectionately. "Did I miss something here?" he asked. "Did we become married or engaged or something while I wasn't paying attention? Or is it just that you've decided to take control of my social life, protect me from bad influences?"

Penny coloured, but didn't say anything immediately. Then she smiled at him. "Well, I guess that now you know how I feel about you, anyway. Yes, damn it, I do want to protect you from people like Margot Stevenson. She has no scruples. They say she picks up two or three sailors at a time on the Santa Monica pier and takes them off to her beach house for incredible orgies. Does that sound like someone you'd like to have a cozy little affair with?"

"No," he said, "you're right. I'm glad you told me. But there is someone around here I would like to have a cozy little affair with. And I bet you can't guess who it is."

Her expression was serious. "No, I haven't the faintest. But if you'd like to go for a walk in the garden, I expect that I could bear to hear all about it."

It was cooler under the trees. They walked along slowly, holding hands, occasionally stopping to kiss. Penny seemed lost in thought, her eyes roving across the sky as if it might hold the answers to her unarticulated questions.

After one particularly long embrace, McDumont began to caress her breasts. She quickly pulled away from him.

"Please, Walter, you mustn't. I'm not ready for that. I have to think. There are things on my mind."

"Why don't you tell me about them?"

"I'd like to, but I can't. It sounds awful, but that's how it is. It isn't anything about you. I like you very much, maybe I'm even in love with you. I don't know, but I can't be involved with you that way now."

He decided to make light of it. "Oh, well, I guess there's always Margot Stevenson..."

"Yes," she said, "I guess there is, I guess there is if you're not the sort of person I think you are." She sounded as though she was about to cry.

He grasped her arms tenderly and kissed her on the forehead. "I'm just kidding, you big dope, I'm just trying to make you jealous. You're worth more than all the Margot Stevensons in the world rolled into one."

"That's a truly appalling image," she said, smiling. "Well, I am jealous, and you'd better remember that. Hell hath no fury like a woman scorned, and so on. Now come on, I should be getting back to the party." She took his arm and they walked back toward the house.

The rest of the afternoon passed in a daze for McDumont. He chatted politely with people whose names he forgot immediately after being introduced to them, and ate strange bits of unknown food circulated by excessively polite waiters, who also proffered glasses of mildly alcoholic fruit punch that he sipped with much enjoyment and little evident effect. Penny was often by his side, smiling constantly and sometimes squeezing his arm or touching his shoulder, and he thought that he had never been so happy.

Even Estelle Bronson seemed to have been affected by the early-summer atmosphere. Saying goodbye to McDumont at the front door, she held his hand for a fraction longer than necessary and said, "You seem to be good for Penny. You must come again." Her husband echoed the sentiment, adding, "Don't you forget about my proposition, young man. I expect to hear from you shortly!"

Penny walked out to the car with him. "So what do you think of dad's idea?" she asked.

"'Dad's idea,' eh? Ho ho ho. Listen, I know you mean well, but I really don't see myself as your father's hired mouthpiece, great guy though he undoubtedly is. Just because I don't go along with the Communist-Party types in class, that doesn't mean I'm ready to become one of the bosses."

"Don't be so dramatic, Walter, it doesn't become you. It was just an idea. Not entirely my idea, either, despite what you seem to think. But it is a job for a writer, and those don't seem to be falling out of the trees these days."

"Can't I just be a bum and let you support me?" He leered at her. "I could be at your beck and call twenty-four hours a day and submit to your every whim."

She punched him lightly on the chest. "It's a tempting thought, but I think I'll demurely decline. You could kiss me goodbye, however— I won't see you again until Tuesday's class."

"That's a depressing thought," he said, reaching for her. "I guess we'd better make this something to remember."

CHAPTER SIX

Tuesday night after class, on their way to the diner, Penny said, "Walter, how do you feel about the zoo?"

"The what?"

"The zoo— they do have zoos in Toronto, don't they?"

"Sure, the good old Riverdale Zoo, now there was a great place to pick up... well, it was a great place. But what brought that into your devious little mind?"

"Oh, just an idea I had. I've been thinking that Paul Junior really doesn't have much of a life these days— that school he goes to is more like a prison, mom doesn't seem to have much time for him, and dad's so busy... what would you think about the two of us taking him to the zoo? I'm sure he'd love to get out of school for a day, too."

"Well, it's not exactly what I had in mind for our next date. But if you think it's a good idea, I'll go along for the ride. Even though your little brother probably shortened my life with that squirt-gun gag."

"You're sweet." He was hugged and kissed on the cheek. "Just for that, I'll pick up the cheque tonight. Just like you used to pick up all those girls at the zoo."

"I did, but they all made monkeys out of me," he said as Penny groaned. "And I sure ain't lion."

They'd decided that Penny would pick him up at his rooming house, since it was on the way to the zoo. "You live *here?*" Paul Junior said as McDumont got into Penny's car. "Boy, what a dump!"

"Is that what they teach you at that expensive school?" he replied. "Making fun of us down-and-outers? Tell me, Paul, is your exalted social position something that you've achieved on your own? Did you buy that house you live in, this car, those expensive duds you've got on?"

"I guess not," the boy finally said, reluctantly.

"I guess you didn't," McDumont said, smiling. "But maybe you did buy that bloody squirt gun you almost drowned me with. What was that thing, anyway, a tommy gun?"

"Yeah, just like the one the Dillinger gang uses! Boy, it's really neat! You should have seen your face when I shot you!"

"Paul," Penny interrupted, "you should apologize to Mr. McDumont for what you did."

Paul looked at McDumont and hung his head. "I'm sorry. I didn't mean to mess up your clothes." Then he became animated again. "But the look on your face— did you really think it was a gun?"

"I sure as heck wasn't going to charge you and find out," Walter replied, chuckling. "But that's all water under the bridge... what's wrong, Penny?" She was bent over the steering wheel, laughing audibly.

"It's those awful puns of yours, Walter, I swear— 'water under the bridge?' I'm surprised you didn't describe Paul as 'a young squirt.'"

It was McDumont's turn to laugh. "I guess it's catching, eh? So much for your hopes of literary greatness. Now where's this zoo? You guys are beginning to get my goat."

They stood in front of the monkey cage and watched as a mother and her young child played with one another. The mother was picking assiduously at the infant's fur, pausing to pay close attention to what she found, then caressing her child's body with vigorous but affectionate motions. The young monkey squirmed, trying to get away, but when put down for a moment it immediately leaped into its mother's arms for another bout of love and personal hygiene. The three human beings watched this absorbing show for several minutes before Paul snorted harshly and shook his fist at the cage.

"Stupid monkey. He could get away if he wanted to, when she lets go of him. I'd be out of there like blue blazes."

Penny looked at him thoughtfully. "I don't think he wants to get away, Paul. I think he appreciates all the attention his mother is giving him."

"Then he's a dummy, that's what he is. I wouldn't put up with all that stupid stuff. I'd break out of that cage, too. I'd run away where no one could find me!"

McDumont laughed. "I don't know about this running away business, though I used to imagine trying it when I was a kid, too. But if you think about it, that's what I've been doing by bumming all around the country. Nobody can find you, that's for sure. You've got no address, no responsibilities, and you don't owe anybody anything. And nobody owes you anything, either."

He looked at Penny and spoke more seriously. "Then, if you're lucky, you find some place you like, a place where you want to stay. After that, you start to worry about how maybe you're so used to running away all the time you don't know how to settle down, you've forgotten what you're supposed to do when you want to become a part of something."

He paused, then laughed again. "That sounds like the kind of junk they feed you in the movies, doesn't it? Like that one a bunch of us snuck into in St. Louis, *It Happened One Night*, that was a pip. Clark Gable as the tough reporter with a heart of mush. Jeez, you guys will think I'm going all sentimental on you."

Penny was smiling at him, but it was Paul who spoke. "Gosh, Mr. McDumont, you've really been around, haven't you? I bet you've done a lot of really neat stuff."

"Yes, tell us about some of that 'neat stuff,'" Penny said. "You've hardly told me a thing. Nothing more than hints about what an exciting life you've led."

"All right, you asked for it," McDumont replied. "But before I do that, let's go get some refreshments at that snack bar over there— this could take quite a while."

"The first thing you have to understand," McDumont said, "is that after you've been on the road for a while you're always tired, hungry, and smelly."

Paul wrinkled his nose. "Yuck, smelly, that's disgusting. Can't you take a bath in a river or something?"

"Well you could, Paul, if you wanted to take the risk of some other bum stealing your stuff while you had a nice soak. And if you had any soap, which nobody ever does, that's about the last thing a real hobo would ever spend his money on. And if the river wasn't full of stuff that would make you dirtier when you got out of it than when you got into it. And if you weren't so darn tired after a day of scrounging for something to eat that you fell asleep in your tracks. No, it's better to stay smelly— you get used to it after a while, and I've seen cops refuse to arrest guys because they couldn't bring themselves to put their hands on somebody who was so filthy."

"But what about your adventures," Paul insisted, "you must have had lots of those!"

"Yes," Penny chimed in, "I want to hear about them, too. All those that aren't too upsetting for the tender sensibilities of we innocent young souls, of course."

McDumont chuckled. "Well, there goes most of my stories. Let's see, what *can* I tell you about...? Okay, there's the time I got arrested for panhandling in this little town in northern Mississippi, I don't even remember the name of the place. But I sure remember that deputy sheriff, a big son of a gun, could have given Crusher Kerrigan a tussle. All he said was, 'You're under arrest for vagrancy, son,' and then he marched me off to the local hoosegow and put me in a cell."

"Golly," said Paul, "you were in jail? What was it like? Did they beat you and make you try to confess to a murder?"

"No, and I think you've been watching too many bad movies. It turned out that this sheriff was lonely. He was an intelligent guy, very sensitive about his size, and looking the way he did and being the law, everybody was afraid of him. This was such a law-abiding town that he never had to arrest anybody except the occasional drunk, and as you can imagine, drunks don't make very good company— they're either plastered out of their skulls or miserable and hung over— that was exactly the way he put it. The real reason he arrested me was because he wanted company, somebody he could talk to and play chess with. Nobody else in town knew how to play."

"Is this really true?" Penny asked sceptically. "It certainly doesn't sound like what I've read about small-town southern sheriffs."

"Oh, it's the truth all right," McDumont said. "And you don't have to tell me this guy was unusual; I've had my run-ins with cops who thought they were holding off the barbarian hordes every time they threw some poor hobo in the slammer. But Sheriff Dennis was different. He got me books from the local library, he left the cell door open so I didn't have to ask him every time I wanted to go to the bathroom, and he was a heck of a cook— I must have put on ten pounds the week I spent in that jail."

"So why did you leave?" Penny asked. "It sounds like paradise compared to life on the road."

"There was just one thing wrong," McDumont said, blushing. "I'm probably the world's worst chess player. Sheriff Dennis tried to teach me, but I couldn't pick it up fast enough. He said he was sorry, but he was going to try to arrest somebody who could give him a decent game."

"Gee," Paul said, "you must be really bad. Even I can play chess."

"That's what I thought, too," McDumont replied. "But Sheriff Dennis spent most of his free time, and he had quite a bit of free time, studying books about chess and playing games against himself. He even played games by mail. We'd start playing, I'd be losing badly, then he'd turn the board around and beat me from what I thought was a hopeless position. I felt really bad about not being able to put up more of a fight, but I never have been very good at games." He laughed. "Maybe it's just as well. If I'd stayed there I'd have turned into a real blimp from eating the sheriff's cooking."

"That's one of the most ridiculous stories I've ever heard," Penny said. "It's so ridiculous that I suppose it's true."

"But didn't you ever get shot at or beat anybody up or anything?" Paul asked. "I thought hoboes were always jumping on trains and stuff."

"Oh, I've been beaten up and pushed around a time or two, but there wasn't anything adventurous about it. It just happened and you tried to forget about it as soon as you could. It's tough being on the road, all right, but it isn't something you enjoy and it isn't something that makes you into a better person." He looked around. "In a way, it's like being in a cage in the zoo. There's not much you can do about it, so you put up with it as best you can and try to figure some way to get out."

"It still sounds pretty good to me," Paul said. "Boy, I wish I could go with you when you leave this crummy town."

"Maybe we'll all go," Penny said lightly, "we'll let Walter take us on a guided tour of all the sights we've never seen. But in the meantime, there are lots of animals here we haven't even looked at yet."

They were homeward bound in Penny's car, McDumont having accepted an invitation to dine at the Bronsons. Paul Junior was napping in the back seat.

Penny turned to him and smiled. "It was a good day, don't you think, Walter? You and Paul seemed to get on very well, considering that you're a rough diamond from the wrong side of the tracks and he's... well, he's from the other side." She frowned and touched his cheek. "That was a silly thing to say, wasn't it? Or do you find it perfectly in keeping with the snobbish character of the clan Bronson?"

"You know, you have this strange habit of asking a whole bunch of questions at the same time and expecting a sensible answer. No, I wouldn't say the Bronsons are snobbish, although your mother probably won't be sponsoring my membership application at the country club. Really, though, your father's been swell, your brother has the right instincts, and if I could only get young Penelope on my side..."

"I suspect that's rather unlikely," she said, running her fingers slowly through his hair. "The fact is that Penelope Bronson prefers suave young men who dress well, have exquisite literary taste, and take her to all the very latest chic night spots. I'm afraid you don't really have much of a chance, Mr. McDumont."

"Oh, well," he said, moving closer to her, "I guess that's that." He nuzzled her ear and kissed her lightly on the cheek. "It was fun while it lasted, though."

"On the other hand... oh yes, that's very nice, don't stop... on the other hand, Miss Bronson has been known to feel sorry for young men smitten with her astonishing beauty and... oh, no, Walter, you will have to stop, we'll have an accident... just a minute, Walter, let me pull over to the side of the road and... we'll... discuss this... further."

As they pulled up at the Bronson's gateway, Paul Junior looked at his watch, yawned, and stretched his arms. "Boy, it sure took a long time to get back from the zoo. Was there a lot of traffic or what?"

"You could say that," McDumont answered. "It definitely was hot and heavy there for a while. I wasn't sure that we ever would get back."

"Nothing an experienced driver couldn't handle," Penny said as she accelerated through the open gate. "Although your clothing appears to be a bit rumpled, Walter. Perhaps you'd like to freshen up once we're inside."

"I've got a scoop for you, toots," McDumont replied. "Somebody messed up your hair, and your lipstick looks like it's been chewed on. I'll race you to the powder room."

Estelle Bronson was very drunk when she came to the dinner table. "Oh, what a nice surprise," she announced when she saw McDumont, her voice so slurred that it took him a moment to understand what words she had used.

"Penny, Paul Junior and Walter had a marvellous day at the zoo," her husband said quickly. "It's the sort of thing we should be doing more of as a family." His wife glanced at him sharply and he lowered his gaze.

"Indeed," Estelle replied, "they do make a touching little family group, don't they? Penny and Mr. McDumont, the proud parents of a strapping young boy." She looked at the three of them in turn. "Let me see, Penny is just about old enough to be Paul's mother, isn't she? There are primitive societies in which women marry and have children very early in life, poor things. And as for you, Mr. McDumont, I imagine you're old enough to serve as the biological father. Or are you already a father? I understand that the lower classes tend to be a bit precocious in that department..."

"For god's sake, Estelle, that's enough," her husband interjected. "Can't we have a nice meal in peace and quiet for a change?"

"Oh, you think it's *enough*, do you? Of course, I've forgotten, you're a father yourself, aren't you? How could I forget that? With the evidence right here in front of me, too." Her voice was shrill, sarcastic.

"May I please be excused?" Paul Junior asked. "I had lots of hot dogs and peanuts and stuff at the zoo. I'm not really very hungry."

"Yes, Paul," his mother said, "you run along. I'm afraid we're not very well supplied in the hot dogs and peanuts department today."

There was silence after the boy had gone. Why does he put up with this? McDumont wondered. Paul Bronson is the president of a bank, he must have a lot of moxie, he didn't get where he is by letting people run roughshod over him. And yet here he is, taking all sorts of grief from his wife without saying boo. He can't look her in the eye; you'd think he was the one who was causing this unpleasant situation. Cripes, if this was what married life was like, maybe it was time to get on the road again.

It was Penny who finally spoke. "I don't think it's very nice for Walter to subject him to our little family problems, mother. And I can't say that I'm enjoying it, either. Would you prefer it if we left?"

"Left?" Estelle Bronson echoed, suddenly pensive. "Left? No, I'm the one that's left, left out of everything that matters." She rose from her chair. "I'm not feeling very well. I think I had better go lie down. Excuse me." She left the room hurriedly.

"Do you think I should go with her?" Paul Bronson asked his daughter.

"No, dad, I don't think that would accomplish anything. You know why..." Penny put her hand to her mouth, shook her head, and turned to McDumont. "I'm sorry, Walter. I thought mother might be cheered up by the fact that I'm going out with a decent young man for a change, but I guess I was wrong."

"It doesn't have anything to do with you, Penny," her father said. "You know that."

"I was just trying to help," she continued as if he hadn't spoken. "That's all I was trying to do."

"I know," her father said. "But I don't know if there's anything we can do to help your mother. I don't think there is anything we can do." He turned his attention to his plate and began to eat slowly, intently.

"I'm sorry," Penny said as they pulled up in front of McDumont's rooming house, "that wasn't very nice for you." They hadn't said much on the way back. Penny seemed lost in thought, and Walter was still trying to figure out the meaning of what he'd seen that evening.

"I don't like to think of you having to live with it," he replied. "Is she always that way, or is there something about me that brings it out in her?"

Penny gripped him hard with both hands. "It isn't you, Walter, believe me. It's something else entirely, something that the Bronsons have to work out for themselves." She kissed him quickly and then pulled away. "I don't know what I'd do if it weren't for you. I can rely on you, can't I? You're not going to jump on a train and leave me, are you?"

"Not on your life," he said gruffly. He drew her to him and kissed her passionately, harshly. He wanted her so badly that he didn't trust himself to speak. Part of him felt like crying, and yet his desire for her was so fierce that he knew he had to keep it under control, had to rein it in and hold the lid down on a violence of feeling that was completely new to him. He didn't know what would happen if he did lose control, and that scared him, scared the hell out of him.

Penny, perhaps sensing this, abruptly broke away from his embrace. "I think we'd better stop, Walter. I think I'm in love with you. But the way things are... I don't know, I'm confused. Talk to me, damn it, tell me what you're thinking about."

He tried to make some sense out of his thoughts. His first reaction was to be flippant, start making jokes. That's what he'd always done in the past whenever some girl tried to get her hooks into him; he'd pull back and act as if it had all been a game, fun while it lasted but not that big a deal. But he couldn't do that now, this wasn't just some girl. Penny was in a class all by herself. Say it, you big lummox— you're in love with her.

"It's hard for me, Penny, I'm not used to being honest about these things." You can say that again, he thought. I haven't been straight with her since the day we met. But that had to be pushed away right now. "There's a part of me that's screaming to get out of here, afraid of getting involved with you. I've never really been serious about anybody, not the way I am about you." He swallowed hard and tried to look at her steadily. "Okay, I'm in love with you. I wish I weren't and I'm glad I am, all at the same time. If you can figure that one out, you're a lot smarter than I am."

Penny smiled. "I can't figure it out because I feel the same way. The last thing my life needs right now is to be in love, but that's what happened. And the funny thing is, I don't know how it happened. One minute I was toodling along, not happy, exactly, but getting along well enough, and the next minute I'm falling for this proletarian dreamboat in my creative-writing class."

She blushed. "I hope this doesn't make you think less of me, Walter, but when I invited you to the diner that night I did imagine that we might have a torrid little student-teacher affair, a spring fling that would snap me out of the doldrums before I said, 'Thank you kindly, good sir, that was just what the doctor ordered, please don't bother to write.' But then I got to know you, and I didn't want it to be that way. Don't ask me what I do want. I can't tell you. But I know that you've become important to me."

"But not so important that you can tell me what's going on with your family." He felt like a bastard saying it, knowing that he wasn't being completely honest himself, but he was long past the point where this was merely some sort of amateur mystery that he was being paid to solve. He wanted to know what was wrong with the Bronsons because he was in love with Penny; he wanted to help her and protect her and be the world to her. And it looked as though he couldn't do that unless he found out what was eating away at her family.

"That's not it," she insisted, "that's not it at all. If I were the only one concerned, I'd tell you in a minute; but it isn't just me, there are other people involved who might be badly hurt. I'm sorry, but that's how it is, and I can't do anything about it."

"I believe you," he eventually said, reluctantly. "But where does that leave us?"

"It leaves us knowing that we love each other, silly, which is something we didn't know before." She kissed him firmly but gently. "And I don't know about you, but that isn't something I say to every Tom, Dick, and Harry I meet. Now you skedaddle. It's late and I'm completely worn out."

"Now that you mention it, so am I. I don't believe I even have enough energy for a goodnight kiss."

"You'd be surprised," Penny said, snuggling into his arms, "you'd be surprised at what you can do when you have to."

Waiting for Chandler to turn up at Rumplemeyer's, McDumont thought about whether or not it was time to level with him. It wasn't fair to Ray, holding back on him; he was paying good money for a job of work and he wasn't getting everything that he was paying for. On the other hand, some of what had happened between McDumont and Penny wasn't anybody's business but theirs.

That was the easy part. But what was he going to say about the odd behaviour of the Bronsons, the tensions that seemed to flare up between them at the drop of a hat? And even if he'd been imagining all that, there was the incontrovertible evidence of what Penny had said about the family's secrets; there was something there, there was no doubt about it. He didn't know what it was, but he knew it was there.

So why didn't he just go ahead and tell Chandler? Partly, McDumont had to admit, it was because he had always been a close-mouthed kind of guy. What people didn't know couldn't hurt you. But here there was more to it than that. Penny was involved, and he wasn't going to do anything that might hurt her. So the question was, what could he tell Ray that wouldn't harm Penny?

Here he came now; he'd better figure out something. "Hi, Ray, what's your pleasure?"

"Hello, Walter. You're buying, are you? A stein of Lowenbrau, then," he said to the waiter who had hurried over. "Let it not be said that Raymond Chandler ever looked a gift horse in the mouth. So how was the zoo? I don't think I've had the pleasure of its acquaintance."

"Oh, we had a pretty good time. It gave me a chance to get to know Paul Junior a little better." McDumont took a sip from his glass. "He's a funny kid, snotty as hell one minute and a little hoodlum the next. You can see he'd be hard to handle."

"How does he get on with his parents?" Chandler asked. "His father was what, forty or so when he was born, and the mother can't be a great deal younger. As far as I'm concerned, anyone who indulges in parenthood at that age is taking quite a chance." He laughed. "Look who's talking, I never had the nerve to indulge in parenthood at any age, what do I know? But I'm still curious about this business of Paul having been kidnapped back East, never having been returned, according to the Boston papers anyway, and then turning up living with his family in Los Angeles. Have any of them said anything about that?"

"No, I think it must have been some kind of an undercover deal. Otherwise I think Penny would have told me about it." You jerk, he thought savagely, keep her out of it, you don't need to brag about your rich girlfriend. Not that there's a hell of a lot to brag about.

"Yes, Penny. You seem to be getting on very well there." He looked at McDumont appraisingly. "You haven't fallen in love with her, have you?"

McDumont didn't say anything.

"I think perhaps you have. My god, is that what's happened? Look, Walter, let me give you some free advice. Girls like Penelope Bronson aren't intended for the likes of you and me; that isn't the way society operates. Think about it. She's used to a certain way of life. Things that she takes for granted are luxuries that you and I can only dream about. The way that you've been living, is that the way you think she wants to live?"

"She isn't like that, she's isn't like that at all."

Chandler shook his head. "You don't understand. It isn't a question of feelings. I'm not saying that she doesn't care for you or you for her. But this isn't a fairy tale, you aren't going to find a pot of gold at the end of the rainbow and live happily ever after. What do her parents think?"

"As a matter of fact, Mr. Know-It-All, her father *has* offered me a job. Writing public-relations stuff for his bank, he thinks I'm just right for it. Working directly under his supervision, too."

Chandler stared at him. "When did this happen?"

"A couple of days ago. I didn't mention it because I don't have any intention of taking him up on it."

"You don't? For god's sake, Walter, you've been offered a job that a lot of people would be willing to kill for, and that's not much of an exaggeration. And it's not just the job. What about Penny? You'd better think about that, too. You'd be putting yourself on a much higher social level if you accepted Bronson's offer."

McDumont sighed. "I don't know if this will make any sense to you, Ray, but I can't accept something that I'd be getting under false pretences. You and I know why I've become involved with the Bronsons; it wouldn't have happened if you hadn't hired me as your half-assed private detective or whatever I am, and I can't very well accept Paul Bronson's generosity when I'm being paid to spy on him. Surely you can see that?"

"Yes, I can. And it seems to me there's a very simple solution. Why don't I just take you off the payroll of Chandler Investigations, Very Limited, and let you continue on your upward climb through Los Angeles society? I'd still like to keep in touch, but if you want to know the truth, you don't strike me as the world's most competent private detective." He chuckled. "You're not supposed to fall in love with the person you're investigating. Every other pulp-magazine story beats that plot line to death."

"Jesus, Ray, you're being swell about this. Would that be okay? I'd feel a lot better about it."

"Not to worry. I've had my fun out of this, and it's even given me some ideas that I think I can use. But now that this odd little relationship has come to an end, Walter, I hope we can still be friends."

"Sure, that's the way I want it, too. Aside from anything else, I'll always be grateful to you for getting me involved in this thing— otherwise I never would have met Penny." Walter looked toward the bar. "Let's get that waiter over here. Tonight all the drinks are on me."

CHAPTER SEVEN

The Prairie sun beat down on the harvesting crew. The air was on fire, it seared his lungs with every breath. His clothes were soaked with sweat, and he was so exhausted that he began to fall behind the tireless, inexorably advancing threshing machines. In the west, a line of dark clouds promised rain. You could hear the thunder now, faint rumblings at first, and then a steady pounding...

Someone was knocking on his door. McDumont got out of bed, still groggy from the vivid dream, and fumbled with the snap lock. It was Penny.

"Walter, you've got to help us! Someone tried to kidnap Paul this morning, you're the first person I thought of. Oh you've got to help, I don't know what to do." She rushed into the room and put her arms around him. She was shaking, her face red and teary-eyed as she held him tightly.

"Whoa, Penny, whoa, hold on a minute. Try to get hold of yourself and tell me about it." He sat her down in the room's only chair. "Stay here for a second while I get decent." He put his bathrobe on over his pyjamas, quickly made the bed, then steered her over to it. When they were sitting down, his arm firmly around her, he said, "All right, tell me what happened."

"It was this morning," she said, her voice still agitated but under better control. "Paul always waits for the school bus in front of the gate. The chauffeur used to drive him, but some of the other boys made fun of him and the headmaster thought it might help his adjustment if he took the bus. It's a small school, the boys are all from this area, and Paul did seem to like taking the bus better."

She paused and wiped her eyes. "But this morning a car pulled up in front of the gate and two men tried to kidnap him. One of them held a gun on the security guard while the other one went after Paul. Thank god Paul put up a fight, he kicked the man in the... where it would hurt the most. Then the school bus came, and the men drove away. But they almost got him, they almost got him, Walter!" Penny began to cry, her face buried in McDumont's chest, her arms wrapped tightly around him.

"It's all right now," he said, "it's all right, don't cry."

"What did the police say?" he asked after she had calmed down.

She glanced at him and then looked away. "We didn't call the police."

He stared at her. "I don't understand. Why wouldn't you call the police? Two guys tried to kidnap your brother and you didn't call the police?"

"No," she said, "we couldn't. And if you give me a minute, I'll tell you why."

"First of all," Penny said, "first of all you have to promise that you will never repeat a word of this to anyone."

He nodded his head. "My lips are sealed. But why all the rigamarole? What the hell kind of mess can you be in when someone tries to snatch your little brother and you can't call the police? It sounds crazy to me."

"Yes," she said, much calmer, "it sounds crazy. Because it is crazy."

She sighed and looked over his shoulder. "I guess it all started, in a way, when I was born. Mother had a very hard time. She almost died.

I don't know what the exact problem was, but it was something that made childbirth very difficult for her. Not impossible, but dangerous.

"And so for a long time I was an only child. But my father desperately wanted a son, even though he knew that mother's life might be in danger if something went wrong. They consulted a lot of doctors. I was too young to understand exactly what was going on, but I knew about the doctors, I often heard them discussing what this doctor and that doctor had said. My mother was afraid to have another child, of course, but she loved my father and she understood how much he wanted a son. So in the end she did become pregnant again."

"And so Paul Junior was born," McDumont said during the pause that followed.

"And so she gave birth to a son," Penny said, looking away. "But again it was a terribly difficult birth. I didn't know this until later, but at one point the doctor told my father that Estelle might die if everything followed its natural course. The child would probably live, but there was a good chance Estelle would die. If they terminated the pregnancy, on the other hand, Estelle would almost certainly survive, although the child would of course be dead."

"That's a hell of a thing," McDumont said. "How did they decide what to do?"

"It wasn't a question of *they*," she answered. "Mother was heavily drugged because of all the pain. She was in and out of consciousness, she had no control over the decision. She could hear them talking about her, talking about how she might die, and she tried to tell them that she wanted to live, she didn't want to sacrifice her life. But they couldn't understand her, that's what they told her later, they couldn't understand what she was saying. It was father who told the doctor not to terminate the pregnancy, to let the child be born."

"And fortunately, both mother and son survived," McDumont said.

"Yes, but Estelle never got over hearing her husband say that the child's life was more important than her own. And even though there have been many times she's made life hell for father since then, you've had a glimpse of that, I can't say that I blame her. Especially after what happened next."

"What was that?" Now the kidnapping, he thought. Jesus Christ, the Bronsons have been through a lot, and you can't say it's over, not after today.

"Estelle didn't want to have anything to do with her son. She refused to care for him. Father tried to make the best of it, he carried on as if this were just some sort of temporary quirk that mother would grow out of— 'post-natal depression' was what they called it, I remember father using that phrase all the time— but she never did. Father had to hire a full-time nurse for the baby. Estelle wouldn't even concern herself with that. She started to drink heavily, too. Most of the time she behaved normally with my father when there were other people around, but at home sometimes she would say terrible things about how he wished she were dead and she wished she were dead, too. And then the baby was kidnapped."

"Kidnapped?" McDumont echoed. "What an awful thing! But at least you got Paul Junior back."

"No," she said, "we did not. The kidnappers demanded a ransom and the ransom money was paid, but the baby was never returned."

McDumont was puzzled. "I don't understand. Paul Junior lives at your house. He's part of your family."

"There is a boy called Paul Junior living at the Bronson house," Penny said. "But he is not the son of my mother and father."

McDumont was stunned. Throughout Penny's account of the Bronsons' troubled family history, he'd been reminding himself that he had to make sure to seem surprised when she told him about the kidnapping, and he thought he'd done a pretty decent job of it. Then he'd had the rug pulled out from under him by what in fact *was* a revelation, and thanks to that little bolt from the blue he felt completely at sea. The boy he'd come to think of as Paul Junior wasn't Paul Junior? It didn't make any kind of sense.

"You've lost me," he finally said.

She looked at him intently. "My father did his best to cope with all of this. He was the one who had to keep the family going, but he was devastated too, in his own way. I think he did come to realize exactly what he had done to his wife, and of course he felt bad about it. He and Estelle had always been a couple of lovebirds; until the birth of their second child they'd been very affectionate with one another. But now she refused to let him touch her, and she insisted on her own bedroom. Father tried to win her back, he paid court to her with flowers and chocolates and everything else he could think of, but it was too late. Mother was either out working on her charity projects or drinking alone in her room. It was as though he didn't have a wife any more."

"But what about the kidnapping?" he asked. "You haven't said what happened to the baby."

"I'm coming to that. But I want you to understand that even before the kidnapping, things had happened that no one was ever going to be able to put right again. It was horrible when the baby was taken away, but that wasn't why everything fell apart. It began long before that, long before."

She paused and looked at him questioningly. "You like my father, don't you?"

"Yes, I do. He's been very nice to me. And this stuff about the baby, well, I don't know that I blame him completely. You said your parents had agreed to try to have another child. It could be that your mother didn't hear what he and the doctor were really talking about. You said she was drugged, she could have misheard."

"That's all true," Penny said, "I've thought it myself. But even if that's how it was, there isn't any doubt about what happened next.

"I said my parents used to be like a couple of lovebirds. Well, after her son was born, Estelle became completely cold toward dad. He did everything he could to win her back, but he couldn't do it. So after a while he stopped trying. And then he became involved with another woman."

"Your father?" McDumont said. "That's really hard to believe."

"It was thirteen years ago, Walter, and dad was still a very attractive man. Plus people knew, sort of, that he and Estelle weren't getting along very well. You can't hide that kind of thing no matter how polite you are to each other in public. So quite a few of Estelle's lady friends started making excuses to meet dad. They'd come to the house under the pretext of seeing how mother and the baby were, or they'd drop in on him at the bank to ask about some investment or other."

McDumont couldn't help laughing. "Well, if it was going to happen, better it should happen that way. 'All in the family,' I suppose, someone like Margot Stevenson, maybe."

"You're right, someone like Margot would have been perfect, although this was back in Boston, remember. They do things a little more discreetly there. Margot would have been a wee bit on the flamboyant side. Anyway, that isn't what happened. No, my father ended up having an affair with someone from the other end of the social spectrum. He became infatuated with a young woman who worked as a secretary at the bank."

"Shocking," McDumont said. "Positively shocking. Maybe she was a relation of mine— a poor relation, of course."

"There wasn't anything funny about it," she said sharply. "Mona Wilson was a calculating little slut who knew very well that this was a chance for her to sleep her way up the social ladder. She'd already been married and divorced at least once— at least that's what she told dad, not that'd I'd take her word that the sun was up without checking— and she claimed that her former husband had treated her very badly. Anyway, when she became pregnant, and I'm sure that she made *sure* she became pregnant, she threatened dad with everything her beady little mind could think of: the police, the newspapers, a beating by her father and her brothers, to make him leave his family and come live with her."

"That's crazy," McDumont interjected. "Queen Victoria's been dead a long time. It wouldn't have been that much of a scandal. Especially since she'd been married before. Why didn't your father just brazen it out?"

"You don't know Boston," Penny said, "it's still awfully conservative. Especially if you're a banker, you're supposed to be holier than thou in every respect. Besides, dad had to take Estelle's feelings into account. He'd hurt her again and this time he was going to do whatever she wanted him to do.

"Mother had been devastated by the kidnapping; it seemed to bring out all the maternal feelings she'd repressed after the child was born. She was sorry that she hadn't behaved as a real mother should; she really regretted it. So when dad told her about Mona Wilson, Estelle was upset, of course, but then she came up with a solution that would satisfy everyone. It was an absolutely idiotic solution, but it was the one that everyone finally agreed on.

"What she decided was that dad would buy the baby from Mona after it was born. This couldn't be done legally, of course, but if you're a very important person with lots of money and influential friends, you can get away with almost anything. Estelle wanted a baby, and by now it was clear that her own baby was never going to be returned to her. So she did the next best thing. She made dad buy Mona's child, made him pay Mona a large sum of money, and then she raised the baby as her own Paul Junior."

"That's the craziest thing I've ever heard," McDumont said. "How in the name of all that's holy did they expect to get away with it?"

"Oh, it was easier than you might think. Mona gave birth to a boy, so that wasn't a problem. The birth took place in a private clinic in Mexico, with the parents registered as dad and 'Mary Smith.' Some time later, legal proceedings were initiated against 'Mary Smith' for deserting her child and its father, and dad became the infant's sole legal guardian. I don't understand all the formalities involved, but whatever they were, the result was that the Bronsons once again had a son named 'Paul

Junior.' And cute little Mona Wilson had a tidy sum of not very hard-earned money."

McDumont shook his head. "And they wonder why people think this is a rotten social system? My god, if someone like me had tried to do anything like that, I'd have had the book thrown at me." He looked at Penny. "Don't you think it's unfair to have one law for the rich and another law for everyone else? Doesn't it bother you that your parents got away with breaking the law just because they could afford to pay people off?"

"It does bother me," Penny said, "I know it's not right. But you're making a mistake if you think that's what happened in this case. The fact of the matter is, my parents didn't get away with it."

"My parents weren't stupid, Walter, they knew that a lot of people had been involved in covering this thing up, no matter how technically legal and above board it all was. So the first thing they did once they had the new baby was to leave Boston and move to Los Angeles. They fabricated a story about adopting a child whose parents had been killed in an automobile accident, and they told people that Estelle's health required that they move to a warmer climate. And they didn't go back to Boston or keep in touch with their friends there. After a while they assumed their secret was safe."

"Which you just said wasn't true."

"Yes, although it certainly seemed to be true for a long time. Years went by without any indication that anyone knew, and the Bronsons seemed to be adjusting very well to their new home. Then Paul Junior began to have problems at school, and Estelle didn't handle it very well. Instead of trying to help him, understand him, she blamed it on his background. And Paul Junior, who had been told that he was adopted, got it into his head that he came from 'bad blood.' And he's been trying to prove it ever since."

"I don't know," McDumont said, "he doesn't strike me as that bad a kid. He was fine when we went to the zoo."

Penny nodded her head. "I know, I can't see it either, but this isn't something that's just a figment of Estelle's imagination. He's done some nasty things in school, he stabbed another boy with a pencil and hurt him quite seriously, and at one of the schools he attended a teacher described him as 'incorrigible.' That's become part of the problem, too, actually; he hasn't been able to settle down anywhere. The school he's at now is very big on discipline, and he seems to be taking to that, although he's still not doing very well in his academic subjects."

"With any luck, maybe that's all it will take. From what you've told me, it's no wonder the kid has problems." McDumont chuckled. "Hell, if you'd known me at the age of sixteen, a high-school dropout who couldn't hold a job, you would have said that I was never going to amount to anything." He frowned. "Not that I ever have amounted to anything."

"Don't be silly. You're already a better writer than a lot of people who've been published. And you're nice, too," she said, ruffling his hair. "In fact, you're much too nice to get mixed up in a crazy situation like this. Wouldn't you like me to just go away and not bother you any more?"

McDumont kissed her. "Not bloody likely, Yank. Sure, your family's in quite a mess, but it doesn't sound completely hopeless. I guess you're going to have to do something about protecting Paul Junior, but it's possible that the rest of it will get better with time, not so much your mother, maybe, but kids can take a lot of confusion and still come out okay. You know that expression, 'time heals all wounds'?"

"I've heard it," she said. "But the problem is, time hasn't healed anything for my family. Rather the reverse, in fact."

"I don't follow you."

"I know you don't. And that's because I haven't finished telling you the rest of the story."

"About two years ago, Mona Wilson got in touch with my father again. She'd come out to California to try to get into the movies— a ridiculous story on the face of it, but quite possibly true, since Mona's IQ is almost certainly lower than her bust measurement— and she'd seen dad's picture in the newspaper. Apparently she tried to start something up again, but dad wasn't having any of it. He told her that was over and done with. She begged him for money, told him that she had spent all of the money she received for the baby and would have to turn to prostitution if he didn't help her, but he was firm."

"She didn't say anything about wanting her son back?" McDumont asked.

"No, not then, although later... but I'm getting ahead of myself. At the same time this was going on, I was hanging around with a pretty fast crowd myself, kids with too much money and too few brains who thought that drinking too much and driving too fast were the ultimate purposes of life." She coloured. "They loved to go *slumming*, too, that's exactly what they called it, the sleazier the better as far as they were concerned. Which is why places such as the Sapphire Club are no stranger to me and mine. Which is also why I happened to run into Mona Wilson and Larry Harmon there for the first time in my life on one memorable evening not too long ago."

"Larry Harmon? He keeps turning up like a bad penny." Now it was Walter's turn to blush. "Sorry, it wasn't one of my dumb puns, it just slipped out. But what was Harmon doing with Mona?" He reddened again. "Stupid question, I suppose, given what you've told me. But how did they know who you were?"

"I can thank my charming escort for that. He'd met Larry somewhere and invited them over to our table for a drink. When he introduced me, you could see Mona's eyes light up like sparklers on the Fourth of July. Larry noticed it, too, and it wasn't long before Mona started dropping coy little hints about how *close* she'd been to my father back in Boston."

"How did you handle it? That must have been pretty embarrassing."

"I was concerned, of course, but as far as I knew, Mona had no legal claim on my family, so I'm afraid I was rather bitchy to her. 'How interesting, darling, I'm afraid father never mentioned your name,' that sort of thing. I certainly wasn't going to let her imply that she had any sort of relationship to the Bronsons." Penny laughed. "I was positively vicious. I made a point of asking Mona about her occupation— she claimed to be a 'model,' of course— and then quizzed her about where she worked, who her agent was, and so on. Her replies were rather pathetic, to say the least, although I thought it was interesting that at one point she referred to Larry Harmon as her 'professional advisor.'"

"Professional advisor? I didn't think cops were allowed to have another job."

"Oh, don't be dense, Walter, the situation was perfectly plain. I asked Jack Diamond about it later and he said yes, Larry was acting as her protector, cops often have this kind of a relationship with prostitutes. They get paid off in sex, and word gets around that the prostitute has a powerful friend in the police department."

"I can believe that, Penny, but you implied before that Harmon was after you in the same way. Why would he think that he had a chance there, given how you feel about him?"

"Mona's big mouth," she said. "She's told him something, although I don't think she's told him the whole story. Larry's always hinting that he knows everything, but if he did I think he'd come right out with it—he's not a subtle guy, that's not his style. He sees what he wants and goes after it." She grimaced. "And what he wants right now is me."

"That bastard," McDumont said. "I'll kill the son of a bitch with my bare hands if I have to."

"No," she said wearily, "you won't, because I can handle him. You don't need to do anything about Larry Harmon. He's the last person in the world I want to antagonize."

He stared at her. "He's the reason why you're afraid to call the police about this kidnapping attempt, isn't he?"

She looked startled. "Yes, that's right. But you can see why. Larry is on the police force; if he found out about this it would be like waving a red flag in front of a bull. He'd squeeze the truth out of Mona and use it for his own purposes."

"Use it to get at you, you mean. I don't know how much faith you can put in Mona, though. She doesn't sound like someone you can rely on."

"She isn't, but at the time she gave up Paul Junior it was made very clear to her that if she tried anything like blackmail, the consequences would be very serious. So in a way it may be a question of whom she fears most, the Bronsons or Larry Harmon."

Now it was McDumont's turn to grimace. "And what if she decides it's Harmon? What if she spills the beans and he tells you that either you... do what he wants or he'll go after your family? What would you do if that happened?"

She looked him straight in the eye. "I would do whatever I thought I had to do, Walter. And nothing and nobody on this earth would be able to stop me."

McDumont didn't know what to think. He'd figured that what was wrong with the Bronson family was some kind of complicated psychological business that only rich and powerful people had the time to indulge in, and now he'd learned that he was dead wrong. They were in serious trouble, and as if that weren't bad enough, Larry Harmon was involved in it, too. He'd talked tough about Harmon, made big noises about killing him, but that was just shooting off his mouth. Harmon scared him. To be honest about it, what McDumont needed was the mindless courage of the pulp-magazine heroes— charge in with guns blazing and fists flying and devil take the hindmost.

Penny was looking at him thoughtfully. "What are you thinking, Walter? It's a terrible mess, isn't it? But I'm so close to it, perhaps I'm missing something. What do you think we should do?"

What I should do is get the hell out of here, he thought. "I don't know, Penny, I wouldn't know where to start." But you do, he said to himself savagely, you start with trying to help the person you love when she has nowhere else to go. "I guess you have to start by protecting Paul Junior," he said. "What about a security service or private detectives?"

"I don't know. Our gate guard was from a private security firm, but he quit after what happened this morning. He said he didn't get paid enough to risk being shot."

"I see his point." He remembered what Chandler had said about private detectives— corrupt, many of them, and if they were ex-cops there was always the chance they'd be pals of Harmon. Then it came to him.

An obvious solution, when you thought about it. And it might even work.

"Come on, Penny, I have to make some phone calls. McDumont's private army is about to go into action."

McDumont got Crusher Kerrigan's number from Jack Diamond. Kerrigan listened to his idea and said, "Yeah, that's jake with me. Pick me up any time after noon." Then Penny phoned her father and arranged for a family meeting at two o'clock.

They gathered on the Bronsons' terrace. Paul Junior seemed none the worse for his experience, was even proud of how he'd defended himself; but his father seemed crushed by this new blow, and Estelle, although doing her best to hide it, was very drunk. The only light relief was provided by Crusher, whose, "Jeez, you really got a nice joint here," even got a laugh from Penny's father.

"I've got a proposal to make," McDumont said when they were all settled. "I've discussed it with Penny, and she thinks it's a good idea. Mr. Kerrigan has also agreed to participate, so I guess it's mainly a question of whether or not the rest of you think this is a good idea." He paused and looked at each of them in turn.

"You go ahead and tell us about it, Walter," Paul Bronson said. "At the moment, I don't know what to do."

"Yes," Estelle added, "I'm very curious myself. I've gotten out of the habit of listening to what *men* have to say." She stared pointedly at her husband, who turned away from her.

"This is the way I see it," McDumont continued. "Paul Junior needs to be protected, and for reasons that we don't need to go into, conventional methods are out of the question." He glanced at Kerrigan, who still seemed to be intrigued by his new surroundings. He hadn't told Crusher why the Bronsons couldn't go to the police, and it looked as though he wouldn't have to— Kerrigan was used to taking it as it came.

He'd do whatever was necessary without worrying too much about the details.

"So what I suggest is this. I'm an experienced driver. I've driven cars, taxis, and farm equipment here, there, and everywhere. You need someone to drive Paul Junior to and from school, and wherever else he needs to go. I can do that."

"That's very good of you, Walter," Paul Bronson said, "but these men today had guns. What about that?"

McDumont nodded. "I'm not a gunman, that's for sure, but I have been around weapons. I was a member of the militia for two years in Toronto, and I did learn my way around a military rifle. I wasn't a bad shot, either. But it's true, guns aren't really my line of territory. That's why I've asked Mr. Kerrigan to give us a hand in that department."

Estelle spoke up. "He's certainly an imposing figure of a man, but how do we know that he would make a competent bodyguard? What exactly are your qualifications, Mr. Kerrigan?"

Crusher made a quick movement with his right hand and flourished a dark blue revolver. Its long barrel gleamed in the afternoon sunshine. "This is my baby," he said, stroking the barrel slowly and affectionately. "Me and baby can take care of ourselves. We been through a lot together, riding a scout car on the border run, keeping the big Eastern mobs out of the local rackets, things like that."

Paul Bronson looked at McDumont quizzically. "What did he say, Walter, I don't quite...?"

"I'll try to translate. Crusher was telling you that he served as a guard for bootleg liquor convoys during Prohibition, and that he has been employed by Los Angeles... business interests to discourage takeover attempts by competitors from other cities. I might add that Mr. Kerrigan's prowess at the latter is particularly admired by his professional colleagues."

"Is that a fact?" Paul Bronson commented. "Well, your recommendation is good enough for me, Walter. What do you think, Estelle?"

"Why not?" she said. "Although we haven't spoken about money. I'm curious as to what valuation Messrs. McDumont and Kerrigan put on their professional services."

"That's the least of my worries," her husband replied, "but I suppose we might as well get it out of the way. What do you think is fair, Walter?"

"I've already discussed this with Crusher, and his fee is twenty-five dollars per day. Very reasonable at the price, I might add."

"Yes, I can imagine," Paul Bronson said. "But what about yourself?"

"I'm doing this for free," McDumont said. "And believe me, I have my reasons."

"How gallant!" Estelle looked at Walter and Penny in turn. "The age of chivalry is *not* dead. Sir Walter will defend us."

"It isn't anything like that," McDumont said. "And even though I'm crazy about Penny, I'm no knight in shining armour." He smiled. "No, if we were going to put it in chess terms, you'd have to say I'm just a pawn in this game. Happy to be one, though."

Penny took his hand. "That sounds like you're fishing for compliments, you big nut, even though I know you aren't. Well, you're going to get them anyway. We all appreciate what you're doing, don't we?"

Paul and Estelle Bronson nodded their heads. "I think it's neat," Paul Junior said. "I just hope those guys try something again."

"I sure hope they don't," McDumont replied. "But if they do, we'll do our best to be ready for them."

CHAPTER EIGHT

Penny and Walter were walking in the Bronsons' garden on the morning after the family meeting. It had been decided that McDumont and Crusher would move into the vacant servants' quarters above the Bronsons' garage, which would save on their travel time to and from work as well as affording better protection for the family. It was a spacious and nicely furnished apartment, more than big enough for the two of them, and so far everyone was pleased with the new arrangement.

"I can't stop worrying about Larry Harmon," McDumont said, as if thinking out loud.

Penny glared. "Do we have to go over this again and again, Walter? How many times do I have to tell you? Larry Harmon has the power to hurt my family very badly. You're going to have to forget about him, I don't want to hear any more about it."

"I understand why you'd say that, but I still think you're completely wrong. You just don't get anywhere with the Larry Harmons of this world by knuckling under. They push and push and keep pushing until you push back. The only thing they understand is force."

She stared at him. "I think I know one of the reasons you're so upset. I shouldn't have said those things about doing whatever I might have to do, should I?"

"No, damn it, you shouldn't have," he said angrily. "How do you think that makes me feel, crazy about you like I don't know what, and then you tell me that if you have to you'll do whatever Harmon wants? How the hell is that supposed to make me feel?"

"I'm sorry," Penny said gently, "it was a very stupid thing to say. And I didn't mean it, not like that. I don't think I could ever go through with it, no matter what the situation was. I mean that, Walter."

She smiled at him ruefully. "In a way, it's the female version of your male bravado— 'a woman's got to do what a woman's got to do' sort of thing, and just as silly as the masculine variety. I really am sorry."

Penny kissed him firmly, almost aggressively. Then she pulled back and looked at him intently. "I love you, Walter McDumont. I don't ever want to hurt you. And I wouldn't have anything to do with Larry Harmon if he were the last man on earth. You can underline the 'anything.' Satisfied?" She kissed him again, harder than before.

"Ecstatic," he said, kissing her back. "It's unanimous, we both love me. But now I want you to listen seriously to something I've done a lot of thinking about. And don't interrupt me until I'm finished. I think I've come up with a way to get Larry Harmon out of our hair."

"For starters," he said, "there's our new friend Crusher Kerrigan."

"Crusher Kerrigan?" she echoed. "Where does he come into this?"

"You should know, you're the one who gave me the idea. Remember when we were at the Sapphire Club, you were telling me about what a terror Crusher was? You said even the police were afraid of him, or words to that effect. Well, if I were to fight Larry Harmon, and Crusher were around to make sure it was a fair fight..."

Penny's eyes widened. "Are you serious? God, my mother called you 'Sir Walter,' and I think it's gone to your head. Why don't you just challenge him to a joust? We could put you on horses and borrow suits of armour from the museum. What about pistols at ten paces?" She shook her head. "I don't believe I'm listening to this. This is utterly insane."

McDumont was angry. "Are you finished? Any more wiseacre remarks you want to get off your chest? Jesus Christ, Penny, do you think I'm just fooling around here? Try to take this seriously!"

She didn't answer him right away. Then she said, "All right, Walter, I'm sorry. Please go on."

"It was you that gave me idea in the first place," he said, still upset. "Were you talking through your hat or not? Who told you what about Crusher and the police?"

"Jack, Jack Diamond. It was something about Larry Harmon and his partner trying to extort money from Diamond. Jack told them that he'd send Crusher after them if he had to, and that was the end of that. That was the sense of the thing, anyway."

"Okay," McDumont said excitedly, "Crusher is now employed by your family. We know Harmon is afraid of him. Why don't we take advantage of the situation and set it up so that I can get Harmon into a fair fight?"

"I suppose it does make some sort of primitive sense," Penny said.

"For that matter, why don't you just sic Crusher on him? Aren't you... worried? Larry Harmon's much bigger than you are, after all."

"The bigger they are... No, Penny, this is *my* beef with Harmon, nobody else's. And I may not look like Jack Dempsey, but I know how to take care of myself."

Then he was twelve years old again, his back against the wall of the school playground, a jeering semi-circle of older kids daring him to fight Sandy Ross. Ross towered over him, hissing obscenities and smacking his hands together. "C'mon, ya little hooligan, what's the matter, you afraid?" he snarled. Then he slapped McDumont contemptuously with his open right hand, looking around at his pals with pride and satisfaction.

Ross had been after him for weeks. McDumont was the new kid in school whose ragged clothing and cocky manner made him an instant target for bullies. Now he'd been cornered, and he was going to have to fight. Okay, that was it. There was no way out.

He took his fear and shoved it away. It couldn't help him. He felt cold and hard, his heart pumping strength into his fists, his mind clear and alert. He laughed. "That the best you can do, Ross? Why don't you go home and beat up your sister? I hear she jumps on every dick in town."

Ross came for him outraged and red-faced, his arms straight out, grasping for a stranglehold. McDumont ducked and sank his fist deep into soft stomach, then brought his knee up savagely into Ross's suddenly agonized face. Half bent over, clutching his stomach with both hands and shaking his head with pain, his enemy was now at Walter's mercy. McDumont punched him in the throat and Ross fell down, first choking for air and then spewing up blood and vomit. His friends shrank back, shock and fear in their expressions.

"Get up, you big piece of shit!" McDumont screamed. He stood over Ross, his body shaking, his fists waving wildly in the air. "Who's next?" he demanded, looking around at the rest of them. "Who's next?"

The high point of my checkered boxing career, McDumont thought. You sure did have your clock cleaned plenty of times after that. But the main thing was to put fear behind you and let your instincts take over. When you grew up the way he had, having to fight for everything you got, you learned that fear could only hurt you, could only hold you back and give you a reason to run away. And he wasn't going to run away from Larry Harmon.

"You're far away somewhere," Penny remarked. "If I weren't leery of provoking another outburst of your wretched puns, I'd say 'A penny for your thoughts.'"

It took him a moment to realize what she'd said. "Well, they aren't worth a plugged nickel, sweetcakes. Not even a thin dime." She groaned. "But you should know me by now, toots. I take no prisoners and give no quarter."

Crusher wasn't crazy about the idea, either. "I seen Harmon work guys over a couple times, Walter. He's one mean son of a bitch. Me, I can take it or leave it alone, it ain't no big deal to me, but Harmon is a guy who digs his work. I've seen him beat some poor slob unconscious and then prop him up so he could slug him some more."

"That's where you come in," McDumont said. "If I do lose, I want you to get me out of there while I've still got my matinée-idol looks. And if he happens to turn up with brass knuckles or a sap or a shiv or whatever, you can take care of that department, too."

"Yeah, no sweat." Crusher looked at McDumont appraisingly. "Maybe you got a shot after all, you look like you can move pretty good. Harmon's used to whacking around guys with a gun on them, either his or Lou's. He don't know what it means to fight fair." He chuckled. "Yeah, this could be good. You want me to set things up, make a phone call?"

"That's right," McDumont said. "Somewhere quiet, no spectators, just you and me and Harmon. Oh, I guess maybe we should let him bring somebody along."

"Not on your life," Kerrigan said. "I'm gonna have enough to do watching Harmon. I ain't got eyes in the back of my head to keep track of nobody else. Nope, this little fandango is gonna be for just the three of us."

"Whatever you say, boss. Did you have a place in mind?"

Kerrigan thought about it. "Yeah. The alley behind the Sapphire Club, there ain't nothing back there, that's what we want. Nice and private, you guys can even kiss and make up after if you want to."

"I kind of doubt that's what we'll be doing," McDumont said thoughtfully. "In fact, I think I'd be kind of disappointed if Harmon didn't feel the same way about this as I do."

Kerrigan made his phone call. Harmon was disbelieving at first, perhaps not remembering who McDumont was, but then suddenly seemed interested. "Yeah, I know who you mean, that punk in the cab. What's his beef? I let the little jerk off easy, I didn't give him that bad a time."

"You been trying to play house with his girlfriend," Crusher said, "and he don't like it. Either you stay away from the Bronson twist or he's gonna have it out with you."

"Stupid little prick needs to learn some manners," Harmon said. "What have you got in mind?"

They set it up for the following afternoon, three p.m. behind the Sapphire Club. Harmon wasn't crazy about not being able to bring Lou along, but Kerrigan was adamant. "I know I can trust me, Larry, but I don't know I can trust Lou. You just be there, lonesome. You ain't, I'm gonna be angry with you. And you know how I get when I get angry."

Crusher put the telephone down with a laugh. "He don't like it, but he'll do it. 'Tell that punk Canuck his ass is grass,' he says. Okay, I told you." He frowned at McDumont. "I know you're a tough guy, you eat cops for breakfast, lunch, and dinner, but could I maybe show you a couple of things? Harmon's taller and heavier than you are, you're gonna to have to dance with him for a little while. You know what fighters mean, they say they're gonna get on their bicycle?"

"Sure, keeping out of a bigger man's reach, then picking your spots."

Kerrigan whistled appreciatively. "You got the lingo, all right. I don't know if you got the sand, but you got the lingo." He looked serious again and began to bob and weave around the room. "Anyway, this is what I'm talking about..."

Jack Diamond clapped McDumont on the shoulder. "Larry needs a good whipping. Give him a couple of shots from me if you can, will you? I didn't tell Curtis and the boys, but they'd be rooting for you too, if they knew about it— Harmon hates coloured people, he's always giving them a hard time, always looking for some excuse to run them in."

"Yeah," McDumont said, "I seem to be the great white hope, all right. What I don't understand is why nobody's done anything about it before. I mean, you have some pretty... important connections, right? You don't have to take any crap from scum like Harmon."

Diamond grinned. "Spit it right out, kid. This joint is mobbed up, isn't that what you're trying to say? Okay, sure, there are guys who have money in this place who might know some very important people. But as long as somebody like Harmon doesn't become too big a pain in the ass, they'll put up with his bullshit. The bastard's got a badge, he isn't just some tinhorn trying to make a play.

"The cops in this town are rotten as hell, but they've got John and Jane Q. Public convinced that they're the only thing between them and the bad guys. And if somebody ices a cop, that's when they crack down on the action, make like they remember what the law is. Which is bad for everybody's business, so it isn't worth bothering with some cockroach like Harmon. If he gets too big for his britches, he'll be taken care of— otherwise, it's live and let live."

"That's one hell of a system," McDumont said.

"It's the system we got. You don't have to like it, but you better believe that it's there."

Crusher joined them. "Harmon's out back waiting for you. He's alone."

"You get out there and make damned sure he stays that way," Diamond said. He looked at McDumont. "You sure you want to go through with this, kid? Nobody would blame you for getting cold feet."

McDumont cleared his throat. "Nuts to that. Harmon is my meat. I've got him right where I want him."

"Yeah," Diamond said, "I guess you do. Well, good luck, kid— I hope you don't need it."

"Thanks. I hope you're right."

Harmon was flexing his muscles, throwing an occasional punch in Crusher's direction, as McDumont came through the door to the alley. Kerrigan stood with his arms folded, the hint of a smile on his face. "Jeez, Larry," he said, "you must of been practising. I ain't seen you move this fast since Toledo Louis shot it out with Fats Fisher over at Slattery's there. You was under a table before anybody else, you could of got hurt if somebody jumped on top of you."

Harmon shrugged. "Fuck you, you mick ham-and-egger. You've got a big mouth that somebody's going to close for you some day. I don't know how you've made it this far."

"It won't be you, flatfoot," Crusher replied. "You won't have no chance. I won't never turn my back on you."

"So this is the guy wants to beat me up," Harmon said, turning to stare at McDumont. He shook his head. "Not that I care, punk, but I let you off easy on that taxi caper, that wasn't anything to wet your pants about. Oh, yeah, you got the hots for the Bronson bimbo, right? She's all class, that baby. After I kick your ass around the block, maybe I'll get some of that. I figure she's tired of screwing those society types, she needs to see what a real man can do."

McDumont laughed. At least it was supposed to be a laugh, but it came out as more of a feral animal sound. "That'll be hard to do, creep, after I get through with you. Besides," he added, mentally apologizing to Penny for what he was about to say, "she told me you weren't her type. She isn't interested in going out with pimps."

"You little prick," Harmon growled. "I was figuring I might let you walk away from this, but now you're dead meat. You're just a little bastard with a big mouth."

"Okay," Kerrigan said, "cut the crap and get this show on the road, I ain't got all night. You guys ready?" They both nodded. "Swell, now remember the rules. No low blows, no hitting a guy when he's down, fists only. I say 'Stop!', you stop." He drew his revolver and leaned back against the wall. "All right, start the ball."

They circled each other warily. Harmon's arms were almost straight down at his side, whereas McDumont had assumed the classic boxer's stance. "Where'd you learn that, punk?" Harmon asked. "That isn't going to help you." He thrust his chin toward McDumont as though he wanted to be hit.

But Kerrigan had told him never to lead, but to let Harmon make the first move and then counterpunch or back away. McDumont was in good shape. Being on the road took the fat off your bones and kept you alert and ready to run; he'd dodged railroad guards and hick cops from coast to coast. He'd let Harmon come to him, he'd tire the big guy out a little.

Suddenly, Harmon was throwing a long, looping left at his head. McDumont ducked it easily, then circled quickly to his left. He did the same with the right jab that immediately followed it.

"Chickenshit little bastard, aren't you?" Harmon said. "Why don't you stand still and fight like a man?"

"Did you want to fight?" McDumont answered. "I thought you were just trying to cool me off, get the air circulating out here. I didn't realize those were punches. Okay, I'm waiting." He backed away, stood still, put his hands on his hips. "Somebody say something about a fight?"

Harmon rushed at him, both arms flailing, breathing audibly now. McDumont circled to his right this time, turning his back to his opponent, saying, "Where the hell is he, Crusher? There was a big fat slob here wanted to fight. Where the hell's he gone to?"

Harmon's arms hung heavily at his sides. His face was flushed, and his chest rose and fell rapidly. "For Christ's sake," he said, "why did you come here if you don't want to fight?"

"Who said I don't want to fight?" McDumont replied. He darted at Harmon, who quickly put his hands up, and then McDumont danced away again. "Come on, pimp, get your ass in gear. You've been spending too much time in the sack, slipping it to all those tramps you've got on the string. Get your dick back in your pants and get on with it."

Harmon reddened and came at him again, more slowly this time, his arms looking to clutch and hold rather than hit. McDumont slapped his outstretched hands away, moved quickly backwards, then feinted an attack. But Harmon had anticipated him, and shot out a quick right jab that smacked solidly off McDumont's left shoulder. He twisted away from the big cop, but his left arm was numb. He could hardly lift it. Harmon closed in, throwing a flurry of punches that couldn't all be blocked. A hard left found McDumont's nose and made it ring with pain.

If Harmon had been in halfway decent shape, that would have been the end of it. But he was panting heavily, telegraphing his punches rather than snapping them off, and McDumont was able to avoid most of them. Even better, his left arm had decided to return to life, and he still had his legs. He could probably run circles around Harmon if he had to.

So why not? He spun to the right and was suddenly behind his opponent's back. McDumont flicked his right hand off the base of Harmon's skull and said, "Tag, pimp, you're it." Harmon turned toward him slowly, laboriously, but again McDumont was behind him. This was getting to be fun. He put everything he had into a quick left-right to the kidneys and Harmon bellowed in rage and pain. McDumont had hurt him; he hadn't been expecting that.

Harmon staggered into a corner and looked at Kerrigan plaintively. "No fair," he gasped, "no fair. You got to make him fight fair."

Crusher rested the barrel of his revolver on his chin and looked thoughtful. "I dunno, he ain't hitting you below the belt or nothing. I don't see nothing wrong with it." He chuckled. "You got to get the lead out of your pants, Larry, that's what your trouble is. Or do you want to call it quits, stop the fight? Maybe we should do that. You ain't walking so good."

"Hell, no. The little bastard got lucky, that's all."

"Yeah, yeah," McDumont interjected, "tell it to the marines. Come on, pimp, get it in gear. The rate you're going, I'll be late for my date with Mona Wilson."

"What do you know about Mona?" Harmon said angrily. "She doesn't do charity work, and she doesn't go with bums."

"You think so? That's not what she told me. She said you were such a lousy lay she had to get her kicks somewhere. She begged me to come over tonight, she said we could play hide the salami after she tucked you in and gave you a nice glass of warm milk."

Screaming obscenities, Harmon stumbled toward McDumont, winding up for a punch with his right hand. But this time McDumont sprang forward, swinging from his heels with a right cross that found cheek and soft bone with a satisfying crunch. Harmon's feet went out from under him and he fell to the ground in a sitting position. A puzzled look appeared on his face.

McDumont's right hand was killing him. He might have broken something. And his legs were beginning to feel funny; he wasn't sure that they would respond to what he told them to do. Stay down, Larry, he thought, please stay down and give up. But after spitting out a mouthful of blood, Harmon was back up on his feet again.

"Lucky punch," he mumbled, shaking his head. "Little bastard hit me with a lucky punch. All right, little bastard, try that again." He lurched toward McDumont.

McDumont stood his ground. His whole right side felt like it had pins and needles in it and he didn't trust himself to move without falling down. "Come and get it, pimp," he snarled. "Come and get it."

Harmon reached him and threw out his arms. Sharp fingernails raked at McDumont's face. There was wetness on his forehead, then warm liquid dripping down into his eyes. He tasted blood on his lips and then all of a sudden it seemed to be at the back of his throat. A funny taste that wasn't like anything he'd ever tasted before. He could hear Kerrigan yelling, "Cut it out! Cut it out!", but Crusher was too far away. Harmon was going to tear him apart.

McDumont thought about Penny, he thought about her with Larry Harmon. He brushed aside Harmon's clawing fingers and smashed first his left hand and then his right into the insanely grimacing face that loomed in front of him, grunting with the effort, willing himself to ignore the fierce pain in his right hand, treating his body as a machine whose sole purpose in life was to destroy this man who threatened everything McDumont cared about.

Suddenly, the face vanished. He looked around dazedly and saw Harmon crumpled on the ground, not moving. His face was a mask of blood and bruises, not immediately recognizable as a human face. McDumont heard someone moaning, knelt on one knee, put his ear near Harmon's mouth. Then he realized that the sounds were coming from his own lips.

He stood up and almost fell down again. He felt Crusher's arms around him. "Jesus H. Christ," Kerrigan said, "I never saw nothing like it. That was a pip. I thought he had you, there at the end, but you really gave it to him."

McDumont didn't feel like a victor. Now that it was over, he only wanted to crawl away somewhere, wanted to forget all the pain he was feeling and go to sleep. He looked down at his hands. They were scraped and bleeding, the fingers bunched in aching fists. They didn't look like his hands.

Kerrigan whistled. "We gotta get you to a doc. I know just the guy. He can take somebody who got put through the ringer and make him look like Valentino, all the fighters use him." He offered McDumont a pocket flask. "Here, take a slug of this."

McDumont took a long swig of the fiery liquid. It was potent all right; it reminded him of the harsh, colourless brew hobo jungle stills produced from rotten fruit and other unsavoury ingredients. "Okay," McDumont said, "but what about Harmon? We shouldn't just leave him here."

"Why the hell not? He woulda done it to you. Nah, I'll tell Jack, he'll take care of it. Come on now, let's get going. You don't want those hands to swell up on you. You got some driving to do tomorrow."

"Hell," McDumont grimaced, "I never thought about that." He held his hands out in front of him. "I don't know what I thought. But I sure as hell never thought it would be like this."

"It was beautiful," Kerrigan said. He pronounced it be-yoo-ti-full. "It was maybe the most beautiful thing I ever seen. I ain't never going to forget it, that's for sure."

"You and me both," McDumont said. "I just hope it's over. I don't ever want to have to do that again for the rest of my life."

The doctor's office was at the rear of a shabby concrete block building on Ventura Boulevard, where the E-Z Credit Finance Company, a "No-Pain" dentist, and the Confidential Detective Agency also had their offices. The screams emanating from behind the dentist's door suggested that at least one of these businesses was engaging in false advertising.

A young, poorly dressed, but very pretty girl was just leaving Doctor Blaine's office. She glanced at them and blushed, then scurried away down the dirty hallway.

"Doc's a good guy to know, you get any babes in trouble," Kerrigan said. "He ain't no butcher, and he don't ask no questions, long as you got the kale."

After applying an astringent liniment to McDumont's forehead and cleaning the blood off his face, Blaine wrapped a light bandage around his head. "You can probably take this off tomorrow morning," he said, "it's a long abrasion but a superficial one." Then the doctor asked McDumont to flex his hands and extend his fingers. "Nothing broken," he concluded, "but I'd avoid pugilism for the next few weeks if I were you. There are some deep bone bruises here that need time to heel." He looked at McDumont appraisingly. "That will be five dollars."

"So how do I look?" McDumont asked as they left the office.

"You ain't gonna win no beauty contests," Kerrigan opined. "But you don't look too bad, considering."

Penny was waiting up for him when they got back to the Bronsons. "Oh, Walter, what happened?" she cried as she ran into his arms.

He winced. "Ouch, Penny, take it easy. I'm okay, appearances to the contrary. I won, I beat him."

She hugged him tightly and then stepped back and looked at him. "Are you sure you're all right? We have a wonderful family doctor. I could telephone him if you like."

"No," McDumont said, "I just need a hot bath and a soft bed."

Suddenly he was incredibly tired. "In fact, I'll skip the bath, just get me to bed." A wave of fatigue swept over his body. He smiled at Penny, stretched out his hands to her, felt himself falling forward. Then there was nothing but blackness.

It was dark and he was in bed. Someone was with him. He sat up and tried to see who it was.

"It's only me, Walter," Penny said. She stroked his face with warm, soft fingers. Then her hand moved lower, caressing his neck and then his chest, pressing him back down on the bed. He didn't seem to be wearing any clothes.

"How did I get here? I don't remember getting undressed. I don't remember anything after I got back to your house."

"Crusher carried you up here, then I did the rest. You were dead to the world."

"There are pyjamas over in the dresser, you know."

"I know. I'm getting to be quite an expert on your sleeping habits." She giggled. "But I like you much better this way. You look very dowdy in pyjamas."

Something occurred to him. "Where is Crusher, anyway?"

"I suggested that he spend the night at his apartment downtown. I thought you might... sleep better that way."

He put his arms around her. Penny didn't seem to be wearing any clothes, either.

"Do you know what you're doing?" he asked. "I don't know what I'm doing. I haven't had the faintest idea what I've been doing since I met you."

"Well," she said after a moment, "I thought it would be nice if we made love. I'll confess I thought about starting without you, but now that you're back in the land of the living we can do it together." She hesitated. "Unless you don't want to, of course."

"You'll have to let me get used to the idea, Penny. I'm nuts about you, but this... this is kind of sudden. I've thought about it so much that everything seems unreal." He laughed. "Maybe I'm still unconscious. Maybe this is all some kind of strange fantasy." He moved his hands up and down her body. "How can I be sure that you're real? Are you sure that you're real?"

"Oh, I'm quite sure," she said, moving on top of him. "But so far you haven't done much besides question my existence. What do I have to do to prove that I'm real?"

"We'll think of something," he said, rising to meet her. "I think my faith is about to be restored."

CHAPTER NINE

It was light out when he woke up. McDumont watched Penny sleep, trying to remember everything that had happened during the night. He decided that there wasn't anything that he wanted to forget.

"Mmm, Walter, good morning." She stirred, stretched, then snuggled against him. "Love you."

"I love you," he said. "Are you wide awake?"

"I think so. Why do you ask?"

"I just wanted to know. So that I could make sure you'd understand what I meant when I got up my nerve and asked you to marry me."

She sat up and looked at him. "You don't have to say that, you know. Just because we spent the night together doesn't mean that we have to get married. Even if we do think we're in love."

"Oh, don't be so damned sophisticated," he said. "And don't think so much. If we aren't in love, nobody ever was." He smiled. "Now give me a straight answer for once in your life. Will you marry me?"

"Yes, I will. On one condition."

"What's that?" he asked warily.

"That you give up wearing pyjamas," she replied, reaching for him. "I refuse to have that incredibly sexy body covered by pyjamas."

"Done," he agreed, embracing her, "but only on the condition that the same goes for you."

She looked puzzled. "That certainly won't be a problem. I've never worn pyjamas in my life. And I most emphatically do not intend to start."

"Good. As you know, we socialists are firm believers in the equality of men and women."

"That's just fine," she said, "but I honestly don't see what it has to do with not wearing pyjamas."

"Simple," he chortled. "That way, no one will be wearing the pants in our family."

Penny groaned. "I should have known there was a pun at the end of it. Is it too late for me to back out of this? I like to think I'm a pretty tolerant person, but I don't know if I can stand a husband who's always making puns."

"Okay," he said, "I'll give you a break. I'll stop making puns as long as you'll agree that we can start making something else." He began to move his lips up and down her body.

"Now that's a wonderful idea, Walter. I think I'm going to like being married to you. Oh yes, in fact I think I'll just... lie back and... yes, yes... enjoy it."

"Wow," said Paul Junior from the back seat, "this is really great."

McDumont and Kerrigan exchanged smiles. They were sitting in the front of the Bronsons's Cadillac, McDumont driving and Kerrigan riding shotgun. It was the first day of the new system, and they were a bit on edge. Paul Junior was bouncing all over the back seat, jabbering a mile a minute, bragging about what they'd do to anyone who tried to stop them.

Finally McDumont said, "Paul, I know this is exciting for you, but Crusher and I need to concentrate if we're going to do our job. Could you maybe be a little quieter?"

"Yeah, kiddo, you need to cut the cackle, know what I mean?" Kerrigan chimed in. "You're going to be flapping your gums and some guy's going to pull up next to us and put a pill in my ear and I ain't going to hear a thing, you know?"

"Gee, I'm sorry. I never thought about that. Do you want me to be the lookout?"

"That's it," McDumont said, "that's just what we need. But you know one thing about lookouts? They have to be absolutely silent, otherwise they can't do their job properly. So when they do have something to report, people will know it's important." He winked at Kerrigan.

"Gotcha," Paul Junior said. "Mum's the word."

"Kid talks pretty good, for a high-class squirt," Kerrigan observed.

"Yeah," McDumont said, "and we can certainly use all the eyes we've got." He looked in the rearview mirror, then checked the mirrors on the left- and right-hand sides. "We don't want these guys to catch us with our pants down."

Kerrigan noticed what he was doing. "You concentrate on what's in front of us, Walter. Leave the peeping around to yours truly. I've got the glims for it, I used to be able to spot an ambush while the rest of the guys thought they were still out for a joy ride."

"Right," McDumont replied, laughing, "I catch your drift."

There was a battered black Ford parked at the intersection of Mountain Drive and Brentwood Boulevard. They could see someone in the driver's seat through the grimy side window. The Ford was facing west on Brentwood, the direction they would normally take to get to Paul Junior's school.

"What do you think?" McDumont asked.

"I think maybe," Kerrigan said. The car matched the description they had been given by the gate guard.

McDumont turned sharply east on Brentwood. "Yeah," Crusher said, "he's making a U-turn. Let's move this jalopy."

McDumont made a quick left, then a right, then a left on to a street that eventually snaked its way back to Brentwood Boulevard. The night before he'd driven around the local area, working out alternate routes between the school and the Bronson house, until he had a map of the neighbourhood firmly fixed in his mind. "Do you see him, is he behind us?"

"Nah, I think you lost him at the second turn. Jeez, these guys ain't too good."

"What you really mean is that I'm a great driver, right?" McDumont said, pretending that his feelings had been hurt. "Bet you didn't have any better on those liquor runs down to the Mexican border."

Kerrigan snorted. "You take this thing through a roadblock with J.

Edgar's boys trying to fill you full of lead, then I'll tell you what a great wheelman you are. But you ain't bad, for a beginner."

"Thanks, I think." McDumont glanced at his watch. "Whoops, we'd better step on it. We don't want Paul Junior to be late on our very first day."

After dropping Paul Junior off at school without further incident, they stopped for coffee at the first diner they saw. "Did you get a look at those guys?" McDumont asked. "I couldn't see much of anything."

"There was at least two of them," Kerrigan said. "I got a look-see when they turned around. And five'll get you ten that ain't no souped-up car, that's for sure. If these guys is trying to pull a snatch job, I think they're playing out of their league."

"Your league, maybe. I don't know about mine." He took a sip of his coffee. "So how'd you get into this business, Crusher? I know you rode a scout car for some bootleggers, was that how you got into it?"

"Yeah, although I was always a wise guy. Guy as big as me, they don't figure you to have no brains, and they always got a use for muscle. I was an enforcer for one of the numbers guys. Some of these mom and pop corner stores, they'd try to hold out on you, I'd go around and make like I was going to tear them apart unless they made their nut every day. They mostly did, usually I just had to come around once and everything was jake, they'd straighten up and fly right."

"What if they didn't?"

Kerrigan shrugged. "That happened, you had to go back and mess the place up a little bit, drop a few bottles on the floor, maybe knock a shelf down." He frowned. "I didn't like that. You could see some of these lames didn't have a pair of nickels to rub together, they was just using the numbers dough to keep their store going. But you got to do what you got to do, know what I mean?"

"Yeah," McDumont said, "I made the mistake of borrowing a few bucks from a loan shark one time, and I ended up paying through the nose. Son of a bitch even came around to my house, scared the hell out of my mother."

"Loan sharks," Kerrigan snorted, "that's for suckers. I didn't mind the numbers. At least somebody wins, they get something out of it."

"Sure, you're right. Tell me about the liquor runs."

"Jeez, you get me started on that we'll be here the rest of the day. There was some pips, all right." Keerigan drained his coffee cup and signalled to the waitress for more. "I guess the time we ran into that ambush south of Dago, that was the hairiest."

"Where's 'Dago'? I never heard of it."

"Jeez, *San Diego*, what do you think? But you don't want to be no square, you say 'Dago,' just like you say 'Frisco,' right? You want to be some guy who bends his pinkie finger when he takes a drink, you say *San Francisco*, polite-like, then everybody'll know you're a real horse's ass."

"I can see this is going to be a real education for me," McDumont said. "So what happened at this ambush, wherever it was?"

"It was the Fourth of July, babe, it was the guy who lit a cigarette in the fireworks factory. I never seen nothing like it. They must of had fifty guys spraying stuff at us, they had tracers, they had flares, they had grenades, you name it, they had it. Guy who was driving our car got it first thing, ratatatatata, right through the windshield, took his goddamned head off, car went into the ditch and I got out about two seconds before they blew it all to hell."

Crusher paused and took a long sip from his coffee cup. "Tracer must have got the gas tank. I don't scare easy, you ask anybody who knows me, but I was sure as hell scared that time. I figured 'Kerrigan, your number is *up*.'"

McDumont's eyes widened. "How'd you get out of it?"

"I got the hell off that road, that's the first thing I did. There was trucks turning over and more trucks slamming into them, some of the guys made it out okay and tried to fight back, but they got cut down before they could do any damage. No, the feds won that one, there wasn't no percentage in hanging around and trying to shoot it out with a goddamned army. I got the hell out of there as quick as I could, made it to the nearest town and laid low for a few days until it all blew over."

"That's some story," McDumont said. "It sounds like you did the smart thing in getting out of there."

"That wasn't the end of it," Kerrigan said sharply. "We knew who done it, a local sheriff on the take who'd decided he'd get in big with the FBI guys by double-crossing us. And we got him good." He rubbed his hands and looked satisfied. "Yeah, we really got him good."

They didn't notice any suspicious cars when they picked Paul Junior up from school, but as they headed east on Brentwood, Kerrigan said, "They're behind us. Same crummy old Ford."

"Do you want me to lose them again?" McDumont asked. "Or should we wait and see what they're up to?"

"Nah, that ain't the way. This is all houses and stuff over here, ain't it?" Kerrigan answered, gesturing to their right.

"Right, mostly narrow little side streets, lots of small bungalows and cars parked everywhere, not a good place to try to lose them."

"We ain't going to lose them," Kerrigan said, rubbing his hands together. "These guys is going to be *found*. Take the next right and goose it."

McDumont turned and then stepped on the accelerator. When the black Ford made the turn, it was quite a bit farther behind them than it had been. "Get down, Paul. Get down on the floor and brace yourself," he said to the boy.

"Okay, make this next right, and then pull across the street," Kerrigan said.

"You want me to block the street?" McDumont asked incredulously.

"You got it, babe. Yeah, turn here, then tromp on 'em." The car screeched to a halt, rubber burning as McDumont hit the brakes hard.

He angled the big Cadillac to block the street, making an almost one-hundred-and-eighty-degree turn so that Paul Junior would have at least some protection if the Ford crashed into them.

Kerrigan was out the door before the car had stopped, revolver in hand. He knelt down behind the hood and rested his gun on top of it.

Their pursuers came careening around the corner. Brakes squealed as the driver tried to avoid colliding with the Cadillac, but the Ford fishtailed out of control and smashed head on into one of the wooden telephone poles that lined the street. Fragments of glass and metal rose in the air, then settled slowly on the pavement. Wisps of steam curled lazily upward from underneath the crumpled hood.

"Holy Moses!" Paul Junior said.

There was no movement from within the Ford. Kerrigan stood up, put his gun away, and warily walked over to the smoking vehicle. He took a look inside and shook his head. "Goddamned stupid amateurs," he said loudly.

McDumont joined him. "Anybody you know?"

Kerrigan snorted contemptuously. "Not on your life. Stupid jerk should have run into us, then he's got a chance. But you take on a telephone pole, you ain't going to do too good." He reached in and shook the driver by the shoulder. "These guys are out for the count, anyway."

"Do you think they're dead?"

"The other rube ain't. I can hear him moaning. I don't know about the driver, though, he really got a whack on the head."

McDumont looked into the car. Both men were above average height, on the thin side, about thirty, he guessed. The driver was losing a fair amount of blood from a gash on the forehead. His blue work shirt was stained with a broad band of red. His passenger was wearing a mechanic's coverall with the name "Gord" stitched in white above its left breast pocket.

"Let's see if they have any identification on them," McDumont said, "we need to find out who these guys are."

They heard a siren in the distance. People were standing in doorways and staring out windows. Others were moving toward the scene of the accident.

"You want cops in on this?" Kerrigan asked.

The big lug isn't as dumb as he looks, McDumont thought. "No, we don't. But let's at least see if there's a name and address on the registration."

He opened the driver's-side door. As required by California law, there was a plastic registration tag attached to the steering column. "Michael Wilson," he read, "427 Boyle Heights Street." He tugged at the plastic holder but it wouldn't come off. "Have you got anything to write with, Crusher? I can't get this darn thing off."

Kerrigan reached into the car and with one hard pull tore the holder loose from the steering column. "That'll really put these birds in with the cops," he said, "maybe they'll spend a little time in a cell."

"Let's get rolling," McDumont said, "I've had all the excitement I want for one day."

"Hell, I was just getting warmed up," Crusher replied. "Couldn't we hang around until these mugs wake up and play patty-cake with them?"

"I don't think so. We sure as hell don't want the police in on this; we don't want Harmon nosing around these guys. Come on, let's go."

They drove away to the sound of approaching sirens.

"Jeez, that was the nuts," Crusher said as they drove back to the Bronson house. "Between watching you beat up on Harmon and playing hide-and-seek with those characters, I ain't had so much fun since Repeal came in. This job's a hell of a lot better than I thought it would be."

"Yeah," Paul Junior chimed in, "that was amazing! Wait till I tell Dad, he'll never believe it!"

"You know, Paul," McDumont said, "maybe we should play down

what happened. Your father's got a lot on his mind. We don't want him worrying any more than he has to. What do you say?"

"Oh okay, but it sure was neat. We showed those creeps what was what."

Kerrigan laughed. "Yeah, *we* sure did, all right. They messed their car up, too. Maybe we seen the last of them."

"I hope we've seen the last of them," McDumont said. He stared intently at the road in front of him, his hands grasping the steering wheel so tightly that the knuckles were turning white. "I've had just about all the excitement I can stand these last couple of days."

"Do you think it's over?" Penny asked. They were sitting on a wrought-iron bench in the Bronsons' garden, looking up at a sky sparkling with stars.

"I hope so. But I don't know." He put his arm around her. "This is one hell of a mess your family's gotten into. You know what I think? Maybe your father should give Mona Wilson some more money. He seems to have enough of it."

"This is the same man who fought Larry Harmon rather than put up with *his* demands? What was that fine little speech, something about 'You don't get anywhere with the Larry Harmons of this world by knuckling under to them'? If I didn't know better, I'd think you had a double standard at work here, Walter— beat up the men but be nice to the little ladies, they're so incapable of looking out for themselves."

"What brought that on? That's not it at all. What bothers me about the Wilsons is that they do have some right on their side. Paul Junior is Mona's child, after all, you can't deny that."

"Yes, and she sold him to the highest bidder, fine mother that she is. You don't really think she's overcome with longing for her son, do you? The little tramp just wants more money, and if we gave her any more there'd never be an end to it."

McDumont shook his head. "True, but wouldn't you rather pay her off, no matter how long it takes, than live with the possibility of Paul being kidnapped? I mean, things worked out fine today, but what if they don't tomorrow? If that car had rammed into us, somebody could have been killed."

He grimaced as something else occurred to him. "Christ, I hadn't thought about it, but now we're not even going to know what kind of car they're driving. Every time somebody pulls up next to us we'll have to figure it could be them."

He hadn't meant to scare her, but he could see that she was shaken by what he had said. When she finally spoke, her voice was deeply agitated, unsure. "I hadn't thought about it that way, Walter, I'm sorry. I don't want anything to happen to you." She clutched him fiercely. "God, I've found the man I want to spend the rest of my life with and I'm expecting him to risk everything for my screwed-up family. You must think I'm completely callous."

He kissed her. "I think we're all under a strain, that's my opinion. But could we talk to your parents about this? I don't think any of us thought this through enough in the first place. It would be one thing if it was just Mona, but she's got at least two other men involved as well."

"Those must be her brothers, from the way you described them," Penny said. "There was a father, too, but he'd be quite old by now."

"Whoever they are, we know they're serious about this. They've put a lot of people's lives, and especially Paul Junior's, in danger. Plus Larry Harmon is snooping around; he might find out about what's happening. So can we go talk to your parents?"

"We'll talk to dad. If it involves Mona, my mother doesn't want to hear about it." Penny turned to look at the house. "His study light is still on, I don't think he's gone to bed yet."

Paul Bronson listened to them without making any comment. If he had seemed withdrawn and abstracted before this, McDumont thought, he now looked completely exhausted and defeated. "Whatever you think," he said when they had finished outlining the reasons why it might be best to negotiate a financial settlement with Mona. "I've made such a mess out of this. But how in the world do you plan to go about it?"

"Crusher and I could pay them a visit, see if we can talk some sense into them." McDumont frowned. "Actually, Crusher wants to go over there and beat the living daylights out of them, but I think he'll do what I tell him— he's used to following orders. And it won't hurt if the Wilsons think we'd just as soon knock them off as pay them off. Anyway, maybe they'll be in the mood to talk after what happened today."

"Let's hope so," Bronson said. "Mona's original demands were absolutely ridiculous. She wanted me to buy her a mansion in Beverley Hills, somewhere she and her shiftless relatives could sit on their rear ends and order the servants around. She comes from a long line of poor New Hampshire farmers; she once told me that her mother made dresses for her out of old flour sacks up until the time she went to high school."

"She did go to high school though, eh? Well, you've got to give her some credit. That couldn't have been easy, given her background."

"You're right, Walter," Bronson said thoughtfully. "It never occurred to me before, but you're absolutely right. Mona certainly isn't stupid, whatever else she is. I suppose that I hired her more for her looks than her clerical skills, but she wasn't a bad secretary."

"Perfectly outstanding in certain departments," Penny said icily.

Her father looked at her as if she had hit him. "I don't expect you to forgive me for what happened, Penny. But I wish you would try to understand that I didn't *want* any of this to happen. I was terribly unhappy and upset, and Mona was there to... to comfort me. Her motives weren't pure, and god knows she isn't, but I can't pretend that I didn't care for her at one time. She may even have saved my life, I don't know."

"While ruining the lives of the rest of us! Oh, hell, dad, that was a rotten thing to say." She went to him and hugged him tightly. He bent over in his chair, his torso almost parallel to the floor, and cried silently but steadily.

When he had regained control of himself, Bronson stood up and walked slowly toward the door. "I'm very tired," he said. "I can't cope with this any more tonight. I'll pay anything within reason to put an end to this. Anything at all."

Four-twenty-seven Boyle Heights Street was a four-storey red brick apartment building on a street that had once had pretensions, but had long ago been forced to give them up. What had begun life as solidly respectable middle-class addresses were now bruised, battered and poorly maintained slum dwellings flanked by overflowing garbage cans, abandoned vehicles, and alleys that the police patrolled only in pairs, and only during the day. In the narrow lobby, a row of unpolished brass mailboxes preserved the anonymity of most of 427's tenants.

"The super'll know," Kerrigan said confidently. "Dumps like this, you got people moving in and out so fast they don't bother to put no names on their doors or mailboxes. But the super always knows, you can count on that."

There was a door marked "SUPERINTENDENT" at the rear of the lobby. Kerrigan rapped on it with a negligent tattoo of his right hand. The sound reverberated through the lobby and sparked a querulous complaint from behind the door. "Hey, it's late, get outa here. Come back in the morning."

The door shook in its frame as Crusher tapped a little harder. "All right, all right," said the now angry voice. The door opened and a short, balding, bleary-eyed man in a dirty grey nightshirt glared at them. "You woke me up, fer Chrissakes. Whaddya want?" he demanded.

"Wilson," Kerrigan said, "you got some people named Wilson living here. What apartment they in?"

The smaller man looked at him craftily. "They friends of yours?"

"Yeah, I heard they was in town and I thought I'd drop in, say hello."

"Kind of a funny time to come calling, it's after midnight. You got any first names for these Wilsons you say you're so friendly with?"

"Aw, come on," McDumont said, "we know them from way back. They'd be upset if they found out we were in town and didn't look them up."

"Yeah, I bet," the superintendent said. "I ain't supposed to give out that kind of information, you know. I could get in trouble..."

McDumont took a five-dollar bill out of his pocket and let it dangle from his fingers. The super's eyes watched it intently. "This make it any easier for you?"

The bill disappeared into an eager hand. "Four-sixteen, top floor off to the right. You go up those stairs over there. You tell them Albie said it was okay. You guys don't need to be so cagey, you know, I'm in on the fix. And you wait till you see that Mona. Man, she's worth every red cent. Who tipped you, anyway, the cab driver?"

"Nah," Crusher said, "some plainclothes dick we met in a bar, Larry something, that was the guy."

"Oh yeah," the superintendent said, smiling, "he'd be the one, all right." A frown crossed his face. "How come Larry didn't give you a little card with the address on it? That's the way he usually handles it, that's what he usually does."

"He did," McDumont said quickly, "but we must have lost it some place. I remembered the street address, but I couldn't think of the rest of it."

"Yeah, I guess that could happen. Anyway, you guys have a real good time." He leered. "That Mona's a swell babe, she can really dish it out, let me tell you." He chuckled loudly and closed the door.

"He thinks we're johns, doesn't he?" McDumont said as they walked up the dark and smelly stairwell. "I didn't pick up on that right away."

"That's what he figures, bo. I should of thought of that, a place like this. But you did good with that stuff about the card."

Yeah, I'm getting to be a great little liar, McDumont thought to himself, I sure am getting a hell of a lot of practise. Maybe I can be a lawyer or a real-estate agent when I grow up. To Crusher, he said, "How do you think we should play this? Is Mona going to be there by herself, or will her brothers be around?"

"I don't figure this bunch could afford two apartments, even in a dump like this," Kerrigan said. "They'll be there, all right, unless the police threw them in the jug. And whoever's up there will be expecting company. Old Albie will have given them the buzz."

"Maybe we should play along a little bit, let them think we're customers," McDumont said thoughtfully. "Check out the lay of the land."

"'Lay of the land,' huh? You looking to cheat on your new mama already?" Crusher laughed. "I thought you two was glued together? You might as well of put up a sign, let the world know you was an item."

McDumont blushed. "It was that obvious, eh? Hell, and I thought I was playing it cool, too. Anyway, I'm sure not looking for another woman, that's not what I meant. I just thought we could come on as if we were johns. We might learn something if they don't know who we are."

"Maybe. But I ain't interested in no hooker, neither. I got big eyes for Cookie and she's got a little time for me lately. So if you're looking for someone to play house with Mona, you're elected."

"Elected I definitely do not want to be," McDumont said. "But maybe it wouldn't hurt if I let myself get nominated."

CHAPTER TEN

The door to 416 was open. A tall, willowy blond woman was silhouetted against the weak light from inside the apartment. She leaned casually against the jamb, her back arched to display a sensuous line of extravagant curves. "Hi, boys," she said. "This must be my lucky day. All alone by the telephone, and now I've got a double date. Come on in and take a load off your feet."

"Hey, good-looking," McDumont replied. Mona was gorgeous, all right, even her cheap dress and sloppily applied make-up couldn't hide that. Her facial features were clear and well-defined, and her body was in the Margot Stevenson class, no doubt about it. For a moment he thought about playing this charade right to the end. What the hell, he liked hookers as a rule. They gave you exactly what you wanted and didn't clown around. Then an image of Penny flashed into his mind and he felt ashamed of himself. What was the matter with him? It was Penny he wanted; he wouldn't touch this cheap tramp with a ten-foot pole.

Not that Mona seemed to be overwhelmingly attracted to him. As they stepped into the apartment's shabby living room, she was staring at Crusher with a combination of amazement and lust, like a kid in a candy store. "You *are* a big one," she purred. "Do you boys have names, or should I just call you Mutt and Jeff?"

"Make it 'Irish,'" Kerrigan said. He smiled. "And you can call my little buddy here 'Scotch.' That's what he claims to be, anyway."

"Scotch and Irish," Mona mused. "Sounds like a couple of whiskies." Her smile brightened. "Say, how about a drink? That would go down swell. I've got a bottle of rye around here somewhere." She leered at them. "Don't you two handsome boys go away now."

"We'll be here," McDumont said, sitting down at one end of a threadbare sofa. He glanced around the room. Mona had gone off into the kitchen, and a short hallway led to what looked like a bedroom and bathroom. There was a closed door off to their right, with the faint murmur of a radio coming from behind it.

McDumont pointed to it and raised his eyebrows. Kerrigan nodded and patted his jacket pocket.

"Here we are." Mona bustled in and put a bottle and three water glasses down on an end table. She filled each glass about half full and handed them around. "Here's to crime, Mr. Irish and Mr. Scotch." She giggled and took a long drink from her glass. Crusher did the same, while McDumont sipped carefully at the strong, harsh fluid. He'd had better liquor from hobo stills.

"Just so you don't get the wrong idea," Mona said, "I'm strictly business. Ten dollars each for a short time, twenty-five for the night, cash in advance. You want something really special, I can make a phone call and get another girl over here. What's your pleasure?"

"We ain't no freaks," Crusher said, standing up. "You take care of my little buddy first. You got a bathroom around here, baby?" He walked over to the closed door and put his hand on the knob.

"Don't go in there!" Mona yelled as he opened the door. But Crusher was already inside the room, holding his revolver on the two surprised men who'd been playing cards at a rickety table, the same pair who had followed them earlier that day. "Don't make any dumb moves," Kerrigan said, moving the gun back and forth between them. "Just come on out slow and join the party."

After Crusher had frisked the Wilson brothers carefully, removing a small pistol from the pocket of Gord's overalls, he shepherded them into the living room. Both men looked as though they'd been in an accident. Gord's forehead was badly bruised, while Michael wore a blood-soaked bandage that came down almost to his eyes.

"Let's get all the Wilsons on the couch," McDumont said. "I always find family gatherings very touching, don't you, Mr. Irish? Especially when they're such a lovely group as the Wilson clan."

"What gives?" Mona snarled when they were all sitting down, the Wilsons bunched together on the sofa. "You guys are going to a hell of a lot of trouble for a freebie. I warn you, one of my best friends is a cop, a detective. You don't want to cross him."

McDumont grinned. "You want to talk about trouble, we're not real crazy about the way your brothers have been driving around this burg. We kind of wanted to talk to them about this bad habit they have of following too closely. They could have an accident if they aren't more careful."

"Yeah," Crusher said, "you guys don't watch out, you're definitely gonna have an accident." He sighted the gun at Gord. "Maybe a permanent accident."

"Are these the men driving for the Bronsons?" Mona asked, looking at her brothers.

Mike looked wearily at McDumont and Kerrigan and shrugged his shoulders. "I dunno, they could be. The big loogan is big enough, all right."

"You think you can scare us?" Mona said. "Well you've got another think coming, you two-bit bastards. That high and mighty Paul Bronson took my kid. He owes me. I was just a kid when it happened, he took advantage of me. He owes me!"

"Jesus, Mona, pipe down," Gord said. "You and your big ideas. You're going to get us all killed, you don't shut your face."

"Bullshit," she snapped. She looked at McDumont and Kerrigan. "Maybe you don't know it, you cheap hoods, but this cop friend of mine has some very important friends in this town. And I bet he'd just love to put the squeeze on the Bronsons. All I have to do is tell him what happened. If I don't get what's coming to me, that's just what I'm going to do!"

"Take it easy," McDumont said. "There's no need to fly off the handle. Paul Bronson is willing to make a deal. He just wants things to be over, that's all. All you have to do is stop bothering him."

"I told you," Mona said triumphantly, glancing at her brothers. "I told you everything would work out." She looked at McDumont intently. "I want twenty thousand dollars, and not a penny less. Then I swear I won't ever bother Mr. Bronson again."

"You better goddamned believe it," Crusher interrupted, letting the revolver slowly traverse the couch. "I had my way, you'd be feeding the fish off the end of Santa Monica pier before you got a plugged nickel." He looked at McDumont. "Why the hell don't we just bump these jerks off and keep the dough ourselves?" he said emphatically. "They ain't worth twenty cents between them."

"Please mister, no," Mike said. "We wasn't trying to hurt you, we was just trying to grab the kid. There wasn't nothing personal about it."

Mona slapped him. "Would you shut up, for god's sake? No wonder you couldn't snatch the kid. I've got more guts than the two of you put together!"

No doubt about that, McDumont thought. If we really were tough guys we'd shoot Mona and then give Gord and Mike a good spanking. "I think Mr. Bronson will agree to that. We'll be in touch about delivering the money. Come on, Irish, let's go. Unless you have something else in mind?"

"Nah," Crusher said, "I need a real drink after that rat piss she served us." He looked at Mona. "So long, babe. Too bad you'll never know what you're missing."

"That'll be the day," she said, "that'll be the day when I miss any of you. You're all a pain in the neck. Goddamned men."

When they were outside the building, McDumont and Kerrigan broke into laughter. "You were great in there, Crusher. I could have sworn you were ready to shoot the lot of them."

"Who says I wouldn't a? Punks like that only understand one thing. Now hows about a drink? We got to get the taste of that stuff out of our systems."

As they got into the Cadillac, there was movement in the front seat of a black sedan parked about twenty feet behind them. After the Cadillac had driven away, the driver's-side door of the sedan opened, and a tall, bulky man stared first at where the Bronsons' car had been, and then at the apartment building. He shook his head and muttered something.

Then the man strode purposefully toward the apartment building, entered, and hurried to the door with "SUPERINTENDENT" on it. He pounded viciously on the door. "Open up, Albie, you stupid fuck!" he screamed. "Open up!"

"Twenty thousand dollars," Paul Bronson said. "I thought she would ask for more. Are you sure she only asked for twenty thousand dollars?"

"That's what she said," McDumont replied. "And you can give all the credit to Crusher. He played the heavy and scared the pants off them."

"Not the most difficult thing in the world to do in Mona's case," Penny observed tartly.

"For crying out loud, Penny, let it rest. She may not be the Virgin Mary, but she's doing the best she can with what she's got. Give her a break."

"That's what I'm afraid of, Walter. Mona seems to bring out the good Samaritan in all you men. I suppose you think she'll take her twenty thousand dollars and start a soup kitchen for the unemployed or something."

"No, I don't think that. I suspect that you won't hear anything from her for a while, and then she'll try to bleed you for another instalment on her retirement plan. But unless you want to have her killed or something, I don't see how you can do anything else."

"We've been over and over this," Paul Bronson said. "I'm sure we've done the right thing. Paul Junior was in danger, and the only intelligent solution was to pay Mona off. Nothing else made sense." He cleared his throat. "And I'm very grateful to both you and Mr. Kerrigan, I don't know what we would have done without you. Which reminds me, Walter, do you think Mr. Kerrigan would agree to stay on and work as our chauffeur on a permanent basis? He seems to be extremely competent at what he does. And I'll do anything to avoid another kidnapping."

"I think he'd like that. Crusher is a lot smarter than most people give him credit for, he knew just how to handle Mona and her brothers. And he likes Paul Junior. Why don't you ask him when he gets here tomorrow morning?"

"I'll do just that." Bronson yawned and stretched his arms. "And now I'm going to go to bed. This has been quite an exhausting evening. I don't think I'll go in to the bank tomorrow. I need a good rest."

"Before you go to bed, dad," Penny said, putting her arm through Walter's, "I've got something very important to tell you. Walter has asked me to marry him, and I've accepted. And we hope that you'll give us your blessing."

"You probably think I haven't noticed what's been going on between you two, don't you? Well, your old father isn't quite that far gone yet. Of course I'll give you my blessing, honey. It's the best thing that's happened in this house since I don't know when." He paused. "Have you told your mother yet?"

"No, I haven't. I wanted to wait for the right moment, but..."

"She's been very upset by this business. Why don't you wait and let me break it to her? I haven't been much use for anything else lately, that's the least I can do."

"If you think that's best, dad. But don't let it go too long. We'd like to get married as soon as possible."

"That's right," McDumont said, "I'm afraid she'll change her mind once she finds out what I'm really like. I've done a pretty good job of fooling her so far."

"Wrong, as usual," Penny replied, punching him lightly on the shoulder. "You're the one who's going to be surprised by what *I'm* really like. No more of this night clubbing and hanging around with disreputable people, for example. I'm really just a homebody. There's nothing I like better than a quiet evening in front of the fire."

"That sounds awfully good to me," McDumont said. "I could do with a quiet evening. One way or the other, my nights have been kind of restless lately."

Next morning Crusher reacted to Paul Bronson's offer with delight. "As long as I don't have to wear no monkey suit," he insisted. "I don't wear no monkey suit for nobody."

"No, that won't be necessary," Paul Bronson said, laughing. "You're quite imposing enough without dressing you up in uniform. You'll note that my comprehension of current American slang is improving, gentlemen."

"He's talking funny again," Kerrigan said to McDumont. "Just when I figure I'm hep to his lingo, he jumps salty on me again."

"I guess I'm going to have to hang around for a while and translate," McDumont said. "All he said was that he was finding it easier to understand you. Why is that so hard to understand?"

"It ain't the words, it's the patter, that's what throws me. But, hey, Mr. Bronson, long as that eagle flies on Friday, you can use all the three-dollar words you want, no sweat."

"Now I'm afraid I'm at a loss, Walter. Am I correct in assuming that Mr. Kerrigan is prepared to accept my offer of employment?"

"That he does, and he also agrees that as long as you pay the piper, you can call the tune."

"Now *you're* talking funny," Crusher said as Bronson nodded. "What's music got to do with this?"

"Darned if I know," McDumont said. "But if you two don't start singing in the same key, you're each going to be hearing a lot of sour notes."

They laughed. "Very harmoniously put," Bronson observed. "Yeah," Kerrigan added, "I can swing with that. Now who's for some java? You guys make talking too much like work."

McDumont had decided that they would continue the driver and bodyguard routine until they were sure the Wilsons were completely out of the picture. He had telephoned Mona and told her that he would be delivering the money as soon as it was ready at Paul Bronson's bank. Mona said, "Sure, yeah. Just make sure you get it in twenties or smaller." You'd think twenty thousand dollars got left on her doorstep every day of the week. She sounded rushed, but what the hell, maybe she had an emergency. He supposed hookers had emergencies; if it wasn't the world's oldest profession it had to be one of the busiest.

Paul Junior and Crusher were in the Cadillac, ready to go, when Penny crept up on McDumont from behind. "I suppose you thought you were going to drive off without saying goodbye, Sir Walter," she chuckled, hugging him tightly and speaking so softly that only he could hear her. "Well, no such luck. I suppose you thought that after your exertions of last night I'd still be asleep."

"And lord knows you should be," he said, turning to ruffle her hair. "Shocking, it was, the lewdness and depravity of my bride to be. If I didn't have work to do, I'd take you inside and show you how strongly I feel about it."

"Well, you couldn't, anyway, I have a meeting at Harrison House this morning. But I'll be back before lunch if you can assure me there's a reason why I might wish to return as quickly as possible."

"Oh, I can do that all right. Wait a minute, darn it, we have to take the money to Mona's place. We probably won't be back until after lunch."

"Hmm, maybe I should come with you. When Mona sees all that money she might want to thank you for it. Thank you the only way she knows how."

"I can control myself. Besides, I'll have Crusher with me. I'm pretty sure he can handle her if it comes down to that."

"You be careful, anyway," she said more seriously. "I don't know what I would do if something bad happened to you. I'm so crazy about you I don't know whether I'm coming or going these days."

Paul Junior honked the horn.

"Well," McDumont said, "I guess I've got to be going." He kissed her quickly. "There'll be plenty more where that came from later."

"Promises, promises." She gave him a final squeeze and watched him walk to the car. She was still watching as the Cadillac accelerated down the driveway.

McDumont and Kerrigan dropped Paul Junior off at his school and headed downtown to Western Fidelity Trust. "I didn't notice anyone following us," McDumont said, "how about you?"

"There was a black car on our tail for a while, but it turned off before we got to the school. There ain't nothing to worry about. Those Wilson boys don't have the stomach for it."

At the bank, they were immediately shown into Paul Bronson's office. "It's all in there," he said, gesturing toward a squat leather satchel. "It's a bit bulky, with all those small bills. But I've counted it twice myself. It's exactly twenty thousand dollars, all twenties or smaller."

Kerrigan picked up the satchel and tossed it in the air a couple of times. "Twenty grand," he mused. "I've seen guys buy the farm for a hell of a lot less."

Bronson looked puzzled. "Are you interested in agricultural real estate, Mr. Kerrigan? There are some very attractive properties available. I'd be happy to put you in touch with a realtor."

McDumont chuckled. "I swear, sometimes you two are like a League of Nations meeting with the translation turned off. No, Crusher isn't looking for country property. If a guy buys the farm, that means he's been killed, he's paid for the ground he died on with his life. I think it's a military expression, maybe British."

"How extraordinary," Bronson said, "he's saying one thing while meaning something else entirely."

"Youse guys sure make a business out of talking," Kerrigan said, continuing to play with the satchel. "But no matter how you slice it, this is one swell bundle of kale."

"What he means..."

"Pardon me, Walter," Bronson interrupted, "but I think I'm beginning to learn Mr. Kerrigan's language." He looked at Crusher. "You said a mouthful, slim. Now maybe you should scram and take the cabbage to the bimbo."

Crusher smiled. "See, you're catching on. It ain't that hard. I think I'm catching your drift, too. If you would be so kind, Mr. McDumont, I believe we have an appointment with a young businesswoman."

They all laughed. "I'll be darned," McDumont said. "There is hope for the human race. If you two can learn to communicate, anything's possible."

Mona answered the door quickly. Behind her they could see suitcases on the floor and dresses on hangers draped over the sofa.

"Checking out, babe?" Kerrigan asked as McDumont handed her the money. "You and your brothers hit the jackpot." He looked over her head. "Gord and Mike around? I wanted to say goodbye, no hard feelings."

"They're out... buying furniture for our new place," she said hurriedly. "I gotta go, they're expecting me." She closed the apartment door and then opened it again. "I guess I should thank you guys for bringing around the money. So thanks. But if I don't see you again, it'll be too soon." The door slammed shut.

"Babe sure is in a hurry," Kerrigan said as they walked back down the stairs.

"You blame her? Getting out of a flea trap like this? I'd be excited about it, too. I lived in too many just like it when I was a kid."

"Yeah, me too. But she seemed kinda nervous."

"She figured we might double cross her, take the money ourselves. That was your idea, remember?"

"I had worse ones, too. I don't like to think about those hillbillies having all that loot."

"I know what you mean," McDumont said. "But look at it this way. With any luck, we've seen the last of them for while."

"I sure as hell hope so," Kerrigan replied. "Those Wilsons ain't got no class at all. Now let's get something to eat. All this talk about money makes me hungry."

They had a long, leisurely lunch at a steak house on Wiltshire Boulevard. Kerrigan wanted to talk about Cookie, the black singer he was crazy about, and McDumont was more than happy to listen. With things going so well with Penny, McDumont felt an expansive wave of affection for anyone who was in love.

"So what's so special about her?" McDumont asked. "You've got to admit you two don't seem like the most likely couple in the world."

"You ain't heard her sing, have you?"

"No, I wanted to ask you about that. I'm a big Bessie Smith and Ma Rainey fan, is she anything like them?"

"Kinda, but she's a little gal, she don't belt it out the way them big mamas do. She sounds like she's whispering to you, just you, but there ain't nothing weak about it. And she don't just do blues, she can swing it, too. I've heard her jam with some of the white cats who work in the studios."

McDumont frowned. "I thought the police didn't allow white and black to play together?"

"They don't, but after hours the musicians make their own rules. That's how I met Cookie, friend of mine who blows bone in Glenn Gray's band invited me along to a session. You were talking about me and Mr. Bronson learning how to communicate, you ought to see how those musicians get along. Colour don't have nothing to do with it, it's strictly what you play that says who you are."

"Sounds great. So you met Cookie, then what happened?"

"I dunno. I don't look twice at her until she starts singing. Then she did 'Them There Eyes,' you know how it starts out, 'I fell in love with you the first time I looked into them there eyes,' and I was gone, Jack. It was like she was talking inside my head. I don't know how to explain it, but she really sent me, so I started trying to hang around with her."

McDumont didn't say anything while Kerrigan took a sip from his coffee cup. He'd never heard the big man talk this way, quietly and thoughtfully without the usual veneer of tough-guy mannerisms, and he was afraid that if he said anything he'd break the spell.

"But it ain't that easy," Kerrigan continued. "You see a black chick with a white guy, you figure she's a pro, and most of the time you'd be right. So somebody like Cookie, trying to make it in the music business, she don't want to be seen with no ofey cats. She knows people will put her down."

"That's rough," McDumont couldn't help saying.

"Yeah. And that ain't the only thing. Some of these so-called 'hep cats,' the white folks who claim to dig jazz so much, they're just as bad as everybody else. I was in the Sapphire Club one night when this rich white son of a bitch said he and his friends wanted to rub Curtis Mosby's head, 'For luck,' he said. Now Curtis, he ain't no Uncle Tom, he smiles and all that but he ain't no shoeshine boy, he don't give you that, 'Yes boss' and 'No boss' jive. But he ain't no dummy, neither. He can't afford to do anything to upset these fat cats who want to treat him like a rabbit's foot or something, he'll lose his job and get a bad rep with the club owners. So he lets them rub his head and it looks like he's all smiles about it."

"Something tells me that wasn't quite the end of the story."

"You got that right." Crusher laughed. "He told me about it later. I just about bust a gut. These white jerks were drinking champagne cocktails faster than the bartender could make them. So Curtis, next time the band takes a break, he goes behind the bar and asks the bartender to give him the bottle of champagne he's using. Then Curtis unbuttons his fly and pees into the bottle. He said it was a pretty good load, too, he'd been drinking a lot of water on the stand. He looks at the bartender and says, 'Make sure you use that for my friends at table so-and-so.'"

"Jesus," McDumont said, almost choking with laughter, "you mean he got away with it, nobody figured it out?"

"Everything was cool. I'm kinda glad I wasn't sitting at that table, though, there was some society types drinking some pretty strange hooch that night. But damn, I ain't told you the best part. All the time Curtis was doing this, standing behind the bar so they couldn't see below his waist, he was smiling and waving at these suckers, being all friendly and nice like he was the best buddy they had in the world."

"I'll be a monkey's uncle," McDumont said, still chuckling. "But we kind of got away from Cookie. You said it was her you wanted to talk about."

"I could talk about her all night, I could talk your goddamned ear off. But to make a long story short, I think we're finally getting someplace. That night I took her home from the Alabam, we finally put each other straight about a couple of things. I told her how it wasn't just the sex bit, I was really crazy about her, I could hear things when she was singing that I hadn't never heard before. And she knew I was telling it how it is. But she's been pushed around by a lot of guys. She was sweet on a white trumpet player one time, but he treated her like dirt. She sure ain't no babe in the woods any more." He cleared his throat. "We just got to go slow, then maybe we'll get some place."

"That's it," McDumont said. "When you've knocked around for a while, trying to play it cool and not get involved, it's hard when you meet someone you really like. You don't know how to be serious. You catch yourself saying phoney things, but you don't know what else to say."

"You and Penny seem to be doing all right."

"Boy, I still can't believe it. I have to pinch myself all the time to make sure that I'm not dreaming." He looked at his watch. "Speaking of dreaming, it's just about time to go pick up Paul Junior. But this has been great, Crusher. I feel like I know you a lot better than I did before."

"Yeah, I don't talk this way much. A big lug like me ain't supposed to have no feelings. Let's go get the squirt. I stay here any longer, I'm going to start getting hungry again."

They picked up Paul Junior and drove back to the Bronson house without incident. As they parked the Cadillac in front of the garage, McDumont said, "That's funny. I don't see Penny's car anywhere. That must have been a long meeting."

"These society types love to jabber," Crusher said. "She's probably telling some girlfriend about this hotshot Canuck she met."

As they walked in the front door, Paul Bronson came to meet them. "Penny isn't with you, is she? I thought perhaps you'd arranged to meet for lunch."

"No," McDumont said, "I didn't know when we'd be back."

"She said she'd be here for lunch. We waited for her until after one o'clock, but she still hasn't returned. I'm getting a bit worried. Harrison House is in a rough neighbourhood."

"Crusher and I can go down there," McDumont said. "Maybe she had car trouble or something."

"It isn't like Penny not to phone, Walter, usually she..." The phone began to ring.

"That'll be her now," McDumont said.

Bronson picked up the receiver and said, "Hello?" He listened for a moment and then collapsed into a chair, clutching his chest. "Walter, Walter," he gasped, holding the receiver out toward him.

"See if you can help Mr. Bronson," McDumont told Crusher. Then he took the phone. "Walter McDumont speaking."

"So it's the little bastard," Larry Harmon's voice snarled. "Hi, little bastard. You're just the guy I want to talk to."

"What do you want, Harmon? What did you say to Mr. Bronson, you stupid prick?"

"It wasn't anything *I* said, fuckface. Listen to this."

There was silence for a moment, and then Penny screamed, "Walter, help me, they've got me..." The sound of a blow cut off her voice.

"How do you like them apples?" Harmon said. "Now shut up and listen to what I'm going to tell you."

CHAPTER ELEVEN

Harmon wanted one hundred thousand dollars. He gave them one day to get it ready, at which point he would call again about the arrangements for delivery. He emphasized that they should not call the police. "If you call the cops, I'll find out," he said, "and you won't ever see Penny Bronson again. Alive. So act smart and keep your mouths shut. Don't even think about marking the money. I know all the tricks. If you try anything you'll be sorry."

"If you touch Penny, you're a dead man," McDumont said into the receiver. "I swear that I'll kill you if it takes the rest of my life to do it."

"You'll do what I goddamned tell you, little bastard, and you'll take it and like it. Hey, Gord, Mike, you know what the little prick said? We touch his sweetie, he's going to kill us. I'm real scared. I'm shaking in my boots."

McDumont heard sardonic laughter in the background. Jesus Christ, he thought, those Wilson birds are in on this, too. That's why Mona was so anxious to get rid of us. She knew what was going to happen.

"Remember what I said, Harmon," McDumont answered. "If anybody harms Penny, you're going to die."

"Aw, gee, I'm terrified," Harmon said. "But I don't know about Mike and Gord. They haven't had a decent piece of ass in so long they might not be able to control themselves. A good-looking dame like the Bronson twist, we might just have to pass her around for a while, keep everyone happy."

McDumont controlled himself. "Just remember what I said," he repeated. "Let me talk to Penny. I want to see if she's all right."

"Oh, I don't think so," Harmon said after a moment. "She tried to tell you where we are. I had to belt her, but she'll be okay. You just get that money ready and keep somebody by the phone." He hung up.

"What are we going to do?" Paul Bronson whimpered after McDumont had told him of Harmon's demands. He was almost doubled over, clutching his chest, having difficulty breathing. McDumont tried to help, but Bronson shrugged him off. After a while he sat up, apparently recovered, and said, "Should we call the police?"

"I don't think so. Harmon's gone crazy, but he's still a cop— we've got to figure he'd find out about it if you called the police. What about the money? Is getting that much cash going to be a problem?"

Bronson thought it over. "I should be able to manage it. I'll have to go down to the bank right away and get started, I'll need to liquidate some investments." He struggled to his feet.

"You sure you feel okay, Mr. Bronson?" Kerrigan asked. "You don't look too good. You maybe want us to call you a doc or something?"

"I'll be all right," Bronson said. "This is something that's got to be done, and I'm the only one who can do it. But you'd better drive me, Walter, I don't think I can manage the car by myself."

"Crusher can do that," McDumont said. "I'm going to stay by the telephone. I want to be here if anything happens."

It's the only thing I can do, he thought. Penny is in terrible danger, and this is the only thing I can do.

An hour later the telephone rang. "My goodness," Chandler said when McDumont answered, "have they got you answering the phone, too? It's Ray, Walter. How are you?"

McDumont explained the situation to him. "It's terrible, Ray. I feel so helpless. I don't know what I would do if anything happened to Penny."

"You could start by damning me to hell," Chandler said grimly. "I started this ball rolling with my stupid curiosity. You wouldn't have had anything to do with this if I weren't such an old busybody."

"No, that's not true. Not the way you mean it, anyway. The Bronsons and Mona Wilson were an accident waiting to happen, I didn't really have anything to do with that. And I'm glad I met Penny, she's so wonderful... but I bet she's sorry she met me, God, I bet she wishes she hadn't..." He couldn't talk any more, he was all choked up.

"I'm so sorry," Chandler said after a moment. "I'd give anything to take this all back. But damn it, Walter, there must be something you can do. Maybe I can help. I'm supposed to have a fairly good brain. What about Harmon? Do you know where he lives?"

"That's the first thing I thought of," McDumont said wearily, "but his phone's been disconnected and there's no new number. You know, this isn't one of your stories, Ray. The good guys don't necessarily win." He couldn't help laughing, crazy though it felt to laugh. "I wish I was one of those pulp-magazine heroes you're so crazy about; I'd find Harmon's hideout, crash in with guns blazing and rescue my girl."

"There must be something," Chandler said, "something that would lead you to where they are. They haven't vanished off the face of the earth. They're out there somewhere. Perhaps you can find them."

"I don't see how," McDumont replied. "The Wilsons were obviously leaving their apartment, and I don't imagine they left a forwarding address." He paused. "Wait a minute, that superintendent, that Albie, he might know something. Damn it, he knew Harmon. He said he was 'in on the fix.' That's the guy I want to talk to."

"If I can help in any way, I want you to call on me, Walter. And I do mean 'any way.' Even if it comes to violence. Harmon has gone off the deep end. You don't know what he might try. I haven't touched a gun since the war but I do know how they work. I used to be pretty good with them."

"I appreciate your offer, Ray, but let's hope it doesn't come to that. Maybe we can get something out of this superintendent character. Or maybe Crusher can, that's his specialty, after all." McDumont laughed grimly. "No, I wouldn't want to be Albie when Crusher gets hold of him. I wouldn't want to be him at all."

McDumont phoned the bank and spoke to Paul Bronson. The arrangements to get the hundred thousand in cash together were progressing satisfactorily. Bronson had told his staff that he needed it for a real estate deal— an unusual but not entirely unknown way of doing business in a community that still had something of the Wild West about it— and they agreed that Paul and Crusher should return to the house immediately, after which McDumont and Kerrigan would go to the Boyle Heights address and see what they could find out. Bronson would stay by the telephone in case the kidnappers called again.

"Please be careful, Walter," Bronson said when they returned. "If this superintendent is associated with Harmon, he could be very dangerous."

"It's the only thing we can do," McDumont said firmly. "Or at least it's the only thing I've been able to think of. We'll be careful, but we have to find out if he knows anything."

When they reached the steps of 427 Boyle Heights Street, Kerrigan paused and said, "You know how to play good cop, bad cop?"

"Sure, like we were doing with the Wilsons. You play the heavy, I make like I'm the voice of reason. Except right now I feel more like playing the bad cop. I'm in the mood to beat the hell out of anybody who crosses me."

"Any way you want to play it, that's jake with me. But you got to remember I ain't real great at playing good guys. I never had much practise."

"Okay, have it your way," McDumont said. "But if you can't scare him, don't be surprised if I have a go."

Crusher snorted. "If that little jerk ain't ratting on his mother two minutes after we get in the place, I'll turn him over to you." He looked at McDumont appraisingly. "That expression on your face, chances are he'll take one gander at that and tell us what we want anyway."

McDumont was about to knock when Kerrigan stopped him. "No," he whispered, "like this." He stepped back, ran at the door, and smashed into it with his left shoulder. The door leapt off its hinges and exploded backwards, revealing a startled Albie lying on a disordered cot.

The little man jumped to his feet. "What the hell do you think you're doing?" he said belligerently.

Crusher picked Albie up by the throat with his left hand and slapped him hard with his right. He slapped him again, and then a third time. The imprint of Kerrigan's hand was large and red on Albie's face.

"All right, all right," McDumont said. "Don't kill him. I want to ask him some questions."

Crusher threw Albie down on the cot. He bounced off the wall and then back onto the rumpled bedding. He held his throat and gasped for air. The back of his head was bleeding. "Whaa..." he said, fighting to get the word out. "Whaa..."

"Larry Harmon and Mona Wilson," McDumont said. "And her brothers, Gord and Mike. Where did they go?"

Albie looked at him in astonishment and shook his head. When he had regained his breath, he said, "Hell, I don't know. They didn't tell me. They just took off, I don't know where they are."

Kerrigan grabbed the front of Albie's shirt and hoisted him up against the wall. "Then you're a dead man," he growled. He tapped Albie's head against the wall, at first gently and then harder. A red circle of blood flowered against the faded wallpaper.

"Hold it, Crusher," McDumont said. My god, he thought, he will kill this guy if I don't stop it. A part of him hadn't been willing to consider this, had believed that no one would refuse to talk when threatened with death. But what if Albie didn't know anything? And what if he did, but was willing to die for it?

"Listen," he said to Albie, sweat beginning to pour off his body, "maybe you don't know where they went. But you must be able to tell us something. What about Mona's brothers? Do you know if either of them had jobs?"

Albie slowly shook his head. "No," he said, in obvious pain, "I don't know nothing. Harmon didn't tell me anything. I don't know, I don't know." His voice was thin and high, like a child's.

McDumont believed him. But Kerrigan was looking at Albie contemptuously, while Albie stared back at him in horror. The little man's bowels had voided, and a terrible smell of fear and excrement filled the room. "You're dead meat, punk," Crusher said, taking out his revolver and pressing it against Albie's forehead.

"Nancy!" Albie suddenly screamed. "Mona's friend Nancy! One of Harmon's hookers. You ask her! Nancy, I got an address for her here somewhere."

Kerrigan dropped him onto the cot. Albie stood up, shakily walked over to a battered wooden desk, and rummaged through its drawers. "Here it is," he said eventually, holding up a crumpled piece of paper. "She and Mona did a sister act sometimes, Harmon ran the two of them. If Mona was busy, I used to send the johns over to Nancy's place."

McDumont took it from him. "Nancy Virdon, 3485 Collins, LE-4593" was scrawled there in bleary pencil. "All right," he said to Crusher, "let's get the hell out of here."

"What about the punk?" Kerrigan asked. "He could be lying, trying to stall us. The minute we leave this rat trap, he could warn this babe we're coming. We got to do something with him."

"No, please," Albie whined, "I told you what I know, I cooperated. I don't want any more trouble."

McDumont hated to admit it, but Crusher was right. Albie was scared of them now, but that didn't mean they could trust him to keep quiet once they were gone. But they didn't have to kill him.

"You stay here with him, Crusher," McDumont said, tightlipped. "I'll go and see if I can find this Virdon dame. If it turns out to be a bum steer, we can take care of this jerk when I get back." *I sound like a cheap hood,* he thought. *What in the name of all that's holy is happening to me?*

"Okay," Kerrigan said. "But don't take too long. Old Albie here get's any riper, I'm going to have to put him in a garbage can and tie down the lid."

"Jesus, mister," Albie said to McDumont, "you can't leave me here with this psycho. You can't just leave me here with him."

McDumont thought about Penny and what might be happening to her. "Shut up!" he said harshly. "You better hope this Nancy knows something. If she doesn't, or if I don't find her, I'm going to let Crusher take care of you. And I'll help him. I swear to God, I'll help him." He turned on his heel and hurried out of the apartment.

Thirty-four-eighty-five Collins Avenue was a small stucco bungalow in a neighbourhood of similar houses, most of which seemed to be well cared for. No one answered the door. McDumont went around to the side and peered in through a curtainless kitchen window. The door to the icebox was open, and debris was scattered around the floor. It didn't look as though anyone lived there.

"Can I help you, young man?" said a high-pitched female voice from behind him.

He turned to find himself being scrutinized by an alert, elderly woman in a beige housecoat who was standing in the yard next door. "I was looking for a Nancy Virdon," he said. "I'm not sure whether it's 'Miss' or 'Mrs.' Can you tell me if she lives here?"

"Oh, she lives here, she certainly does," she said maliciously. "The carryings on in that house... now I can't tell you if she's married or not, but if she is, she doesn't live with her husband." She coloured. "Or if she does, he's a very... strange sort of husband." She regained her composure. "But why are you looking for her, if I may ask?"

He said the first thing that popped into his head. "It's an insurance matter, Nancy Virdon is making a claim against the company I represent." Think fast, he told himself, this woman is just itching to tell me all about the disreputable Nancy. "She claims to have been injured in an automobile accident, a broken leg and other injuries."

"Hah!" the woman said. "She doesn't have a broken leg any more than I do." She glanced down at her legs as if for confirmation. "She was racing around here this morning. Two of those men who visit her picked her up in a car."

"What kind of car was it?"

"A black sedan, a beat-up old black sedan. I don't know enough about cars to tell you what kind. But they sure left in a hurry, let me tell you." She thought for a moment. "I've seen those men before, they were around here quite a bit. More than most of the others, I reckon. It looked as though she was moving, they were carrying out her clothes and things." She frowned. "If you could call them clothes, some of the things she wore. I swear, Herbert must be rolling in his grave at what's gone on in that house. Herbert, that's my late husband, God rest his soul, he wouldn't have stood for it. He would have told those people what's what!" she said emphatically.

"I don't suppose you have any idea where they went? The company will want to know."

He could see that the idea of an insurance company on Nancy Virdon's trail appealed to her. "No I don't, young man, I wouldn't have the faintest idea, but I can tell you who would. Oh, yes, I can tell you who would!"

He waited, but she seemed to be gloating. "And who would that be, ma'am?" he finally asked.

"Sam Reilly, that's who! He lives across the street, just over there." She pointed to a yellow bungalow numbered 3480. "Sam Reilly's no stranger to that Nancy, no siree!"

"Thank you very much," McDumont said, "you've been a great help. I'll go see Mr. Reilly."

"Always glad to help, young man. But don't you let anyone tell you that Nancy broke her leg. She shouldn't get away with it, by golly, she shouldn't!"

"She won't get away with it," he said grimly. "You can bet your life on that."

Sam Reilly's bungalow had a neglected air about it. The grass needed cutting, and the concrete steps leading up to the verandah were chipped and cracked. McDumont was about to knock on the front door when it opened before him.

A small, wizened, bespectacled man in a dirty grey cardigan looked at Walter curiously. "I seen you talking to that sourpuss across the street," he said. "When I seen her pointing at my place, I figured I was in for it. You're from the city, huh? I know the goddamned grass is too long. I'll get around to cutting it one of these days. But it ain't easy when you're on your own, it ain't so goddamned easy, young fella."

I wonder if he's Crusher's father, McDumont thought. He sounds like he could be. He didn't look like he'd be all that thrilled to cooperate with an insurance company investigator, anyway, that obviously wasn't the right tack to take. No, given what he knew about Nancy Virdon, Reilly was probably one of her customers. Even though the guy looked like he'd be bowled over by a stiff breeze.

So good-time Charlies together, then. "No, you got me wrong, pal, I'm just trying to connect with Nancy. I'm from out of town, we had some swell times, Nancy and I, but it looks like she moved. You know where she went?"

"Travelling salesman, ain't ya?" When McDumont nodded his head, Reilly guffawed and slapped him on the shoulder. "Yes sir, I can always tell. After I was in the army I was on the road myself until a few years ago. It's the berries, there ain't nothing like it." He smiled broadly. "We got more than that in common, too. You wouldn't think it to look at me, but I can still cut the old mustard even if the goddamned Krauts did fill my ass full of shrapnel." He laughed. "They got me on the other side, I wouldn't be doing no loving, but this way I got partial disability, that cheque sure comes in handy." His good mood abandoned him. "Nancy didn't say nothing to me about where she was going, though, she didn't say a thing. I guess she was in too much of a hurry."

"So you don't know where she is," McDumont said wearily.

"I don't have no address for her." Reilly looked at him quizzically.

"But if you're so tight with Nancy, how come you don't know where she hangs out? You must of met her there the first time, right? Come to think of it, I ain't never seen you around here. You sure we're talking about the same party?"

"Oh, yeah," McDumont said, thinking furiously, "I got her number from another guy. I'd call her, she'd usually come to my hotel room, I was only out here once or twice." That seemed to satisfy Reilly, so he went on. "So where's this place she hangs out at? Somewhere around here?"

"Nah, it's over on Melrose, joint called Barney's. It don't look like much, but that's where the dolls are, you looking to pitch a little woo. Place is always full of cops, too, there must be a hell of a payoff." He paused. "You see Nancy, you tell her Sam wants to see her." He leered. "You make sure and tell her I been saving something up for her, and I ain't talking about my army pension."

"I'll do that," McDumont said. "You won't mind if I take care of my business with her first, though?"

"Hell, no," Reilly chortled. "I know what it's like on the road. After a hard day, the first thing you need to do is relax, you got to get your mind ready for tomorrow. Then the next day you're ready to go out there and knock them dead."

When McDumont returned to Boyle Heights Street, Albie was gone. "He figured he was gonna get it caught in the meatgrinder no matter what happened," Kerrigan said. "He's got a sister in Pasadena, he took a cab over there. He's gonna lay low for a while."

"You don't think he'll try to get in touch with Harmon or the rest of them?"

"Nah, Albie learned his lesson. I told him what we did to that fink sheriff I was telling you about, just in case he didn't get the message. You don't got to worry none about Albie. He's going to be a real good boy."

"I'm glad he's out of the way. Anyhow, Nancy Virdon scrammed out of her house this morning, but I think I know where we can find her. A place called Barney's. Ever heard of it?"

Crusher snorted. "That figures. The squares love that joint, they get to hang out with cops and get their ashes hauled at the same time. What they don't know is that most of the dough they spend on the floozies goes right into some cop's pocket. Yeah, Barney's would be the place, all right." He frowned. "Trouble is, I ain't gonna be much help to you in there. A lot of those cops know me, and most of them are friends of Larry's. They see me, they're gonna know I ain't there on the pussy patrol. They're gonna wonder."

"They don't know who I am," McDumont said, "except for that guy Lou, and he didn't get much of a look at me. Harmon is going to be laying low, he won't be in there." He thought for a moment. "I'll ask Ray to go with me. We'll be a couple of salesmen from hicksville who heard about Nancy from a friend. That's probably how she gets a lot of her dates, anyway."

"You be careful, you go in Barney's," Kerrigan said. "It ain't gonna be like having tea with the Bronsons. Some of those cops are mean, specially when they get drinking, and they stick together. You get in a fight in there, it won't be no fair fight. They'll 'Hey, Rube!' you."

"I won't get in any fights," McDumont replied. "I'm just looking for a good time, mister," he drawled in an imitation country-boy accent. "Say, you got any good-time gals in this here town?"

Chandler said he'd be happy to keep McDumont company. "You're going to think I'm an old fussbudget, Walter, but have you thought about what you're going to wear?"

"What I'm going to wear?"

"Yes, if we're going to be a couple of out-of-town businessmen, we're going to have to dress the part. Now, I've got an old horse blanket of a jacket around here somewhere, I bought it when I was three sheets to the wind. That will do for me. But you won't be able to wear the outfits I bought you, they're not right for the person you're going to be impersonating."

"So I suppose it's back to your tailor's again," McDumont said dejectedly. "Just when I thought I'd seen the last of them, too. Wearing that blue blazer over my slacks with an open-necked shirt, I was taken for an insurance investigator *and* a travelling salesman today."

"I'm sure you still looked much too urbane," Chandler said, laughing. "But we won't be visiting my regular tailor, in any case. No, we'll be travelling in the opposite direction, both geographically and sartorially. I'll pick you up in half an hour."

They drove out Fairfax to a large barn of a building topped by a giant revolving sign for "Sid's Suits." The sides of the building were plastered with banners advertising the remarkable bargains to be found inside. "'Jacket and two pairs pants $19'?" McDumont read. "I wonder if they're guaranteed not to dissolve in the rain?"

"Probably not," Chandler said. "But that's the idea, old chap. The cheaper and gaudier the better. And this will be my treat, I quite enjoy being your wardrobe consultant."

"I always knew there was something weird about you. Maybe you were a clothing salesman in a previous existence."

"Them's fighting words, partner," Chandler said, smiling. "Come on, this will only hurt for a little while."

One advantage of Sid's Suits, McDumont decided once they were inside, was that Sid's cheapness extended to not hiring many employees; if you looked as though you knew what you were looking for, the harried salesmen were happy to let you alone. Just as well, he thought, I wouldn't take most of the stuff in here if they were giving it away.

Chandler was working his way through a rack of stunningly garish sports jackets. "Would you look at that?... amazing, I've never seen the like... ah, now here's something truly exceptional!" He took one of the jackets off the rack and held it up against McDumont's body. "Try this on, Walter. I think it's exactly what we're looking for."

McDumont stared at the mirror in disbelief. The garment's primary colour was red, a flash your lights and whir your sirens red, a red so red that it made his normally neutral complexion look pink and shiny. The jacket also featured small irregular splotches of yellow and green, which gave the whole an effect of mustard and relish spilled on a red fire engine. It was the ugliest thing he had ever seen.

"Ray, it's the ugliest thing I've ever seen."

Chandler smiled. "I take your point, although there are paintings hanging in our local art galleries that might give it a run for its money. Yes, I think it's just what we want. Now, as for accessories... actually, your jacket is so remarkably vulgar that it's going to overwhelm whatever you wear with it. But something dark and shiny in the pants department should complement it nicely. And then one of Sid's inimitable floral-patterned neckties. Yes, that should do it. Come on, lad, buck up, it'll soon be over."

"It won't be too soon for me," McDumont groaned. "Just when I was starting to hang around in respectable circles, too." Chandler held out a dark blue necktie smothered in large pink flowers. "Oh no," McDumont said, "if you think I'm going to wear that you're crazy!"

McDumont glared down at the tie. The pink flowers seemed to be moving up toward his neck. "I feel like a goddamned clown," he said plaintively.

"Jeez," Kerrigan said from the back seat of Chandler's Desoto coupe, "I think you look kinda sharp. I'm gonna go out to Sid's, see if he's got that jacket in my size."

"I don't imagine he will," McDumont said. "Somebody would have called the fire department by now, they would have hosed it down with a couple of pumpers." He looked at Chandler. "So who are we tonight, anyway? What innocent community are we going to slander by claiming to be from it?"

"Somewhere Middle Western, I should think, although we don't need to be from the same town. Better if we weren't, perhaps. Did you spend any time in the Midwest on your travels across the states?"

"Not much. I was mainly in the South and Southwest. Wait a minute. How about Cairo, Illinois? I hoboed around there a little bit. It's the kind of place most of the people still have straw in their hair."

"That should do nicely for you, then. I think I'll choose Omaha, Nebraska, I actually was there as a child." He spoke over his shoulder. "Are you coming in with us, Mr. Kerrigan? I'm sure you could pass as a Chicagoan without any difficulty."

"Yeah, Chi town. I broke a little bread there. My kinda town. But I better play possum out here, I ain't exactly no stranger to Barney's. If you guys get in a jam I'll be in there like Flynn."

"Tell me, Mr. Kerrigan," Chandler said thoughtfully, "would you have any objection to my using you as the model for a character in one of my stories? I'll change the minor details, of course. No one will connect you with it. But would it be all right if I did that?"

"You want to use me as a *model*? You mean you want me to pose for a painting or something? I don't know about that."

"No, no," Chandler said, laughing, "nothing of the kind. This is a story I'm writing about a detective in Los Angeles. Fiction, not a true story. I'd like to make someone like you one of the characters in it, that's all."

Crusher thought about it. "Yeah, that's okay with me, except I don't want you to make me no private dick. Any of my friends heard about that, I'd never live it down."

"Not to worry, I won't. But I would like to talk to you about it some other time when we can sit down and get to know each other. Would that be possible?"

"Yeah, no sweat." Crusher leaned forward in the back seat and said, "That's Barney's right up there. The parking lot's in behind, off that driveway on the right."

They parked the car and Chandler and McDumont got out. "Don't you guys worry," Kerrigan assured them. "I'll be right out here if you need me."

"I hope to hell we don't," McDumont said. "We need to find Nancy Virdon, and then get her to lead us to Harmon. If anybody figures out who we are, we're sunk. Come on, Ray, let's get on with it. And let's stick with our own goddamned first names. I'm sick and tired of pretending to be someone I'm not."

CHAPTER TWELVE

Barney's was jumping, all right, there was no other word for it. The night club consisted of one big, long, low-ceilinged room, a small bar to the left and a row of leather-padded banquettes to the right. Most of the remaining space was crammed with wooden tables and chairs, placed just far enough apart for the scurrying waiters to thread their way between them.

Several faces turned to look as McDumont and Chandler came through the door. They were cop faces, faces that looked at you and then through you with an arrogance that proclaimed their easy superiority. Just as well, McDumont thought. It was when those stares stopped and fixed themselves on you that trouble was just around the corner.

They sat down at a small table toward the back. A waiter hurried up. "What's your pleasure, gents?"

"A couple of beers," McDumont said, spreading his arms expansively. "And say, a good buddy of mine told me this was a real *hot* joint, you know what I mean?"

"You mean you wouldn't mind a little company," the waiter said, flashing him a quick smile. "Sure, I think that can be arranged."

"My buddy told me to ask for Nancy, that's who he said, Nancy."

"Nancy, huh? You know, she ain't been in tonight, which is kind of unusual— maybe she's sick or something, I don't know. Tell you what, I'll go see if she's around."

When he came back with their beers he said, "Sorry, gents, I don't see Nancy no place. But Marcia and Gale, they're a couple of real good-looking ladies, they got some time on their hands. You want me to send them over?"

When McDumont hesitated, Chandler said, "Sounds bloody good to me, mate. Let's have a look at the lassies. I feel like getting my leg over tonight."

"English, huh?" the waiter said. "The dames really go for that, they think it's classy. I'll send them over." He hurried off.

"What the hell kind of an accent was that?" McDumont asked. "You sounded like a Cockney who'd grown up in Scotland."

"You Canadians would be aware of that, but the Yanks don't know a Cockney from a kipper. I've seen characters from the East End of London pass themselves off as lords and ladies, no one here has a clue. But I'm supposed to be a salesman, *in trade* as my relatives would genteelly observe, so I'm nonetheless going to try to mask my usual very proper diction, thank you very much. I want to sound authentic in case we do run into someone from the old country. So gorblimey, guv, Bob's your uncle!" He took a sip of his beer and made a face. "Hoot mon, laddie, this stuff makes the Shanty Lounge's brew taste like bloody ambrosia. Mind how you go."

"We do run into any one from the auld sod," McDumont said, "we're in serious trouble. You're going to have to pretend you lost your voice suddenly— if they hear that sorry attempt at merry olde English we're for it."

Two women sat down at their table. One was a medium-sized brunette, the other a small redhead. Their eyes suggested that they'd seen it all, but their smiles announced that they were willing to have another look. "You the boys looking for company?" the brunette asked.

"That's right, baby," McDumont replied. "Me and Ray here just got into town, and we're ready to roar. What's your pleasure, ladies?"

"The usual," they chorused to the hovering waiter.

"I think we should all be introduced," Chandler said. "In England, that's where I'm from originally, you always have to be introduced to people first, then you can go on about your business. So I'm Ray, and the good-looking young chap on my left is Walter. We're so very pleased to meet you ladies. We look forward to a most mutually rewarding acquaintance."

"Ain't he a riot?" the brunette said to the redhead. "Whatever you say, sweetie, you're buying. I'm Marcia, and this cute little old thing on *my* left is Gale."

"Any friends of yours are friends of ours," Gale said, batting her eyes at them. "In fact," she continued, giggling, "most of *my* friends are friends of just everybody else. Isn't that simply a riot?" McDumont figured that she had at least half a load on.

"Let's keep it professional, sweetie," Marcia admonished. "Willie said these gentlemen were asking for Nancy, and Nancy would want us to show her friends a good time."

"You're darn tooting," McDumont put in, "Nancy's a swell old girl. That's what Clem said, Ray, you remember? He said Nancy was a swell old girl." *If I pretend to be drunk,* he thought, *maybe I can get away with this oh-for-the-love-of-Nancy jazz— I don't want to seem too interested in her, but I do want to find out where the hell she is.*

"Indubitably, old chum, indubitably, but a bird in the hand, eh, what? A nudge is as good as a wink, am I right, old crumpet?" He turned to the women. "You must excuse young Walter, he was so looking forward to seeing this Nancy he's heard so much about. You know how stubborn these young chaps can be. But don't take any notice of him."

"Well *excuse me*," Gale huffed, "I guess I know when I'm not wanted." She pushed her chair back and stood up.

Marcia grabbed her hand and tried to pull her back into the chair.

"Take it easy, honey, he didn't mean anything by it. Come on, sit down, have a drink. Don't take it so serious. These are nice guys, I can tell."

"She isn't Nancy," McDumont snivelled, "she just isn't Nancy." He felt completely ridiculous, but if they could get rid of one of the women, looking for Nancy would make a little more sense...

Gale tore her hand away. "You're welcome to her, you son of a bitch. I hope she gives you a dose." She walked away quickly, beginning to cry.

"Jeez, I'm sorry," Marcia said. "You'll have to excuse Gale, she hasn't been too... popular lately. You want me to get another girl, or get lost, or what?"

"Oh, no, love," Chandler put in quickly, "you're a bit of all right with me. But I don't know about me mate here, he's not himself tonight. Tell me, is there any chance this Nancy person will be here later? I know Walter, when he gets in one of his moods there's no stopping him. It'll be Nancy or nobody for him this evening."

"Well, I could ask around. But you got to pay for my time... tell you what, you order a bottle of champagne, that should make it jake. I'll go see what I can find out. You stay here and see if you can sober up your friend."

"Oh, he isn't that drunk. He just gets this way when he's been on the road too long. He'll be fine by the time he gets back to Illinois."

"Nancy," McDumont moaned, "I want to see Nancy."

"Illinois, huh?" she said. "Okay, you just order that champagne and I'll be back in a jiff."

"Quite a remarkable performance," Chandler said when she had gone. "If I didn't know better, I'd have been convinced that you were a drunken idiot with an absurd crush on a woman you'd never met. But what if Nancy doesn't show up?"

"The only thing I can do is skulk off to our supposed hotel room and mourn my lonely fate, that's obvious." McDumont chuckled. "You, however, who have already declared your interest in Marcia, will have to carry on and remain 'in character,' as I believe they say in the theatre. Have a good time, *sweetie*, give her a kiss from me."

"Don't think I won't, old sausage. Marcia may not be a film star, but she looks to me like someone who enjoys her work. All right then, what's the plan of action if Nancy should decide to turn up?"

"We'll cross that bridge when we come to it. The main thing is to find her."

"I hope you know what the hell you're doing, Walter. Ah, our faithful servant has not abandoned us," Chandler said, as their waiter suddenly reappeared. "A bottle of champagne, if you please, my good fellow, and make sure it's the best in the house."

Marcia wasn't long in returning. "You're a lucky boy, sweetie," she said, patting McDumont on the hand, "Nancy phoned in a while ago and said she'd be in later. She moved to a new place today and she's getting things fixed up, but she should be along soon. So dry your eyes and drink up, mister. This could be your lucky night."

For the next half hour they made desultory small talk punctuated by Marcia's occasional hints about the need to keep the flow of drinks coming. "I get a percentage, sweeties, it keeps a poor girl in lipstick and things." McDumont found himself liking her, thinking about what she'd be like in bed. You could relax with hookers because the old will-we-won't-we question had already been settled. Then he thought about what might be happening to Penny and had to fight to keep himself under control, because part of him wanted to get Kerrigan's gun and turn Barney's upside down. Somebody here must know where the hell Harmon was.

"There she is!" Marcia stood up and waved. "Nancy, over here!"

Nancy Virdon walked slowly toward them, the mechanics of her hip movements drawing appreciative stares from other tables. Her closely cropped black hair didn't do much for her stubby nose and full lips, but the action below the neck was something else again: it was provocative, aggressive, it said maybe you can take me and maybe you can make me, but you'll never break me. Her hips seemed to give an even harder bump and grind when a sharp wolf whistle cut through the general clamour.

"So you've heard about me, have ya?" she said to McDumont after Marcia had introduced them. "Nothing too dirty, I hope," she giggled.

"No, no, nothing like that, just that you were a swell girl, lots of laughs. My friend heard I was going to L.A., he said you've got to look up Nancy, she's the cat's meow."

"Now that you lovebirds have finally found each other," Marcia said, "the night isn't getting any younger. How about it, Ray, do you want to come back to my place and pitch a little woo? Just tip the waiter twenty bucks and we'll be on our way."

"Oh yes, very much indeed. I'll see you back at the hotel, Walter. And don't do anything I wouldn't do, old bean. Tallyho, all!" The grin on Chandler's face looked like it was about to split. He was enjoying every minute of this farce.

Which left McDumont with Nancy. What the hell, a man's got to do etcetera. "So what do you say, baby? I bet you can pitch some pretty nice woo yourself. I sure would like to find out." He gave her his best leer, and threw in a wink for good measure. You can't say I'm not giving it everything I've got, he thought wryly.

"Sure, honey, but my place is kind of a mess, I just moved in. How about your hotel? I bet it's real nice."

"Oh, it is, but..." But what, idiot? How can you explain not taking a hooker to a hotel room? They go together like bacon and eggs, or cops and jail cells. The answer came to him in a flash, and he couldn't help chuckling out loud. "That's not so good, see. Ray and I are sharing a room and he... well, let me put it this way, old Ray is getting a little over the hill in the romance department. It isn't going to be too long before he's sacked out in one of those beds trying to catch up on his beauty sleep."

She stared at him so blankly that he thought he was going to have to spell it out to her, but then she got it. "Oh, yeah? Gee, three's a crowd, ain't it? Okay, honey, come on. Take care of the waiter and we'll get a cab to my place. You'll just have to excuse the mess."

Outside, Kerrigan was sitting in the front seat of Chandler's car. As Nancy scanned the street for a taxi, McDumont made a follow-me motion with his head, and was relieved to see Crusher nod vigorously.

When they got into a cab a few seconds later, Kerrigan pulled out and followed them.

"Thirty-seven Bunker Hill," Nancy said to the driver. Then she moved close to McDumont and put her hand in his groin. "We're going to have a real nice time, honey. You just wait and see."

He was embarrassed that his body responded to her, but what else was there for him to do? He was a john, a guy looking for a hot time in the old town tonight, a visiting fireman who wanted his fire put out. He was going to have to go through with it, so he might as well try and enjoy it.

But try though he did, he couldn't turn his brain off. Inside Nancy's apartment, he had to force himself to play his part in the familiar game of the desirer and the desired. He told her that he liked to have the lights completely off, and as they coupled quickly and vigorously he tried to think only about Penny, about her and about how he was doing this to try to rescue her. At one point he even laughed, when it occurred to him that many men went to prostitutes to forget about the women they lived with, and here he was going to a prostitute and trying to remember the woman he loved.

Afterwards, while getting dressed, he tried to be as enthusiastic as possible. "That was great, Nancy, that was really great. I sure am glad I waited around for you."

"You don't have to be in such a hurry, sugar," she said, patting the mattress beside her. "The night is young. I bet you've got plenty more where that came from. Why don't you stay a little while?"

Aside from anything else, he thought, Larry's liable to walk in on me in what would be one hell of a compromising position. "I'd like to," he said, "but I've got to get on the road early tomorrow. I'll catch you next time I'm in town, baby, you can bet your life on that. Let me have your phone number so I can call you."

"Sure, honey, here you go." She gave him a business card-sized slip of paper with a telephone number on it. "You be sure to call as soon as you get in town, though, a girl gets... busy sometimes."

Kerrigan was parked down the block. McDumont got into the car on the passenger side.

Crusher was looking at him with dramatically raised eyebrows. "I figured it out," he said, "I figured out what you're doing, but I got to say you got a funny way of doing things. Why didn't you just turn her over to me? I would of got where Harmon is out of her."

"I thought about it, believe me. If anybody thinks I enjoyed that, they're crazy. But we don't know for sure that she knows where Harmon is. He wouldn't necessarily tell her about something this big."

Kerrigan thought it over. "Yeah," he finally said, "maybe you're right." He laughed. "But you got a hell of a way of doing things, just the same. So you figure Harmon'll turn up here?"

"I don't know. He's Mona's pimp, Nancy is pals with Mona, you'd figure Harmon has some kind of deal going with Nancy. The guys who moved her sure sound like the Wilson brothers, too." He snapped his fingers. "Yes, damn it, those Wilsons are too dumb to come in out of the rain. They'd never think of something like that themselves. I bet they were following Harmon's orders. They must have been."

"And you could be talking through your hat," Kerrigan said. "Even if it's like you say, Harmon ain't stupid. He ain't gonna come waltzing around here just so you can find out where his hideout is. All he's got to do is lie low. He'd be nuts to go anywhere at all."

"Yeah, I know. But what else are we going to do? If you've got any better ideas, I'd sure like to hear them."

Crusher tapped him on the shoulder. "Nah, you're doing okay. At least we got a chance this way. Harmon don't show up, I'll go see the broad, see what she knows. Maybe she'll spill without too much trouble. She's probably in love with you, she ain't used to nice guys."

McDumont glared at him. "Can that love stuff. That had nothing to do with love. Shut up about it, would you, please?"

Kerrigan didn't reply. After a couple of minutes he yawned, stretched, and then said, "I don't know about you, but I need some coffee and sandwiches. There's an all-night diner back at the corner. How about I get us some eats?"

"Good idea." McDumont took out his wallet and gave Crusher a five-dollar bill. "You know, you might as well get enough to see us through till morning. We could be in for a long night."

They took turns dozing. At eight a.m. McDumont went to the diner and phoned Paul Bronson.

"Harmon called last night, Walter. We're supposed to drop the money off in a park near Topanga Canyon this evening. He gave me detailed instructions. Did you have any luck at your end?"

"Yes and no. We got a line on one of Harmon's lady friends, but I don't know if it's going to pay off. We'll be back at your house by the afternoon, anyway."

He phoned Chandler and told him what was going on. "We've still got your car, Ray. We might need it for a while yet. Do you want to pick it up at the Bronsons', or what?"

"Not to worry, old bean. I was planning on a dull day at home. These late nights take it out of us elderly chaps. How did things go with Nancy?"

"We know where she lives, but nobody else has shown yet. Crusher and I are parked down the block from her apartment building. We'll see what happens."

"My goodness, a *stakeout*, how exciting. Except that it's usually the police who stake someone out, and here you are staking out the police. Unusual, to say the least."

"You're determined to make this into one of your stories, aren't you? Well, Ray, nobody would believe this cockeyed mess if you did write it up— it's too nuts to be true." McDumont glanced at his watch and said, "Look, I've got to be getting back. I'll call you later."

"Don't worry about the car, Walter. Just be careful... and don't follow anyone too closely. I seem to recall you have a tendency to do that."

"Yes, boss. But Crusher's a professional at this stuff. He'll know just how to work it. Talk to you later."

McDumont bought two large containers of coffee and a dozen doughnuts before returning to the car. After he told Crusher about Harmon's call, they ate and drank in silence. Time was running out. If something didn't happen pretty soon they'd have to pay the ransom money and hope for the best.

A little after ten o'clock, a black sedan pulled up in front of the apartment building and Gord and Mike Wilson got out. They hurried inside and in a minute or two came out again, this time dragging Nancy Virdon and a large suitcase along with them. She was fighting them, jerking from side to side; it was obvious that she didn't want to go anywhere. They forced her into the back seat and Gord Wilson got in with her. As the sedan drove off, one of the back doors opened slightly but was then quickly pulled shut.

Crusher started the engine and eased out into the light mid-morning traffic. The black sedan was weaving all over the road, and they could see movement through the rear window. Kerrigan had to drive very slowly to keep from passing the Wilsons' car.

"Christ," McDumont said, "they're going to see us."

"No, they ain't. They got their hands full with Nancy, they ain't got time to worry about nothing else." He chuckled and looked at McDumont. "Good thing you didn't spend the night in there, Walter. She wouldn't be up to nothing this morning."

"Shut up and drive, you big lug. I told you I didn't want to hear any more about Nancy!"

"Okay," Crusher said, laughing. "But you got to hand it to her. She's keeping those boys so busy they wouldn't notice a paddy wagon sitting on their tail."

The sedan was heading east on Cahuenga Boulevard, making better time, though still subject to sudden changes in direction. Kerrigan dropped back and kept a car or two between them and the sedan.

Traffic thinned out as they continued heading east. Kerrigan slowed down until the sedan was barely in view. "I know, I know," he said as McDumont looked at him questioningly, "it ain't good. But what else are we gonna do? They make us, we ain't got no chance of finding out where they're going. Anyway, there ain't that many places to turn off here. We ain't gonna lose them."

The country was getting hillier, and they were losing sight of the sedan whenever it went over a crest in front of them. Then, when they topped one particularly long rise, the road before them was empty.

"Where the hell are they?" McDumont yelled. "Do you think they sped up? Did they spot us?"

"Keep your goddamned pants on," Crusher snarled, braking to a halt before a road sign. "County Road 14" it announced. There were arrows pointing left and right to the two gravel tracks that branched off the highway.

"Great," McDumont said, "they must have gone one way or the other. Now we have a fifty-percent chance of catching up with them. You want me to flip a coin, or what?"

"Nah, I want you to use those things you got on top of your nose, eyes I think they call them. You quit running your mouth and take a gander out there, you'll know which way to go."

McDumont looked at the two tracks. There was a small but perceptible cloud of dust hanging over the one on the left.

"Left, huh?" he said sheepishly.

"You're smarter than you look, kid. Now don't jump salty on me again. We got to take it real easy from here on."

They drove slowly over the road's crunchy gravel surface. They passed a couple of weatherbeaten farmhouses, then a rundown shack in front of which a woman was doing her laundry in a large grey washtub. She stared at them without expression, then finished wringing out a shirt and pinned it up on the clothesline that ran between the shack and a scraggly willow tree.

"This is real classy," Kerrigan said. "Don't look like these people got a pot to piss in."

"It's a good place to hide out, though— not exactly on the highway to anywhere. These farms sure don't look very prosperous. I bet a lot of them have been abandoned."

"We just need one that ain't." Kerrigan was peering intently through the windshield. "And maybe this is it."

They had topped a long, low rise. In front of them, they could see for miles as the road cut through a valley nestled between rolling hills. To their right, the sun glinted off something moving toward a house and barn set in a large clearing.

"This is it," Kerrigan said. He pulled the car off the road to the left. "They come back again this way they'll see us, but I can't do nothing about that. We're out of sight of that house, anyway."

They got out of the car and moved across the road. The land between them and the house was fairly heavily treed. They should be able to approach it without being seen. "What do you think?" McDumont asked. Even though it was cool and windy, sweat was pouring off his body.

"I think we better go have a gander," Kerrigan said. "That's what we're here for, right?"

"Right. That's what we're here for." McDumont swallowed heavily and hunched his shoulders. "Let's go."

It took them about half an hour to reach the edge of the clearing. For the last fifty yards, the tree cover became much thinner, so they had to get down on their hands and knees and crawl slowly and carefully. They stopped when they came to a wire fence beyond which there were only weeds and brown wisps of grass.

The house was less than a hundred feet in front of them. It was a squat, grey structure, a storey-and-a-half of ramshackle sprawl that looked as though a good wind would knock it over. There were two cars parked in front, the black sedan and a smarter green roadster. Off to the right, a large barn and some empty wire pens were visible.

"You want to try to get any closer, maybe try to make a play?" Kerrigan asked.

"No, we can't do that, Penny's in there." McDumont was sweating so hard that his vision was blurred. Christ, he was scared. Now that they knew where Penny had been taken, the full reality of the situation was coming home to him. It could be that he was going to have to go up against at least three armed men, one of whom he knew would kill him without compunction. This wasn't some fight in a schoolyard or an alley, where the worst thing that could happen was you got your clock cleaned. This was something else. And he didn't know if he had the stomach for it.

Kerrigan was looking at him. Maybe McDumont's fear was so obvious that Crusher could see it. "Okay, Walt, come on. We know where they are, anyway."

"No." He said it through clenched teeth, but he said it. "Let's wait and see if we can find out anything. Let's just wait and see."

They could glimpse movement through the house's opaque windows, but that was about all. Smoke was curling up from a chimney at the rear of the house; maybe somebody was cooking a meal. That could be why they'd gone to get Nancy. She might be a great cook or something, not that either she or Mona looked like they knew how to boil water. McDumont realized that he had no idea as to whether Penny could cook or not, he hadn't even thought about it when he'd asked her to marry him. Not that it made any difference. He was crazy about her no matter what... oh, shut up, he told himself savagely, think about something else. Think about how you're going to get her away from those goons in there. Do something useful.

Then Harmon came out the front door, stretching his arms and looking up at the sky with a smile on his face. *I could kill him right now,*

McDumont thought, and it wouldn't bother me at all. He had stopped sweating. He concentrated on Harmon, tried to visualize what he would look like with bullets smashing into his body, liking the image more and more until Kerrigan tapped him hard on the shoulder.

"Don't breathe so goddamned loud," he whispered. "You sound like a locomotive."

"Sorry, I was thinking about something. Something I'm going to enjoy doing."

Harmon went back inside. They could hear what sounded like a door banging shut somewhere in the rear of the house, but they couldn't see anything from where they were. "Let's move over to the right," McDumont said, "maybe we can get a better view."

They crawled slowly along the fenceline, which curved up toward the barn and led them to a point where they had a partial view of the back of the farmhouse. There was a lot of debris scattered around, scraps of lumber and pieces of old furniture, a rusty bedspring against a wall. There was a small woodpile with an ax leaning against it, and they could hear the clatter of dishes through the back screen door.

"Okay," Kerrigan whispered, "sounds like they're making lunch. Maybe this would be a good time to move in on them." He took his gun out and sighted it at the back door. "We get a little closer, I can nail Harmon easy. Them Wilson punks ain't got no sand, they'll be pushovers."

"We can't do it, Crusher, it's too risky," McDumont said quickly. He paused and made a deliberate effort to speak more calmly. "No, the ransom's all arranged. Let's get Penny back and then we can go after Harmon."

McDumont didn't like the way Kerrigan was looking at him. There was something between surprise and contempt in his face; he'd expected McDumont to want to go charging in there. Well, he wanted to, but it was too damned dangerous. Somebody could get hurt. Yeah, "somebody," he said to himself viciously, you mean your own chickenshit ass. You're afraid, why don't you admit it?

They made their way carefully back to the car and drove to the Bronson house, neither saying a word. As they pulled into the driveway, McDumont blurted out, "What I said before about guns was crap. I don't really know anything about them. They never let us fire those rifles. We learned how to take them apart and put them together again, but that was all. We never got to fire them."

Kerrigan looked at him appraisingly. "There ain't a hell of a lot to it, you want to learn. I could teach you easy, wouldn't take too long." He pulled to a stop in front of the house. "Far as that goes, rifle ain't going to do you much good in this kind of a deal, where you got to go in places and get guys. You want to know what to do, I can show you."

McDumont thought about it. "Yeah, that would be swell. I guess the first thing to do is to buy a gun. Where do you get a gun in this town, anyway?"

"Now you're cooking," Kerrigan said, laughing. "One thing I know about is where to get guns. Come on, we'll take a ride. This guy I know has got guns like Carter's got pills."

"Sure. I'll just run in and tell Paul Bronson what we're doing. It can't be any worse than going to Ray's tailor." McDumont laughed. "Your very own custom-tailored gun, the final touch in the well-dressed man's ensemble for an exciting evening out. Do you think we can get one that won't clash with the rest of my wardrobe?"

Kerrigan looked at him quizzically. "I don't know what the hell you're talking about, Walter. But one thing I do know, you want a gun, my friend Frankie is the man you want to see."

CHAPTER THIRTEEN

Frank's Gun Shop was an unprepossessing storefront on Broadway, just south of Fairfax. Frank himself was a large, jovial man whose eyes lit up as they walked in the door. "Crusher! Where the hell you been? I ain't seen you for ages. I figured you must of retired or something."

"Nah, I just been taking it easy lately, things has been kinda quiet since Repeal, everybody's too goddamned busy raking in the loot. But I want you should meet my friend Walter. He ain't no shooter, but he needs a little weight because of something that came up."

"Okay," Frankie said. "A thirty-two would be about right, what do you think? Nice and light, not much recoil, goes where you point it."

"I don't know," Crusher replied, "I was thinking a thirty-eight. You got to hit a guy just right with a thirty-two, otherwise you ain't going to stop him."

"Yeah, but you still got to hit him first," Frankie interrupted, "and your standard thirty-eight bucks like a son of a bitch. No offense, Walter, but Crusher here, he's built like a brick shithouse, he don't realize most guys ain't built like him."

"No offense taken," McDumont said, "but it sounds like I should try these things out for myself, see what's best."

"Yeah," said Frankie, "I got a firing range down in the basement. Lemme lock up and we'll go shoot a few."

One end of Frankie's basement was set up with black, man-sized targets propped against a tall pile of sandbags. The three men stood about twenty-five feet away from them as Frankie deftly loaded two revolvers, then handed one to McDumont.

"This is a thirty-eight, fully loaded. Six shots. Hold it out at arm's length, take your aim, and then let her go— yeah, hold her steady, that's good."

The target seemed to loom over McDumont, dark and menacing. He didn't see how he could miss it. He closed his eyes and pulled the trigger.

In the basement's confined space the explosion was deafening, and its force threw his hand straight up into the air. He shook his head and stared at the target, wondering exactly where he had hit it.

"I told you," Frankie said, "the kick's too big for him."

McDumont looked at him in disbelief. "What are you talking about? Let's go take a look, I bet I hit something. How could I miss?"

Kerrigan chuckled. "You hit something, champ. Any time we got to shoot some sandbags, I want you on my side. Look up to the left there."

About five feet to the left of the target, and not quite as high above it, a small rivulet of sand trickled slowly downward. McDumont couldn't believe his eyes. If he wasn't able to hit a stationary target from this range...

"Nothing to worry about," Frankie said, patting McDumont on the shoulder, "you just got to use the right gun. Here, give this thirty-two a try."

They exchanged revolvers and McDumont took aim with the thirty-two. Remembering how the heavier calibre weapon had bucked upward, he tried to lower the barrel slightly at the moment of firing.

The noise wasn't so loud this time, and although the revolver shuddered it wasn't so violently that it tried to tear itself out of his hand. "Thataboy," Frankie said, "keep shooting, you got the idea."

He fired five more rounds and then the hammer clicked on an empty chamber. "Whoa, hoss," Kerrigan said, "hold your fire and let me see if you hit anything."

Crusher examined the target from head to toe and then started to laugh.

"I missed again?" McDumont said sulkily, shaking his head. "Maybe I should get a shotgun or a blunderbuss or something."

"You didn't miss with all of them, anyway," Kerrigan said, still laughing. "You got this guy in the right foot, he ain't going to be walking so good. Hit him in the left arm, too— guy was left-handed that would be a hell of a shot. But listen, Walter, seriously, maybe you should give this gun stuff a pass. Some guys just ain't no good with them."

"Shut up and pass the ammunition, Crusher," McDumont said. "If a big lug like you can figure out how to use one of these things, I'm betting that a little more practise should make me as good as Wild Bill Hickock."

Half an hour later, McDumont was prepared to admit that he wasn't ready to go to work as a professional gunman. It hadn't taken him long to get to the point where he was hitting the target with about half of his shots, but after that he didn't make any progress. He didn't feel comfortable with guns; part of him simply didn't want to have anything to do with them; and if he wasn't any good shooting at targets, what was he going to do when there was a human being at the other end?

Crusher and Frankie didn't say much, but it was obvious that they weren't impressed by McDumont's attempts at marksmanship. Who could blame them? Here he was trying to learn something in a few minutes that they'd spent years of their life perfecting. Who did he think he was kidding? He was way out of his league.

"Okay," McDumont said after another volley of random hits and wild misses, "I might as well stop wasting everybody's time. Wrap this thing up and throw in a lot of ammunition. Maybe I'll get a chance to practise some more."

"Not when I'm around," Kerrigan said. Then, seeing McDumont's grimace, he tried to laugh it off. "Come on, Walter. You can dish it out, but sometimes you got to take it. Hitting a target don't mean nothing. Those rookie cops, they got a marksmanship test to pass before they put on their badge, but half of them still ain't no good once they're out on the street. Come on, we got to get to work anyway, we got things to do."

They arrived back at the Bronson house a little after three. Paul Bronson was in bed. He looked old and beaten down, as if everything that had been happening had suddenly caught up with him. "You'll have to take over now, Walter," he said in a frail and quivering voice. "This is too much for me, my heart won't stand it."

"Don't worry, it's all going to work out. You rest, I'll take care of things."

McDumont sat at the kitchen table with Crusher, the telephone and a pencil and note pad in front of them, waiting for the phone to ring. The money was in a black leather satchel on the floor. Funny how little space one hundred thousand dollars took up. You'd think that much money would deserve a special place all to itself, some kind of strongbox or something.

They drank coffee and ate sandwiches, not saying much, McDumont trying to look anywhere but at the phone. Which didn't keep him from willing it to ring. Ring, goddamn it, get it over with. Much more of this and he was going to be in the same shape as Paul Bronson.

The telephone finally rang at six-thirty.

"Hello."

"Hey, little bastard, what do you say? Let me talk to mister moneybags. He's got something for me."

"Mr. Bronson is sick, he's in bed. You can talk to me."

Harmon whistled. "So it's like that, huh? Okay, you listen then, and listen good. I'm not fooling around. Any funny business about the money, you mark it or try to follow me, your girlfriend is going to be one dead little pussycat. You hear what I'm saying?"

"I understand."

"All right, this is how it's going to work. You drive out the Sierra Highway to Pacifica, then you keep going another couple of miles until you see the turn-off for Morgansville. You go left down that road till you come to a bridge that crosses a small stream. There's a dirt track runs along the other side of it, you can only go one way. You go a hundred yards or so and you'll see an old shack. You stop there and put the money inside the door. Then you turn around and go back the way you came. You'll be under observation from the time you leave the highway. I see anything doesn't look right, any suspicious cars or people, your girlfriend is dead. You got that? D-E-A-D!"

McDumont swallowed hard. "I understand."

"You goddamned well better. And you come alone, you hear me? Leave that fucker Kerrigan at home. You go out there by yourself."

"I'll be alone."

"Okay, you start driving now, you should be out there in an hour. You don't make it like I told you, your girlfriend don't make it, either."

"What about Penny? When will you let her go?"

"Soon as I get the money, I'll drop her off in L.A. somewhere. Course I might want to give her a little... goodbye kiss first, yeah, that might take a while."

"If you've touched her..."

"Aw, jeez, little bastard, what are you going to do, kill me? You aren't going to do anything. You want to see your girlfriend again, you do what I told you, no more, no less." The line went dead.

McDumont hurriedly explained the situation to Crusher as he grabbed the satchel and rushed out to the car. "I don't like it," Kerrigan said. "There ain't no way to cover you out there. How about I get down on the floor in the back of the car? There ought to be enough room."

"No, we've got to do exactly what he says. We can't give him an excuse to hurt Penny. You stay here by the phone, I've got to get going."

Crusher rested both hands gently on McDumont's shoulders. "You watch your step, Walter. Harmon is one tricky son of a bitch. You got your revolver? You got those cartridges?"

McDumont patted the shoulder holster that Frank had showed him how to wear. "I've got them, all right. The cartridges are on the front seat there next to the money. For all the good any of this stuff is likely to do me."

"Just be ready to use them. You remember what we were telling you—you point that gun the right place, the bullets'll go where you point it."

"Sure, sure, I know, how the hell could I forget? You guys sounded like schoolteachers or something. Now let me get out of here, I can't waste any more time."

"You take your time," Crusher said, "take your time, and watch out for yourself." He looked over McDumont's shoulder. "You're a right guy. I don't want nothing to happen to a right guy."

"You and me both," McDumont replied, tapping Kerrigan lightly on the chest. "Go on, you big lug, ride herd on that phone. I'll be back before you know it, and then Penny will be back. It won't be long before all this is over." He got in the car and started the motor.

Kerrigan watched the car speed down the driveway. "I don't trust that Harmon," he said out loud. "He's a dirty son of a bitch, and I don't trust him."

McDumont tried to keep his mind on the road, but he couldn't help thinking about Penny and what might be happening to her. Held prisoner in that house full of pimps and prostitutes and lowlifes, with Harmon implying that he was going to... Jesus, he'd better face it. Harmon had been after her anyway, and now she was completely at his mercy.

What if it *had* happened? He'd never felt about anyone like he felt about Penny. What if Harmon had been with her, had forced himself on her? He had to face it, that was probably what had happened.

It wouldn't mean anything, though, it wouldn't mean anything more than when he had gone to bed with Nancy Virdon. That kind of sex was like being hungry, you got an appetite and you ate, no big deal.

What if it had happened? He wasn't Penny's first lover, and she sure as hell wasn't his. He'd been around; he was no plaster saint up on a pedestal. That woman downstairs in the rooming house in Toronto, she'd been married, for Christ's sake. Afterwards he saw her on the stairs with her husband, looking like butter wouldn't melt in her mouth. And that teenaged hooker in Cairo, Illinois, taking on all comers at a quarter a time in that dirty boxcar, the straw and the smell of animals, he would have lined up again if he'd had another two bits on him. So what, so what? It didn't mean anything, it was something your body needed, it was just like scratching an itch, that's all it was.

He pounded on the steering wheel with his right hand. Who the hell did he think he was kidding? The idea of Penny and Harmon together tore him up, he'd start to visualize it and have to force himself to stop, try to just concentrate on Penny by herself, how wonderful she was, how much he loved her. That was the answer, just think about how much you loved her, not about how some filthy pig of a cop... no, he'd drive himself crazy if he kept on thinking about it. That way was madness, a hatred that would take possession of him, lead him to places he didn't want to go.

He was past Pacifica, the turn-off should be coming up soon. The sun was almost down, shadows lengthened across the road, he flicked the lights on and saw a gas station and a cluster of houses ahead. This must be Morgansville. He turned left onto a road that soon ran out of macadam and settled for crushed stone that pinged loudly off the car's undercarriage. He had to slow down or it would scratch the paint all to hell. There was the bridge, a narrow wooden one-lane job. There was a little park with a bandshell running along the stream on the near side. He drove across the bridge and saw the dirt track leading off to the right, just the way Harmon had described it.

He stopped and rolled down the driver's-side window. Over the engine's quiet purr there was an insect symphony warming up for their evening concert, its more excitable members already dancing in his headlights. He turned onto the dirt track, going very slowly, tree branches and bushes swishing against the side of the car. He didn't want to miss the shack.

Was that...? Yes, it must be. Something had flattened down the vegetation in front of it; otherwise he might never have seen the dilapidated structure. He drove slowly past it and then turned the car around, having to reverse and go forward several times in the narrow lane, then stopped and got out, leaving the headlights on so that he'd be able to see where he was going. Carrying the satchel with both hands, he walked toward the shack, swivelling his head around to see if he could make out anything else. Harmon had said he'd be under observation, though, he'd better not waste any time.

The battered wooden door to the shack was almost off its hinges, and protested loudly when he pulled it open. He glanced around quickly but saw only some rusting tin cans and scraps of newspaper. It didn't look like anyone had used the shack for a long time. He put the satchel down and shivered. This was a lonely place to be on a dark night. He wanted to get back to the car and get out of there.

As he hurried out the door, his right foot hit a loose board and he stumbled down onto his knees. From the darkness in front of him he heard a booming gunshot, and the air fluttered as something whirred quickly over his head. Out of the corner of his eye he saw an orange flash on the other side of the stream and there was a loud 'tock' against the wall of the shack behind him. He'd better get the hell out of there. He crawled quickly to the shelter of the car; the car was in between him and the gunfire.

He put his head gingerly around the right front tire. This time he saw the flash clearly as a bullet whined off the dirt in front of him. The shots were coming from the top of the bandshell across the stream. He had to get the goddamned headlights off, that was the first thing he had to do. He was a sitting duck while they were still on.

He opened the passenger-side door just wide enough to get through and wriggled toward the dashboard. Another shot tore through the front window and suddenly there was glass all over the place. Maybe he should just get the hell out of there. He forced his body forward another couple of feet and then reached up and turned off the headlight switch. A bullet screamed angrily over his head.

For a moment there was silence. Then Harmon's voice came bellowing across the stream. "How you doing, McDumont, you little bastard? You're in some fix, huh? How do you like these apples, you little prick?"

McDumont picked up the box of cartridges and stuffed them inside his shirt, then took the revolver out of its shoulder holster. He wanted to answer back, but if he kept quiet maybe Harmon would think he'd been hit and come in closer to where McDumont could get a shot at him. He made sure the revolver was loaded and then eased back out the door, leaving it ajar in case he needed to get inside in a hurry.

"Gord! Mike! Get your asses down there and see what the hell's going on!"

"Aw, Larry, what if he's got a gun? We ain't gonna go down there." Whoever answered was back up the track between McDumont and the road. But the voice in the dark didn't sound real happy about it. There was fear in that voice.

"Get down there, you spineless pieces of shit! He hasn't got a gun and Kerrigan isn't with him. You got nothing to be afraid of. Besides, I think I might have hit him; he's a mouthy little bastard and there hasn't been a peep out of him. Go on, I'll cover you."

So the Wilsons were going to come down the road. They wouldn't come through the bush; it was dark and they'd make too much noise coming that way. They'd walk down the road, and they'd come slowly and cautiously, probably one on each side. If McDumont got in the car and drove through them... but then Harmon would have a clear shot, he'd probably be dead before he got down the track. The Wilsons would be firing at him, too. No, he'd better stay put, he was pretty well under cover here. He'd just stay where he was and let them come to him.

They sure were taking their own sweet... what was that, had he heard something? He stared hard down the road. Yes, there was movement. He could make out a tall, dark shape slowly coming toward him on the right-hand side. He gripped the revolver harder and told himself this was just another kind of target practise, you just pointed the gun where you wanted the bullets to go and then pulled the trigger. That was all, point and pull, anybody could do it.

McDumont yanked open the door, dove inside, and flicked on the headlights. Then he threw himself backward just in time to avoid the bullets that came smashing through what was left of the windshield and tore their way into the front seat. He scrambled behind the door, using it for cover, and looked up the road.

The Wilsons were running away. They'd been closer to the car than he'd thought they were, running bunched together in the middle of the road. He could see guns in their hands. They were yelling, too. He didn't know what they were saying, but they were yelling.

McDumont pointed the revolver in their direction and pulled the trigger six times. He saw one of the men stumble, then fall down. It must have been Mike, because now Gord was standing over him, screaming, "Shoot the lights, get the fucking lights." He didn't stop, he just kept yelling it over and over. McDumont wished he would shut up. It was annoying having to listen to that over and over again. Why didn't he just shut up?

McDumont reached into his shirt and took out the box of cartridges. He broke the revolver open and reloaded. It was really very simple. You took a cartridge out of the box and put it in one of the chambers of the revolver. You did this six times, then you pointed the gun and pulled the trigger. It wasn't difficult, anybody could do it.

A series of explosions played across the front of the car. First the left headlight and then the right headlight flickered and went out. Bullets ripped into the hood. Harmon was going for the engine, making sure that McDumont would never drive out of there. Harmon shot out both the tires on the driver's side and the vehicle gave a sudden lurch, began to settle that way. The car was sure taking a beating. McDumont hoped the Bronsons had lots of insurance. At this rate it wouldn't be long before there wasn't anything left of their car. Harmon was going to shoot it to pieces and McDumont was going to have to find a new place to hide.

"Jesus Christ, Larry, come here and help me! Mike's hit bad! You've got to help me." Gord was going to lose his voice if he kept screaming. Somebody should help shut him up. McDumont finished reloading and pointed the revolver in the direction from which Gord's voice seemed to be coming. He pulled the trigger six times and then listened to see if it had worked. Nope, Gord was still yelling his head off.

"Larry! For the love of God, help me! He's shooting the hell out of us! You got to come help!"

McDumont broke open the revolver and began to reload. Nothing to it, you took a cartridge out of the box...

"All right, I'm coming, keep your shirt on. If he comes up the road you kill him, you hear me? Use your goddamned gun and kill him! Now shut the fuck up, he can hear where you are. I'm going to get the car."

At least Gord had shut up. McDumont didn't have to shoot at Gord any more, that was something. Then an understanding of what he had been doing came flooding in and he felt sick to his stomach. What was he thinking about? He had to get the hell out of there. For a moment he thought about going back to the shack and taking the money, but the satchel was bulky and he wanted to get away in a hurry, the money would slow him down. Anyway, it was time to leave, there wasn't any sense in staying around.

McDumont crawled behind the car and looked carefully up the road on the driver's side. There were lights in the distance, slowly getting bigger. That must be Harmon coming. Keeping as low as he could, McDumont walked quickly in the opposite direction and then veered off to the right, gingerly picking his way through the strip of bush and small trees that separated the road from the stream.

When he heard voices off to his right, Harmon's loud and angry, the Wilsons' quieter and whining, he left the cover of the trees and picked his way down to the stream. He couldn't see very well, but he could hear the water bubbling along, as if it was in a hurry to get somewhere. Well, so was he, damn it. A little water never hurt anyone.

He eased his feet into the water and gasped at the cold of it, then nearly stumbled as the bottom dropped out from under him and he was in up to his waist. Christ, they must have heard that splash, he'd better keep going. It wasn't that much deeper in the middle of the stream, but he had to lean against the force of the current, it must have snowed up in the mountains or something. Then he was in shallower water and walking up the opposite bank, shoes squelching and pants completely soaked, the night air cold against his shivering skin.

McDumont glanced behind him and saw headlights slowly moving down the road. That would be Harmon picking up the ransom money. For a moment he thought about going back and shooting Harmon, killing him, then making the Wilsons take him to where Penny was being held. That's what would happen in one of Chandler's stories, the hero wouldn't be freezing his butt off out in the bushes. Well, McDumont was no hero, he'd just try to get out of here alive and live to fight another day. What was that, a quotation or something? He'd seen it somewhere, "He who fights and runs away lives to fight another day." Penny would know who wrote that, he had to get back and find her. That was why he was running away from Harmon rather than toward him.

He kept going away from the stream, through a little cleared area with picnic tables and outdoor fireplaces. Then he was in the woods and had to take it really slow, holding his hands out in front of him to ward off branches that brushed at his face. Off to his right, he could see a small patch of light approach and then recede as the sound of a car motor passed. Keep going, he prayed, keep going and don't try to pull any more tricky stuff. With any luck he'd never see those guys again in his life. Funny, Harmon had tried to kill him, but he didn't feel any overwhelming desire for revenge. Just let him have Penny back and they'd try to put the whole thing behind them.

But first he had to get back, and that might not be so easy. He crashed and flailed his way through another few yards of forest. At this rate he wouldn't make it home for Christmas. He should have stayed in the Boy Scouts, damn it. So what if they were all goody-goodies who looked down on poor kids like McDumont? At least he might have learned his way around the goddamned woods. If he'd stayed in the Boy Scouts he wouldn't be wandering around in the dark like a lost soul with a gun in his hand. A gun. Jesus Christ, he was still holding the goddamned gun. It must have got soaked back there in the stream, he wondered if it would even work. He put it back in the shoulder holster. He never wanted to see the bloody thing again.

He angled right toward the road and after a couple of minutes came out on it all too suddenly. If they'd stopped the car and were waiting for him he was a sitting duck. He couldn't see anything, they would have been in a hurry to get out of there, they had to get Mike to a hospital. But wait a minute, there'd be questions if they took him to a hospital. Gunshot wounds were supposed to be reported to the police. There wasn't any point worrying about it, anyway, if Harmon had doubled back and waited for McDumont he was dead. There was no way he could get back to Morgansville without following the road.

He tried to walk as slowly and quietly as he could. Why make it easy for them? His waterlogged shoes made more noise than the rest of him. He wondered if Ray knew a good shoe store. He probably did, McDumont would go there and treat himself to a new pair of shoes as soon as this was over. He shook his head and tried to concentrate on the road in front of him. He was on the macadam now, it was easier walking than on the crushed stone.

He kept trudging forward until he saw lights ahead, then slowed and moved over to the edge of the road. Morgansville wasn't much of a town. There were only a few cars on the street, and no signs of life. One of the lights resolved into a naked bulb on top of a phone booth and McDumont collapsed into it, fumbling for change in his wet pants pocket.

"Hello." Kerrigan answered in the middle of the first ring, his voice hard and anxious.

"It's me, Walter. You've got to come and get me."

"You should of been back here already. Where the hell you been? What happened, you have an accident?"

"Harmon tried to pull a double cross. He shot the hell out of the car and he tried to shoot the hell out of me. He had it all set up."

"I knew I should of come with you. That son of a bitch, I'll take him apart with my bare hands! What about the money?"

"Harmon's got it, I couldn't stop him." This must sound pretty pathetic to Crusher, McDumont thought. "But I shot one of the Wilsons, it sounded like Mike might have been hurt pretty bad."

Kerrigan snorted. "Those sons of bitches, I'd like to fit them all with cement overcoats. So where the hell are you?"

McDumont told him and then put down the telephone and sagged against the wall of the booth. Suddenly all he wanted to do was go to sleep. There wasn't anything more he could do tonight, he didn't even have the energy to stand up, go outside, and try to conceal himself in the event that Harmon decided to return. McDumont stared at the road along which Kerrigan would be coming and tried to keep awake. He'd wait for Crusher, Crusher would take him home and he'd be safe again. He stared at the road and willed his eyes to stay open. This was no time to fall asleep. Crusher would be here soon, and then the night would be over.

CHAPTER FOURTEEN

They were sitting around the kitchen table, waiting for the phone to ring. McDumont and Kerrigan had gotten back around midnight, McDumont napping in the car. Now he was watching the phone and willing himself to stay awake. It had to ring soon. Harmon had the money, what more could he want?

You know what it is, McDumont thought for the thousandth time that night, and you're going to accept it, you're going to make yourself accept it and come to terms with it, because all you want is for Penny to live. That's the only thing you care about. You want her to come back to you. Nothing else matters.

At some point McDumont must have fallen asleep, because the next thing he knew he had woken with a start and sunlight was streaming through the window. Morning. He tried to rub the sleep out of his eyes and said, "What happened, Crusher?"

"Nothing happened. The phone ain't rung, and I'll bet you dollars to doughnuts it ain't going to ring. That son of a bitch Harmon ain't going to let Penny go. She'd make one hell of a witness if he ever got caught. He ain't never going to let her go."

McDumont swallowed hard. "Do you think he'll kill her?"

Kerrigan looked away. "I don't say he'd kill her, not right away, anyhow. But I don't figure he'll ever let her go."

"Jesus Christ," McDumont said, burying his head in his hands. "What the hell are we going to do?"

"We know where they are," Kerrigan said grimly. "And Harmon don't know we know. I figure we got to go out there and kill the son of a bitch. I don't see no other way."

"You think he's still there? They could have gone some place else, they might not be there at all."

"Maybe. But you said you shot Mike, maybe shot him pretty bad, and you don't want to move around no guys what got bullets in them. They got to rest, keep quiet. You don't start moving them around."

"Harmon's a killer," McDumont said after a moment. "He tried to kill me, killing doesn't seem to bother him. What's to keep him from getting rid of Mike, or just leaving him behind?"

Kerrigan laughed. "If it was just Mike and Gord, I wouldn't argue with you. But you saw that Mona, she ain't going to let something like that happen to her brother without kicking up one hell of a fuss. She's a tough baby, and I can tell you, I seen a few."

"So you figure they'll stay put?"

"Why the hell not? Far as Harmon knows, he's sitting pretty."

"All right," McDumont said, "we'll go after him." He paused. "I don't know why the hell I'm assuming you'll go with me. This isn't any of your business. There's no reason why you should get involved."

Kerrigan snorted. "You just try and keep me out of it, fella. These Bronsons hired me as a bodyguard, and I got my professional reputation to think of. Ain't nobody going to say Crusher Kerrigan can't cut it no more."

"I hadn't thought of that," McDumont said bitterly. "Bums like me, we're professional screw-ups, everybody expects us to take off when things get hot. Hell, that's what I do, take off when things get hot. That's what I'd like to do. Far as that goes, why the hell don't you tell me to get lost? You don't want a bum like me on your side, I'll just screw up the works."

Crusher looked at McDumont sharply. "I seen enough bums in my time. And you ain't one. That wasn't no bum that duked it out with Harmon."

"No, it was a scared kid who got lucky. But getting shot at... Jesus, Crusher, that frightened the hell out of me. I think about it now and I don't even want to go out the door, I'm afraid Harmon might be laying for me out there. I look out a window and I see the glass exploding, bullets coming through it, Harmon firing away, trying to kill me. While it was happening, it was like I was in a trance, or numb. I wasn't thinking about it, but when it comes back to me now I start shivering." McDumont held out his right hand. It was steady for a moment and then started to shake. "You see that? I can't even keep my goddamned hand steady."

Kerrigan didn't say anything. Then he chuckled lightly and smiled at McDumont. "You know something? I ain't never told nobody this, and you better not pass it along, neither. But when I was just starting out in this business, an old geezer who was short on his numbers payoff put a slug in me." He rolled up the shirtsleeve on his right arm and tapped a small area of discoloured skin. "Right there, it must have been a forty-five or something, you could see through the hole. And you know what I did?"

McDumont stared at him. "You probably tied the guy in a knot and made him eat his gun. Or maybe *you* ate his gun. I don't know, what did you do?"

"Nah, nothing like that. I got my rod out all right, but then I took one look at the daylight coming through my arm and I fainted. Just like that, fainted dead away. Guy was so scared, he thought he'd killed me, he fainted, too. Customer came in and called the cops, reported two dead palookas had knocked each other off in a gun battle. I came to later in the hospital, figured I'd died and gone to heaven. Doc told me later I'd been out so long they thought I was in a coma.

"So don't try to give me some song and dance about what you're going to do and what I'm going to do. You don't know nothing until you get in there and start doing it, and then you ain't got no control over it, anyway. I seen you take Harmon. That's good enough for me."

McDumont opened his mouth, then closed it. Crusher was right, there was no way to tell how you were going to react in a crisis. Unless you ran away, of course, if you saw one coming you could always run away from it. This one here, Christ, you sure as hell could see it coming, coming right at you...

The telephone rang. McDumont snatched at it and said, "Harmon?"

"It's Ray, Walter. I just wanted to know how things are going. Have you paid the ransom money yet?"

McDumont told him what had happened.

"What are you going to do?" Chandler asked.

"Kerrigan and I are going to go out there and try to get her back, Ray. That's all that we can do."

"No, it isn't. You count me in on this. Wait for me, I'll be right over."

"Ray, I appreciate how you feel, but I don't think..."

"No, you don't have to do all the thinking, Walter. You're going to let me do some of it. I'm going to pull rank on you— I didn't spend all my time in the service trying to debauch the sergeant's daughter, you know. Are you and Kerrigan armed?"

"Yes."

"Good, I'll get my old Lee-Enfield out of mothballs and we'll have at them."

"Your old what?"

"Lee-Enfield. A finer rifle God never made. Steady and dependable, as lots of chaps named Hans and Fritz could tell you, if they were still alive. It's quite a remarkable weapon. Still used in competitive shooting, I believe."

"Well, we've got competition, that's for sure. But you don't have to do this, you don't have to get involved."

Chandler snorted. "Stop talking like the beleaguered sheriff in a town full of outlaws. That plot's so old even Hollywood will give it up one of these days. You need all the help you can get. I'm coming along, and you're going to stay there and wait for me. That's an order."

Chandler looked at the map McDumont had sketched on a sheet of typing paper. "How far is it from the crest of the hill down to the farmhouse?" he asked.

McDumont looked at Kerrigan. "What do you think? Two hundred yards?"

"Maybe. I ain't so good at figuring stuff like that." He looked at Chandler and grinned. "About right for what you're thinking, though."

Chandler smiled back. "I'm glad that two of us know what's going on."

McDumont glared. "What's the big deal? So it's around two hundred yards from the hill to the house. So what? Somebody's still going to have to go down there after them."

"More work for the PBIs," Chandler said. "That's the 'Poor Bloody Infantry' to you lot. Yes, somebody will have to go down there. But if you put a man with a Lee-Enfield on that hill, he can command the whole situation."

"Don't forget that Harmon's got a rifle, too," McDumont said. "And he knows how to use it."

"That's as may be," Chandler said. "But shooting uphill from that distance is a different matter entirely, especially if Harmon is using one of the lighter repeating-action rifles, which would be my guess. In any event, the man who's under the gun is always at a disadvantage. You can take that from me."

Kerrigan cleared his throat. "Meaning no offense or nothing, there's been a little water under the bridge since the war ended. When's the last time you did any shooting?"

"10:59 a.m. on the morning of November 11, 1918, one minute before the Armistice took effect, and quite a shoot it was— our commanding officer ordered us to empty our weapons at the German lines. Chap was a bit of a nutter, we just raised our rifles in the air and tried not to hit anything." He chuckled. "But I take your point, a certain amount of practise would be desirable, though I suspect it's like riding a bicycle—not the sort of thing one forgets."

"I got just the place," Kerrigan said. "I'll give Frankie a call."

"Good. You know," Chandler said, looking thoughtful, "I never imagined that I'd use this again. I kept my rifle as a souvenir, a lot of the fellows did. We weren't supposed to bring them back with us, but it was easy enough if you contributed a sufficient amount to the supply sergeant's retirement fund. I had the gun up on the wall for a while, I used to take it down and fiddle around with it, but I never thought I'd have a reason to use it again." He looked at them in turn. "But enough nostalgia. We should start making a sensible plan."

McDumont checked his watch. "By the time we get you some shooting practise and have something to eat and get out there, it'll be after dark. Maybe that would be a good time, we can get right up to the house without being seen."

"I dunno about that," Crusher said. "You start running around in the dark, first thing you know you lose touch with your buddies. You can shoot each other just as easy as anybody else if you ain't careful."

"I agree," Chandler said. "On the other hand, they have at least two automobiles out there. We have to do something about them. Why don't we immobilize their cars during the night and then see if we can pick off Harmon? With him out of the picture, it should be much easier to deal with the Wilsons."

Kerrigan smiled and nodded. "I like that. Especially the part about picking off Harmon. He already tried to sandbag Walter, he don't deserve no chance."

"We've got to be careful about Penny," McDumont said. "We can't just shoot up that house. She's in there, too."

Chandler patted him on the shoulder. "There won't be any need for that if we can get Harmon. And we can maximize our chances if Mr. Kerrigan can get down to the farmhouse, perhaps behind one of the cars, while it's still dark. If I can't snipe Harmon from the top of the hill, Kerrigan might be able to pick him off from up close."

"Yeah, now you're talking," Crusher said. "I'm going to give Frankie a call, we're going to get you some shooting practice, then we're going to murder a couple of great big steaks. Just thinking about blasting Harmon gives me one hell of an appetite."

It didn't take Chandler long to get what he called "my old shooting eye" back. His third clip was centred in the middle of the target's chest in an area no bigger than a clenched fist. "You got the touch," Frankie said. "You squeeze that trigger like you were stroking a tit. You got some time, maybe you could give Walter here a few lessons."

"Time is what we haven't got," McDumont said. "We've got to get this show on the road. Come on, you old soldiers. We've got a long night ahead of us."

They had dinner at a steakhouse on North Hollywood, nobody saying much, eating slowly and methodically and leaving their plates so clean that the waitress made a joke out of it, told them they were good boys and could stay up late if they wanted to. She winked as she said it, maybe she wouldn't mind staying up with them. But something in the way they looked at her shut her right up. After that it was all business and, "Would you care for any dessert, gentlemen?"

They drove out to the farm in Chandler's car. Crusher took it easy, staying at or just a little under the speed limit. The last thing they needed was some nosy cop getting interested in them. After they turned off the highway onto the county road, there were no lights showing in any of the houses they passed. The car's two narrow yellow beams cut the way through a darkness that surrounded them like a palpable thing, like something waiting and watching to see what they were going to do.

As they started up the hill that overlooked the farmhouse, Kerrigan turned off the headlights and slowed to a crawl. "Got to take it *real* easy," he said. "Sound travels at night. We got to do everything extra careful from now on."

Crusher pulled off the road at the same place as before, driving deep into the bushes and small trees until they couldn't go any farther. "Careful with the doors," he whispered as they got out of the car. "Just leave them open. If we need to get the hell out of here every second counts."

Then they were ready to go. The moon was only about a quarter full, but it was a cloudless night and they could see fairly well. And be seen, if anyone was on the lookout for them, McDumont thought. But maybe they wouldn't even bother with that, they had no reason to suspect that anyone knew where they were.

They started walking up the hill, Kerrigan leading, McDumont and then Chandler behind them. As they neared the top, Kerrigan stopped and waited for them. "Hands and knees from here on. Over the ridge one by one and take it as slow as you can. They got anybody on watch down there, this is where he's going to be looking."

Kerrigan disappeared over the ridge inch by inch; one minute you thought he'd grown into the dark landscape and the next he was gone. McDumont tried to imitate him, moving only one part of his body at a time, as slowly as possible, but it wasn't easy. If there was someone on the other side with a gun he'd be a sitting duck, inching along so slowly. He'd be better off running, it would be harder to hit a running man.

Calm down, he told himself fiercely. Take a deep breath, get hold of yourself. He concentrated on keeping track of Crusher, who was crawling a little faster now that he was over the ridge. Then McDumont felt something on his right leg, it felt like somebody's hand. Quickly he rolled over and turned around. What the hell...?

Chandler had his finger to his lips, he was shushing McDumont, telling him that he'd made too much noise in moving so abruptly. Then Chandler tapped himself on the chest and pointed to his left, where a deadfall of twisted tree limbs rose up out of the semi-gloom on the hillside. He repeated his motions and McDumont nodded back. Chandler was going to position himself behind the fallen trees, they'd make a good spot from which to cover the farm.

Chandler gave him a wave and a thumb's-up signal and then faded slowly out of sight. Lucky guy, McDumont thought. He gets to stay up here and pick his spots. We've got to go down there and take them on face to face. Then he felt ashamed of himself. Ray didn't have to be here, this sure as hell wasn't his fight. He didn't have a personal stake in it the way McDumont and Crusher did... Christ, where the hell was Crusher? He didn't have a clue, and he'd better find out quickly.

McDumont turned back toward the farmhouse and stared intently into the darkness. He'd have to start moving toward it again, that was the first step. He began to crawl forward, as slowly and deliberately as he could. The last thing he wanted was to surprise Kerrigan and maybe get shot for his trouble.

So where the hell was Crusher? Why couldn't he have waited? McDumont was on his own. He could see the farmhouse from where he was, those black shapes in front of it must be the cars. What was he supposed to do, charge down there? What was it Chandler had said about the cars, something about immobilizing them? Was McDumont supposed to do that? Or was Crusher going to do it? Christ, you'd think they would have told him, how was he supposed to know what to do?

He heard a low whistle off to his right. It could have been a bird. Yeah, that would be a laugh. Hello Mr. Bird, want to go shoot some bad guys? But it was too dark and too early for birds. It had to be Kerrigan. Or somebody else, maybe Harmon, playing him for a sucker. Wouldn't staying where he was be the smart thing to do? No, it had to be Crusher. Move toward it, you cowardly son of a bitch, get yourself over there and see what's going on.

Then he saw a big hand waving at him. It had to be Crusher, the only other things that size that looked like hands were baseball mitts. He'd go over to Kerrigan. Maybe they'd gotten to first base. There you go. How scared could he be if he could come up with a crummy pun like that? They drove Penny crazy. Jesus, Penny, that's what this was about. Get over there and get on with it, now.

Crusher was waiting for him behind the row of bushes that were the last decent cover before the mown-down area around the house. "What took you so long?" he whispered. "I heard a crash, sounded like you fell."

"No, that was Ray telling me he was going to get behind some cover just below the ridge, over to the left there." McDumont pointed to about where he thought Chandler had gone. "Startled me, that was all, came up behind me too fast." He could hear himself whine as he whispered.

"Okay, okay, it's no big deal, nobody in the house did nothing. Listen, I'm going down to fix those cars. You stay here and keep your eyes peeled. Give me a whistle if you see anybody come outside. You know how to whistle, don't you?"

"What the hell kind of a question is that? Of course I know how to whistle. You just put your lips together and blow."

"Jeez, don't get sore. Some guys don't know how, they never learned.

Anyway, keep a good lookout— I'm going to have to make a little noise, somebody might hear."

"Just be careful. If I do see anything, have you got any requests? We're out in the great outdoors here, how about my original hot-jazz rendition of 'Petting in the Park,' you know that real catchy tune from *42nd Street*, 'Pettin' in the park, ooh-ooh'..."

Crusher shook his head. "At least you got your sense of humour back. No, skip the hot jazz. We don't want the birds getting all excited. Just give me three or four high notes and be damned sure they're loud. Make like Hot Lips Page or somebody." Then he stretched out flat on his stomach and began to move down the hill.

McDumont could see him all the way. It took Kerrigan about ten minutes to reach the cars, one parked behind and a little to the right of the other from where McDumont was sitting. The one farthest away was quite a bit smaller; that must be Harmon's roadster. The one closest to him was the Wilsons' sedan. It shouldn't take much to put that old heap out of commission.

Crusher was out of sight. He must be working on the roadster, McDumont heard faint clunks and scrapes. How *did* you sabotage a car, anyway? Take out the battery? But that would mean opening the hood and taking a chance on making too much noise. What could you do to a car without opening the hood? Slashing the tires would keep it from going far, but if somebody was desperate enough they could still drive on the wheel rims, it wasn't like you'd completely disabled it.

Draining the oil would be better. Yes, it was messy and it took a while, but you could do it from underneath, and once it was done the engine would tear itself apart if you started the car. But you needed a wrench, didn't you? You always saw mechanics working under cars with wrenches, and Kerrigan wouldn't have those with him. McDumont chuckled, had to stop himself from laughing out loud. If Crusher couldn't do it with those hands of his, it probably couldn't be done with any tool mere humans had invented; besides, he could always bite the drive shaft in half with his teeth, or maybe pull the wheels off and throw them into the shrubbery.

McDumont was daydreaming, thoughts all over the place, he'd better concentrate on what he was supposed to be doing. Kerrigan was moving around the Wilsons' jalopy. That was good, that meant he'd finished with Harmon's roadster. There wasn't a sign of life from the house, they'd probably been celebrating getting the ransom money. Celebrating. Christ, what would people like that do when they came into the chips, made the big score that every lowlife dreamed about and most never came close to achieving? Oh, turn your goddamned mind off, you know what probably happened, there wasn't anything you could have done about it. It's what happens now that counts. Get your bloody brain concentrating, you're supposed to be looking out for Crusher and you're not doing a very good job of it.

There was movement in front of him and Kerrigan was there, pulling himself slowly and wearily through the clump of bushes. Then he stretched out at full length, breathing heavily and rubbing his hands on the grass as if he were trying to bury them under the ground.

"What happened?" McDumont asked after a while. "Did everything go okay?"

"Kinda. Yeah, I mean those cars ain't going nowhere. I ripped the oil lines loose, I couldn't see to do nothing else, and it was messy as hell. Tore up my hands, though, right one hurts like a son of a bitch."

"Let me take a look." Even in the dim light, McDumont could see that it was serious. A deep gash in Crusher's palm was bleeding steadily through the oil and grease. He had to bandage it, but what was he going to use? He dug into his pocket and pulled out his handkerchief, it should still be clean, he couldn't remember using it. He tied a knot around Kerrigan's thumb, spread the handkerchief over the wound and patted it down, then pulled it around the hand and tied the other end to the thumb. By the time he finished the last knot, the part of the handkerchief over the wound was soaked with blood. He should get Crusher to a hospital. But Kerrigan had already pulled his hand away and taken out his gun; he was sighting it at the house and squeezing on the trigger. "What the hell are you doing?" McDumont whispered fiercely. "Are you nuts?"

"Just seeing how bad it was," Crusher said, his lips pulled back over his teeth in an agonized grimace. "Gun butt keeps the bandage in place. You got to give it that." But Crusher's right arm suddenly buckled and fell heavily to his side. He stared at it for a moment and then turned and looked at McDumont. "I don't know if I can pull the trigger. There's goddamned blood all over the place and my fingers keep sliding around. I can maybe get by with a two-handed grip, but I ain't used to it, that's going to throw my aim off some. Anyway, I ain't going to be able to pick nobody off from no distance, that's for goddamned sure." He turned his head and spat into the bushes.

So they couldn't just wait for Harmon to saunter outside, McDumont thought, not unless Ray... but that was a much longer shot. Besides, they couldn't count on Harmon being the first one outside, and if it was anybody else they'd see what had happened to the cars and raise the alarm. "Should I get Ray to come down here?" he asked Crusher.

Kerrigan thought it over. "I guess you better," he finally said. "But that means you and I are probably going to have to go in there. You thought about that?"

"Yeah, I thought about it," McDumont said. He'd been trying hard to keep the possibility at the back of his mind, but it didn't take a genius to figure out the logical person to approach the house and see what could be done was him. He'd have Crusher with him, and that was good; but there was now much less chance of picking Harmon off beforehand, and that wasn't so good. But what the hell, he was taking this one step at a time. That was the only way he could keep going; the next thing he had to do was retrace his steps and find Chandler. That wouldn't be hard, he knew right where he was.

All he had to do was make sure that Ray didn't shoot him. "I'll be back in a minute," he said, and moved off up the hill.

You could get awfully sick of crawling around on the ground in the dark. If anything, it was even harder propelling yourself uphill with gravity working against you. Then he could see the deadfall off to his right. No sign of Chandler, but he was in there with his trigger finger itching. Who'd ever have figured old Ray for a dead shot? Just went to show you, some mousy little guy jumps in your cab and says, 'Follow that car,' you'd never guess that he was hell with a rifle and knew his way around the ladies and in general wasn't as square as he looked.

Something was trying to joggle McDumont's memory, something about that first cab ride... not as square as he looked, that was it. Chandler had whistled an Ellington tune, what was it? The one with the Bubber Miley solo, "East St. Louis Toodle-oo," yeah, that had surprised him. He'd pegged Ray as strictly from squaresville. But since they'd neglected to select a password for their little band of adventurers, Ellington had to be it.

McDumont whistled the first part of the melody toward the deadfall, trying not to be too loud. Nothing happened. He did it again. This time he heard muffled laughter, and then the sound of someone approaching him. "Advance and be recognized," he heard Chandler say. "You're either Walter McDumont or an unknown Ellington fan, either of which makes you okay in my book."

McDumont told him about Crusher. "Bloody hell," Chandler said. "I thought this was going too smoothly. Just like the army, draw up a plan that covers everything down to the last detail and then throw the useless thing out the window when things go wrong." He paused for a moment. "I'd better get down there then, hadn't I? If we can't rely on Kerrigan's shooting ability, I'm going to have to cover you from up close." He scowled. "Back in the poor bloody infantry again. You'd think old ma Chandler would have raised smarter children."

"Listen, Ray, you don't have to..."

"Stuff it, Walter, I know exactly what I have to do. Unlike your sorry self, nothing but good intentions and high ideals. Oh, listen to me, I don't know what I'm saying, don't pay any attention to me. This is all my fault anyway. I apologize, Walter, I'm a scared old fogey who should be home in bed hiding under the covers. All of a sudden I'm in the middle of something I should be writing about rather than involved in."

"But you were in the war, Ray, you're no coward..."

"What do you know about it? All that bravado about shooting people, do you think that's how I really felt? I was scared all the time, scared firing at little gray shapes that kept coming at you, scared stumbling across no-man's-land with shells exploding everywhere around you and the bloody mud sucking at your boots. It was the bloody mud that killed you, you couldn't go anywhere fast enough to keep away from the bloody shells." Chandler stopped and took several deep breaths. "So don't treat me like a hero. There's something that has to be done, so let's just take ourselves down the hill and do it."

By the time they got back to Crusher, the sky was lightening in the East. McDumont looked at his watch. It was a little after five. The night had passed quickly. He shuddered. They could do with some sunshine, it was chilly out here. He glanced at Kerrigan and Chandler, who were looking at the farmhouse. Ray was sighting his rifle on the front door. Crusher was staring at the house as if hypnotized, as though he were trying to commit it to memory.

"Are we just going to wait?" McDumont asked when he couldn't stand the silence any longer.

CHAPTER FIFTEEN

It was Kerrigan who finally answered. "Nah, we got to go in there. Catch them sleeping, don't give them no chance to go for their guns, wrap this thing up." He cocked his head at McDumont. "You ready?"

"Ready as I'll ever be." He took the revolver out of his jacket pocket. "Let's go."

"And the best of British luck," Chandler said. "I'll move up to where the automobiles are once you get inside the house. Give me a shout if you want me in there."

They eased their way through the bushes and walked slowly toward the house. As they passed the cars, McDumont glanced curiously at the oily stains spreading from underneath their dark, metallic bodies. They were bleeding to death, spilling their life's blood on to the barren ground, some of Kerrigan's mixed in with it. He shivered and tried to pull his jacket collar tighter. It was cold out. He wished the goddamned sun would start doing what it was supposed to do.

A flight of four wooden steps led up to a small porch and then the front door. "You first, you're lighter," Kerrigan whispered to him, and he nodded back. He put his weight gingerly on the first step. It creaked, he'd have to take it easy. There was a crack in the third step. He'd avoid that one entirely, he should be able to reach the top one and boost the rest of his body up onto it. He wobbled, but Crusher steadied him, there, he'd made it, the door was right in front of him.

There was just the one door, a small window set in it at eye level, but so dirty that he couldn't make out what was on the other side. The knob turned easily in his hand. He pushed the door open and gently eased it back against the wall. There was a hallway running straight ahead, stairs up to the second floor about halfway down, a passageway leading to what looked like the kitchen at the back. Nearer to him there were closed doors off to the left and right. He heard snoring coming from behind the one on the left.

He turned and beckoned to Kerrigan. "There's somebody in there," he whispered when Crusher was alongside him. "You hear that?"

Kerrigan looked at him and smiled. It was a terrible smile. Crusher's hand must be killing him, but McDumont knew that it was supposed to be a smile. "We got a bird in the hand, pally," he muttered, "you get in there and I'll be right behind you."

The door stuck a little bit as McDumont opened it. He had to give it a nudge with his shoulder and exert some upward pressure on the knob; he couldn't help making some noise. There was light coming from his left, filtering through a window with the shade pulled most of the way down. He could make out a bed against the far wall. It looked like there were two— no, better make that three— people in it. Whoever was in the middle was starting to toss and turn. It looked like a woman, she must have heard him. McDumont stopped and put his hand out behind him, holding it palm up to tell Crusher that he should stop, stay back.

The woman sat up. Nancy Virdon stared at him. She could probably see him better than he could see her, there was more light where he was. He smiled at her and waved his left hand, keeping his right hand with the gun in it down at his side where she couldn't see it. She hesitated and finally waved back, then looked to either side of her and put her hands in the air with a "What can I tell you?" expression. McDumont could see now that it was the Wilson brothers in bed with her. He kept smiling, but he was at a loss as to what to do next. What would Emily Post prescribe as the proper etiquette in this situation? He guessed that Emily would be as puzzled as he was.

He heard movement behind him, and then Kerrigan pushed him aside. Crusher pointed his gun at Nancy and said, "Don't make a sound!" in a harsh whisper.

She took one look at him and screamed.

Gord and Mike sat up with a start. "Don't..." Kerrigan started to say, but it was already too late. Gord, on the side nearest the window, hit the floor running and dove right through the glass in the window. One minute he was there and then he was gone. They could hear his feet pounding on the porch. McDumont stared after him, open-mouthed. Then a rifle boomed from outside, and then again, but now something was going on at the other end of the room. Mike was frantically tearing at some clothes flung over a chair. He must not be hurt too bad, McDumont thought with relief. Then Crusher was yelling at Mike, saying "Don't move! Don't move!", but Wilson had found a gun and turned toward them. Then Mike was lifted up and smashed against the wall as Kerrigan shot him three times from close range, the body squirming as the bullets thudded home, then collapsing in a motionless heap on the floor.

They heard feet pounding overhead. Crusher ran to the door and fired toward the top of the staircase. "Missed the son of a bitch," he said disgustedly, coming back into the room. "You get over here and keep a lookout. Harmon'll think twice about coming down them stairs, but keep your eyes peeled."

Nancy was still screaming. Crusher moved to the bed and slapped her hard across the face. The force of the blow flung her back against the headboard. "Shut up," he said, grabbing her by the throat. "Shut up or you'll get what your boyfriend got." He took her by the arm and pulled her over to where Mike Wilson's body was lying. "Tell us where the rest of them are."

"Mona's across the hall," she sobbed. "Larry's upstairs. He took the Bronson woman up there last night and said he didn't want anybody to bother him. That's all I know, honest." She stared at McDumont and swallowed, regained control over herself. "What the hell are you doing here, Walter? What's going on? Are you with the cops or what? Larry said the fix was in, there wouldn't be any cops around here."

"I'll bet that's what he said," McDumont replied grimly. "No, we aren't cops. You must know what Harmon's doing. You can't be that stupid. Did you think this was a vacation in the country or something?" He kept taking quick glances at the top of the stairway, but there was no sign of Harmon, who must realize the way was effectively blocked. There hadn't been any signs of life from Mona's room, either. She must be lying low. Just as well, the last thing they needed was somebody else to worry about.

Nancy shook her head. "I don't know. Larry doesn't tell me anything. It was only last night Gord and Mike told me about the kidnapping. I didn't have anything to do with it. You got to let me go, I didn't have a thing to do with it."

McDumont looked at Kerrigan. "She's probably right, you know? Why don't we let her go? She told us what she knows. We don't have any more use for her."

"She saw me kill that guy," Crusher said, reloading. "You think she ain't going to spill it?"

McDumont was angry. "What the hell are you going to do, kill her in cold blood? Mike was different, he was trying to kill you. So what if she saw you? I saw you. Are you going to shoot me, too?"

Kerrigan looked at him appraisingly. "You're part of it, Walter. You came in here with me, armed, you're what the shysters call an accessory. Her, she's just a dumb broad. I don't care whether you got a soft spot for her or what. She saw what she saw and she ain't got no reason to keep it quiet."

"I swear I'll never tell," Nancy said, "I swear it. Just let me go. I'll leave town, you'll never see me again."

"Crusher," McDumont said, "you weren't hired to kill innocent people. The Bronsons wouldn't countenance murder. You couldn't help shooting Mike, that was self-defence whatever the law says. But this is something else. Remember what you said about me being an accessory? I've got something to say about it, too." He was grasping at straws, but he couldn't let Kerrigan do this terrible thing. There were limits, there had to be limits or you might just as well be an animal. Nancy didn't deserve to die just because she happened to be in the wrong place at the wrong time.

Crusher looked at him. "You still don't get it, Walter? I guess you better think about it some more. I'm going to tie her to the bed here, we still got work to do. We'll settle this later."

There was the sound of a rifle shot from outside, and glass shattered somewhere above them. "Harmon!" Kerrigan said. He went to the window and raised the shade that was still dangling over where Gord had made his sudden exit, being careful to keep his body off to the side. Then he waved his hand and yelled, "Ray! What's going on?"

"Harmon tried to get out an upstairs window," Chandler replied. "But the boys and I have got all of them covered, you don't need to worry about it."

"Smart," Crusher said, nodding his head. "Harmon'll think we've got the place surrounded. He won't try that again." He glanced at the ceiling. "You hear him walking around up there? Maybe I can pop him through the floor."

"Don't!" McDumont said quickly. "You don't know for sure it's him. It could be Penny."

"Yeah, okay." Kerrigan put his head out the window and looked to the right. "Gord ain't going anywhere, anyway. Ray ain't lost his shooting eye. He's a good man to have along."

"Is Gord dead?" McDumont asked.

"If he ain't, he's doing a damned good imitation of it. Hell of a shot, hit a running man like that."

McDumont flushed. "Jesus, I'm sorry. All I've done is try to keep you from gunning down Nancy and maybe shooting Penny, pardon me. Why don't we just kill everybody and get it over with? Or maybe you'd like me to go across the hall and shoot Mona. Then I'd be a killer, too, we could form a club and have meetings. What is it they call that bunch in New York, 'Murder Incorporated?' Hell, maybe we could set up a branch in Los Angeles. You and Ray must be eligible, and you could sponsor me if I still haven't killed anybody by the time this is over."

McDumont didn't really know what he was saying, but this was how he felt. He had seen people killed and knew it wasn't right, but how were you going to stop it? What had gone so terribly wrong that he was holding a gun in his hand in a room where a man had been shot to death, and another man was probably dead or dying outside?

Crusher was standing next to him. "You forgotten why we're here? You remember who's upstairs?"

"No," McDumont snarled, "I haven't forgotten." But you had, he thought, for a moment there you were ready to run away. When Crusher shot Mike, something in you died along with him. You lost something that you didn't even know you had. Not your innocence; you'd lost that growing up a slum kid, lost it in the hobo jungles where the strong preyed on the weak and nobody felt sorry for the loser. No, when you saw Mike die you understood that you were going to die, too, you realized death was always with you and your world could end at any time, at any moment, and it would have no more meaning and importance than any other trivial event in a universe that had always planned to go on without you.

Kerrigan was looking at him in a funny way; some of this must have shown on his face. Then McDumont knew that he wasn't going to run away. There was still Penny, and she was his world. If something happened to her, he wouldn't want to live. He had to keep going. He had to save her life to save his own. That was all there was to it.

"Cover me," he said to Crusher. "I'm going to see what Mona's up to."

The door to Mona's room was open part of the way. She must have been curious about what was happening. Kerrigan eased out into the hallway and searched the staircase with his gun, but there was no sign of Harmon. He must be trying to figure out how the hell he's going to get out of this, McDumont thought. That'll give the son of a bitch something to worry about. Then McDumont ran across the hall and shoved open the door.

Mona was standing just behind it. There was no light on, just patches of sunlight filtering through the tattered shades that partially covered the windows. She raised her arm and pointed a small, silvery gun at him. "Close the door behind you," she said in a firm, no-nonsense voice. She motioned with the gun. "Then go over there and sit down on the bed."

He did as he was ordered, moving deliberately, trying to decide what to do. She could have shot him as he came through the door, so she must still be making up her mind about the situation. If she'd heard everything that had been going on, she knew she was in a tough spot, trapped in a house surrounded by armed men who'd already killed her brothers. On the other hand, she might not know that Mike and Gord were dead. He'd just have to play it by ear.

"Your brothers have been shot," McDumont said. That might break her down. Maybe she wasn't as tough as she looked.

Her arm stiffened, the gun pointing straight at him. "How bad?" she asked. "There was a hell of a lot of shooting. I heard Kerrigan's voice. Who else is over there?"

"They both got shot," McDumont said, "I don't know how bad. I've been watching out for Harmon. We've got some of Crusher's pals with us, they're all around the house. There's no chance you or Harmon are going to get away."

She stared at him. Her nostrils flared, her eyebrows raised, the gun continued to point right at him. She's such a beautiful woman, he thought irrelevantly, this is a hell of a way for her to end up. Then he almost laughed. He was the one who was looking death in the face, he must have some weird masochistic kink somewhere if he got a thrill from being threatened by a desirable woman. But there it was, he even had an erection. This was a great time to find out Doctor Freud was right about the relationship between sex and death.

"I didn't have anything to do with it," she finally said. "It was all Larry's idea. He grabbed the Bronson chick and made me come out here with him." She paused, thinking. "It was my brothers, too. They were in on it, they made me come out here."

So much for Wilson family feeling, McDumont thought. "Sure," he said, "I can see that would be how it was. So why don't you put the gun down? Relax. We'll get out of here, nobody needs to know you were even here at all."

Mona thought it over. "Get Kerrigan," she said. "I want to hear it from him. He's a hard guy, he's probably the one who shot my brothers." Something must have shown on McDumont's face, because then she said, "I figured that's what happened. Now you stand up, and take your time about it. Go over to that door and open it enough to make yourself heard. Tell Kerrigan to come in here, and make sure that's all you tell him. After that, you go back and sit on the bed. Try anything funny and I'll shoot you."

McDumont did as he'd been told. Kerrigan was in the doorway across the hall, his gun waiting for Harmon to show on the staircase.

He nodded at McDumont's message and motioned him to get back from the door. Then he looked back into the room where Nancy was tied and said, "You stay right there. Make a move and you're dead." McDumont turned around, walked to the bed, and sat down.

Crusher came through the door quickly, then stopped when he saw Mona pointing her gun at him. He shifted his own gun to his left hand and grasped it by the barrel, holding it out away from his body. "What do you say, babe?" he asked in a light tone of voice. "Don't shoot. You don't know me good enough to shoot me. You still look good. Maybe we can break a little bread together when this is over."

"You shot my brothers, didn't you," she said. It was more of a statement than a question.

Kerrigan looked at McDumont, then back at Mona. "I shot Mike, yeah. I didn't have no choice. I told him not to go for his gun, but he wouldn't listen. Nothing personal, babe, but I didn't have no choice."

"I bet," she said. "What about Gord, what happened to him?"

"Crusher didn't have anything to do with that," McDumont said quickly. "One of the guys outside shot him. He was making a break for it."

"One of your friends," Mona said, speaking to Kerrigan.

"Well, kinda. Yeah, you could say that."

"You murdering bastard," she said. She pulled the trigger and the gun made a funny popping sound, like a little motor scooter backfiring. Crusher smiled at her, as if he were contemptuous of such a pathetic gun, smiled while he put his own massive weapon back in his right hand and took aim at Mona. She fired twice more before Kerrigan's revolver crashed and she was flung back against the wall, doubled over and folding her arms around the red stain spreading rapidly down the front of her dress.

Crusher was still smiling. Then he slowly fell to his knees, twisted sideways, and stretched out on the floor on his back. He turned his head so that he could see McDumont. "I told you, Walter. Always watch the broads." A convulsion passed through his body and the look on his face changed to one of fear, his eyes widening as he saw something that he seemed to be afraid of, his teeth making an audible grinding noise that filled the room with anguished sound. Another spasm gripped him and he was still, his eyes staring without comprehension at the dimness. McDumont knelt over him and looked at the three small holes in his chest. They'd hardly bled at all, you wouldn't think a big guy like Kerrigan would take any notice of them.

But he was dead. There was no pulse, no sign of life at all. McDumont went over to Mona and took a quick look at her, but she had died almost instantly. The bullet had torn a massive hole in the middle of her body and there wasn't anything he could do for her. Not that he was doing much good for anybody. They were all dying. It was like playing tag when you were a child, you started out part of a big bunch of kids and then one by one the size of the group diminished. The idea was to be the last one left.

He shook his head, tried to start thinking again. He should feel sorrier than he did for Crusher. McDumont would probably be dead by now if the big lug hadn't come along with him, but he couldn't forget that Kerrigan had wanted to murder Nancy Virdon. Crusher really had wanted to kill her, get rid of her the way you'd swat an insect.

McDumont realized that he simply hadn't understood the meaning of all that talk about bootleggers and the numbers racket. He hadn't connected it to real violence; he'd thought it was colourful and exciting. What was it Kerrigan had said about the sheriff who'd double-crossed his gang? "We got him good!" And what was that but another way of saying that they'd killed him? It must not have been your garden-variety killing, either, it must have been pretty spectacular if Crusher remembered it so fondly. No, McDumont couldn't feel that sorry about what had happened to Kerrigan: someone who had lived by violence had died by it. There wasn't any other way to look at it.

He went to the doorway and glanced cautiously up the stairs. Still no sign of life from Harmon, but then there wasn't any reason to expect one. McDumont and his friends supposedly had him surrounded. He had to think of something... all right, he'd start small, he'd try to get Nancy Virdon out of there. Enough people had already been hurt.

He ran across the hallway and found Nancy cowering on a corner of the bed. "Please don't kill me," she whimpered as he untied her. "I just want to get out of here. I won't talk, please don't kill me."

"Get dressed," McDumont said. "Nobody's going to kill you." Then he frowned. "Why the hell were you here in the first place, unless your idea of a good time is to be the filling in a Wilson brothers' sandwich?" His face was burning, where the hell had that come from? Was he jealous?

That was what Nancy seemed to think. She'd gone from stark terror to simpering cuteness in the blink of an eye. "I knew you liked me, Walter, I can always tell. Larry made me come out here. I'm one heck of a good cook and Mona doesn't know a pot from a piano." Then she looked frightened again. "What happened to Mona? I heard shooting..."

"She's dead. There isn't anything you can do for her. Now finish getting your clothes on, and hurry up about it." He softened his tone. "Is there somewhere you can go, somewhere out of the city?"

"I've got a sister in Phoenix, divorced but she still uses her ex-husband's name. Nobody could trace me there. After today," she said, shuddering and glancing at Mike Wilson's body, "I won't be back, I don't ever want to come back here."

When she had finished dressing, he took her over to the window and looked out. Chandler saw them and waved. McDumont pointed to Nancy and made pushing-away motions, then helped her through the window. She edged to the right and then took off in a sprint up the driveway.

Ray was trying to get McDumont's attention, pointing toward the house and cocking his head quizzically. McDumont would have liked to have Chandler with him, but that might give Harmon a chance to get away through an upstairs window. McDumont shook his head vigorously and held his palm up. He wanted Ray to remain right where he was.

And then he couldn't put it off any longer. He had to do something about Harmon. Maybe he should try to talk to him. Then he heard a shout from upstairs. It sounded as though Harmon wanted to talk to him.

McDumont warily peeked around the edge of the door frame. The first thing he saw was Penny, standing at the top of the stairs, her face expressionless. It was as if she were staring at him but not seeing him. There were bruises on her face and her arms were twisted behind her, as though she might be handcuffed. Harmon's left arm was around her neck, and he was standing right behind her. There was a gun in his right hand and he was holding it to her head.

"You're going to let us get out of here," Harmon said. "We're going to walk down these stairs, and I don't want any monkey business. Anybody shoots at me, I'm going to kill her."

"Are you all right, Penny?" McDumont asked.

She nodded her head but didn't say anything. Harmon leered at McDumont over her shoulder. "Your girlfriend thinks she's a tough little mama, but I showed her what's what. Why don't you tell the little bastard what we were doing last night, baby? He probably don't know what you high-class chicks can get up to when you meet a real man."

Penny turned her head and spat in Harmon's face. He laughed and grabbed her hair with his left hand, then roughly yanked her head backward. He moved the barrel of his gun across her throat. "Still full of the old pizzazz, huh? Well, we'll see about that after we get out of here." He looked at McDumont. "Now you get out of my way, little bastard. Get outside and keep away from those cars. Keep your friends away from them, too."

"Kerrigan fixed them," McDumont said, "he drained all the oil out of them. Why don't you give up? The Wilsons are dead, and you're surrounded by armed men."

Harmon laughed. "You got one son of a bitch out front who can shoot, but that's all I seen. Where's Kerrigan? He should be backing your play here. You aren't man enough for it."

"Don't worry about Crusher," McDumont said. "He's here if I need him. Put your gun down and let Penny go. You can stay here if you want to. Set her free and then go back up the stairs. I just want to get her out of here."

Harmon shook his head. "I don't think so. I think she's my ace in the hole and you're showing deuces. You back up out that door. We're coming down."

"I'm not going anywhere," McDumont said. He moved out into the hallway, keeping his gun down at his side. "Give up, Harmon. Let Penny go. Let's put an end to it." He meant it. He'd let Harmon go if that would bring Penny back to him. He couldn't bear to see her like this.

Harmon reddened and pointed his gun at McDumont. "You asked for it, little bastard!"

Penny tore her head away from Harmon's grasp and sank her teeth into his right hand. He screamed as the gun went off, the bullet thwacking into the wall beside McDumont, then clubbed at Penny with the barrel and caught her across the face. Her knees buckled and she fell awkwardly down the stairs, handcuffs glinting as she rolled over on her back. Harmon brought his gun up again and aimed it at McDumont.

McDumont sighted down the barrel of the revolver and began to pull the trigger. It was easy, he'd done it before. You just aimed at the middle of the target and tried to keep your hand steady. You kept pulling the trigger until you'd fired all the bullets. There, he heard a click. Now you broke the cylinder open and reloaded, put the bullets in quickly and deftly. He'd always been good with his hands, "high dexterity" they'd called it, he'd learned how to type faster than anyone else in his grade-nine class. The teacher hadn't believed it, she'd thought he must be cheating, but he wasn't. He was good with his hands. Look how smoothly and easily these bullets went in.

He snapped the cylinder shut and aimed the revolver up the staircase again. But there wasn't anything to shoot at. Harmon wasn't there. Then he looked at the bottom of the stairs. Harmon had fallen on top of Penny, who was trying to squirm away from him. But his weight was on her legs, and with her hands cuffed behind her she couldn't move very well. Harmon was moaning, babbling away about something or other. McDumont tried to ignore it. He didn't care what Harmon had to say.

He pulled Penny out from underneath Harmon's body, picking up Harmon's gun and throwing it behind him, and then held her to him tightly. He was crying. Why was he crying? He should be happy she was all right. But maybe she wasn't, she'd been hit and then had fallen down the stairs. He looked into her face anxiously. Her eyes were closed, and there was a red welt across her nose and cheeks where Harmon had pistol-whipped her. Her mouth was bleeding, too. "Can you hear me, Penny? Are you hurt? Open your eyes if you can hear me."

Her eyes opened. She looked at McDumont as if she'd never seen him before, then turned to look at Harmon. "The keys to the handcuffs are in one of his jacket pockets," she said in an emotionless voice.

McDumont went to get them. Harmon was bleeding from wounds in his stomach and right shoulder. Another bullet had creased his skull and opened up a thin line of red over his left ear. He was starting to move around, tossing his head this way and that, saying he was going to "Get them all and kill them, kill them all, kill every one of them," but they were just words. McDumont didn't have to listen. He unlocked the handcuffs and helped Penny stand up. He wanted to hold her close again, but she broke away, rubbing her wrists furiously. They must hurt her. Then he heard someone coming through the door behind him and turned to greet Chandler. Ray was looking past McDumont, breaking into a grin, then he was looking somewhere else and frowning. "I think you'd better put that down," he said.

Penny was standing over Harmon with his gun in her hand. He was still talking, talking about how he was going to get them all, kill everybody. Then he opened his eyes and saw Penny. He shook his head, focused on her, smiled. "You back for more, baby? I knew you couldn't stay away."

Penny stared at him. Then she dropped to one knee and shoved the gun barrel in his mouth. Harmon's eyes widened. He was trying to say something, something important.

She pulled the trigger. Harmon's head changed shape. It wasn't a head any more. Penny stood up and dropped the gun on the floor. Then she walked over to Walter and embraced him. "Hold me," she said. "Please don't say anything, just hold me and don't let go." After a while she began to cry, and some time after that McDumont walked her slowly out the front door, across the farmyard and into the bush and trees, speaking to her quietly, telling her how much he loved her, telling her how glad he was that she was alive, telling her that he would never leave her, telling her that they would always be together.

Chandler had gone to get the car. McDumont was still holding Penny, stroking her face, saying, "It's over, it's all over," repeating it, trying to make himself believe it.

"I don't know if I'll ever get over this," she said after a while. "I don't think I'll ever be able to forget it."

"We've got time," McDumont told her gently. "You and me, we've got nothing but time."